KT-103-119

WITHDRAWN

9030 00007 3175 5

Sweet

ALYSIA CONSTANTINE

interlude press • new york

LONDON BOROUGH OF WANDSWORTH	
9030 00007 3175 5	
Askews & Holts	
AF	
	WW20010494

Copyright © 2016 Alysia Constantine
All Rights Reserved
ISBN 13: 978-1-941530-61-0 (trade)
ISBN 13: 978-1-941530-62-7 (ebook)
Published by Interlude Press, New York
http://interludepress.com
This is a work of fiction. Names, characters, and places are either a product
of the author's imagination or are used fictitiously. Any resemblance
to real persons, either living or dead, is entirely coincidental.
All trademarks and registered trademarks are the
property of their respective owners.
Book design and Cover illustrations by CB Messer

10 9 8 7 6 5 4 3 2 1

interlude ✦ press • new york

For my love, B—, who is the brightest and most beautiful person I know.

One

THIS IS NOT A STORY with a beautiful first line or the perfect symmetry of a beginning and ending wrapped tightly together like a present from the Fates. This is not a story about love at first sight; there will be no perfect first kiss, no white horse and sunset, no prince, no glass shoe. In fact, in this story, nothing very important happens—it is a very unimportant story about two very unimportant people who find one another. Yes, there will be some kisses in this story, and also cupcakes and lost keys and other secretly beautiful small things, but nothing that changes the world or shifts the ground under anyone's feet.

Except for this moment, on a winding side street in the West Village of New York City, on a slippery and too-chilly spring morning soundtracked by the wet whoosh and spray of taxis hissing over damp pavement, when the woman with the red umbrella comes rushing out of a nail salon in a flap of still-sodden overcoat, with her cell phone and umbrella stem clamped precariously between cheek and shoulder and her eyes trained on her wet painted nails, and bangs directly into Teddy Flores.

Teddy, too, had been a dark flurry of wet trench coat and wool gabardine and barely balanced coffee, with his newspaper clutched over his head in a vain attempt to prevent his hair from re-coiling into ringlets around his face in the spring rain. He was late. He was always late, because the hurry and the thinking forward—*get there get there get there*—stopped him from thinking too much about how miserable it was to actually *be* there, in that world of gray wool and blue carpet and steel and linoleum and fluorescence and sticky notes and very sharp pencils and meetings in which too many men cleared too many throats and shuffled too many folders and nobody said anything that anyone—least of all Teddy—cared the least bit about.

If you knew Teddy Flores in high school—a bright boy with a bright smile, flickering eyes and doglike devotion to joy, who had so many friends and so much waterfall energy, who saw his future opening before him like a stage curtain pulling back, saw his future like that spot of light into which he was always about to step, a boy sparkling and muscle-ready and about to burst open—if you knew that boy in high school, you would ask him how it was that he ended up this way, gray and hushed and soft as wet flannel. But most people are too bored or too polite to ask such questions of a man like him: one CPA among a team of CPAs, in a big department of an overgrown company occupying a single floor of a plate glass building on a crowded block in a city so large and harried and full of everything under the sun that nothing—certainly not he—was remarkable enough for it to stop its bluster for even one quiet second.

It's not that nobody cared about him, for Teddy still had loving parents, good friends, familiar and welcoming faces at his regular haunts (coffee, laundry, Chinese takeout). It's simply that everyone, including Teddy, was in such a rush, with so many errands to run and so many important things to think about. And his story wasn't much to tell. It was a slow slipping down into mediocrity, as if Teddy were being very gently crushed under a quietly building avalanche of nods and agreements and the gradual understanding, finally, after many discussions, of the difference between what was *fun* and what was *practical* and what it meant to *grow up and take care of yourself.*

But all of this is an untold story and will stay that way; and that is for the best, because it will soon change, and because it will interest neither you, nor I, nor Teddy himself, whose only thought in this moment was that he must *get there get there get there* until the crash with the wet-nailed woman knocked that out of him, knocked him flat back onto the watery concrete. He fell with a small, surprised "ooof!" and almost laughed out loud at the ridiculousness of the sound he made, like the butt of a slapstick stunt in a Stooges movie. His coffee splashed up and was gone; the paper cup skittered into the gutter and rolled under a parked car; his shirtfront became a clinging Rorschach blot he could only read as *ruin* and *wreck of a morning.*

"Damn! I am so sorry!" the woman said as her umbrella flipped past them both and went skipping down the sidewalk, cheerfully leaving her behind to soak in the rain. She extended her hand, and when Teddy, still spinning and stunned, didn't take it, she grabbed his collar and pulled him to his feet. She dusted his shoulders and then laughed at herself, pushing back the wet hair that flopped in her eyes. "Well, that's useless! I'm so, so sorry. Are you okay?"

Teddy nodded. The cold and wet had soaked through the seat of his trousers, soaked through his underwear, was soaking into the muscles of his thighs in a way that made his whole body ache.

"*God*, look at you! I really messed you up! You're wearing your coffee, too!" She smiled at him, a very white smile, a very straight smile, and Teddy tried to grin back, but her hands were clutching his shoulders and the rain was starting to slide down the collar of his shirt like little slivers of ice.

"It's really fine," he said, forcing a stiff smile. "Are you okay?"

"I'm an idiot," the woman said, pushing her hair back again and letting her hand drop to his bicep. "And I'm buying you a new coffee."

Teddy opened his mouth to protest, but the woman tightened her grip on his arm and pulled him into the doorway of a little shop. Gold letters above her head on the glass of the door, in a very simple font, read, without elaboration: BUTTERMILK. She turned toward him, raised her eyebrows and threw herself back against the door so it shuddered open and the little bells that hung above the door shimmered a silvery tingle down his spine. She nodded once and yanked Teddy into the warm, sugary air of the bakery.

"Sit," she told him and shoved him onto a stool. "How do you take it?"

"What?" Teddy said.

"Hey, Irene," said the bored girl behind the counter. "Back already?" She was dreadlocked and pierced in a number of places, with black tattoos curling over every exposed inch of her skin.

"I," Irene said, making a grand gesture toward Teddy, "just accidentally slammed into this gentleman here and ruined his morning and I am buying him a new coffee. And I'm late, so I'm running." She slapped a wad of cash onto the counter. "Whatever he wants. The rest for you, sweetie, for the tip cup." She turned to Teddy and squeezed his arm again. "Tell 'Trice your coffee order. She looks like she might bite, but she never has, not once. Here's my card, so that you can call me and we can have a drink sometime, and someday we'll tell all our friends about our perfectly adorable romcom first encounter, when we met cute and then I bought you a coffee and you couldn't stop thinking about me and asked me out and then the rest is history, but I've got to be rude and run *right now because I am extremely late!*" She shouted the last words over her shoulder as she whipped out the door with a shiver of bells and cold air.

"So, that was Hurricane Irene," the girl said, smiling at Teddy. "I think she likes you, because she never, ever tips. She was trying to impress you. You'll have pretty babies with pretty eyes."

"I don't..." Teddy started to say, but the girl raised her hand, laughing at him.

"I totally know. I live in Chelsea. I work in a pastry shop. My boss coordinates his socks and his pocket squares, and my best friend breeds teacup Dobermans. But Irene usually can't tell the difference between a man and a fire hydrant, let alone pick up on the subtleties of homosexual semaphore. *She* has no idea. Nor does she probably care," she added with a smirk, flipping a large paper cup in the air and catching it with a flourish. "How do you take it?"

"What?" Teddy asked again.

"Your coffee," the girl said, enunciating slowly. "What are you drinking?"

Teddy felt dumb and cold and still as a stone. Why couldn't he catch up? Everything seemed to be moving so fast around him, everyone seemed to be talking at high speed, but the warm air smelled like cinnamon and had wound itself around his neck and cheeks like a scarf, and he simply wanted to sit and breathe it in.

"Black, please, just plain coffee."

He was slowly thawing. The stools and the counters were of old softened wood, dry and warm; jewel-toned fruits and mounds of frothy pastel sugar glinted from the display cases in the dim light—the entire shop front, he noticed now, was lit mostly by daylight from the large plate glass window, aided by a few old lamps with heavy velvet shades that drooped with ornate tasseled trim. Strings of colored glass beads criss-crossed overhead, glittering and shaking slightly with faint vibration. Some of the wooden stools were loosely topped with well-worn velvet cushions, and the walls were hung with gauzy fabrics in rich, delicious colors: fuchsia, pumpkin, vermillion. No fluorescents anywhere. It was cozy, even romantic, and he wanted to linger, snug in the glittering semi-dark, all day.

"Black, please," he said again, more sure of himself.

"You got it, sailor," the girl said, flipping the cup again. She turned her back and filled the cup, then slid it toward him across the counter, along with a stack of napkins. "Here, dry off."

"Thank you," he said, but she was already gone; the door at the back of the room was still swinging in her wake.

Teddy sat on a stool and placed the coffee carefully on the table in front of him. He began to pat himself with the napkins, first drying his face and neck and then attempting to clean the brown blotch on his shirt.

"You're just rubbing it in." The girl had returned and was leaning against the counter and staring at him with widened brown eyes. "Just let it be. It's already gone. That shirt is a done deal, my friend." She whistled and swept her hand through the air like a plane taking a nosedive.

Teddy grimaced at her and continued to blot. It was a good shirt. Was.

"Here," she said, "a consolation prize." In front of her on the counter was a petite, perfectly pale yellow cupcake topped with a swoop of the lightest-looking white frosting. A little bramble of shredded basil and a thin twist of sugared lemon rind curled across the top. She pushed the little cake toward him with her finger.

"No," Teddy said. "Thanks. But it's too early for that much—"

"It is never too early for something this good. This is sunshine and fluffy clouds and bunnies and happiness for your mouth," the girl said seriously. "Well, maybe not the bunnies, because, well, gross. But, you know…"

Teddy looked dubious, but he did stop blotting.

"Meyer lemon and olive oil cupcake. Whipped cream and ricotta frosting. A little basil in there. Didn't even put them in the case yet. Totally fresh. My boss might be uptight and totally crazy and use enough hairspray to punch a Cleveland-sized hole in the ozone, but he is a genius with food. You will never taste anything more beautiful.

On the house. Seriously. Eeeeeeaaaaaaat," she wheedled, poking the cupcake forward.

Teddy had to laugh, because a girl by whom, under other circumstances, he might have been quite frightened was trying to force upon him the most dainty-looking cupcake he'd ever seen.

"Okay," he said and took the cupcake. The girl clapped her hands and bounced on her toes. She watched as he carefully peeled the paper from the cake and opened his mouth. "Just for you," he said and winked (when did he ever wink?) before taking a gentle bite.

You may have experienced a moment like this, sometime in your life, when you were filled with light and magic and you knew—completely and without question, all-of-a-sudden and with your whole body—when you knew *something* you could not quite put into words. A moment when you felt the sure click of a key turned in a lock, after which the whole mechanism of your life slid into place, and the door, the one your back had once pressed against, sprang open, and you felt the wild, pitching expanse of possibilities suddenly rolling out in front of you. A moment when, in the back of your throat, a small voice that might have been your own whispered desperately, *turn around turn around!*

It was simply a cupcake. A cupcake, Teddy reasoned, cannot change your life. Not even a cupcake as gloriously, floatingly light and exquisite as this one. It must be the warming up, the coffee and the sugar, and the being-out-of-the-rain and the halting of the rush, and the jarring of the fall he'd taken and the sneak of a head cold coming on, but he felt it: a burning like a little flame as the bite went down. It settled like a sun in his belly and embered there and spread heat in waves that rippled through his bones and muscles and through his skin in curling-out rays, and he thought, for a moment, that he must be glowing with it. All the strings of bells and beads, all the lamp tassels and the passementeries looped over the doorknobs, everything seemed to rock and twinkle with a whispering rustle and a soft, musical jingle. It was as if the whole little bakery was laughing with him.

"Mmmmmmhh," he groaned and rolled his eyes closed because he knew the girl was watching, and something inside him said *show her how glowing and good it is* and, without thinking, he did. He fanned his hand near his mouth and tipped his head back, a decent kind of ecstasy, for her benefit alone.

"I know!" she shouted, and slapped the counter with the flat of her hand, clearly pleased. "Like sunshine, right?"

"Ohhhh." Teddy moaned around another bite. "Like sunshine, yeah. Bright. Tangy. But underneath there's a kind of green taste, a little planty, a little spicy and not too sweet, either, just"—here he stole another bite, took a moment to chew and swallow—"just *perfectly*—"

"I *know!*" the girl squealed. Her hands were clasped on the far lip of the counter, and she had pulled herself across it toward Teddy and was leaning so far forward she was practically lying on her stomach. "I told you, he's a genius." With that, she turned toward the kitchen and hollered, "And I know you're listening, but I mean it anyway! You're a genius, darling!" From the kitchen, as if in answer, came a sudden clatter of metal. She turned back to Teddy and whispered, "I hid four of them for myself, to take home. Don't," she winked at him as she slid off the counter and turned on her heel, "don't you dare tell the boss man!"

With that, she was gone again through the swinging door at the back of the bakery. In her wake, the kitchen expelled a puff of hot, spiced air, and all the bells and hanging beads shook lightly.

Teddy sat, half a cupcake in one hand, his other hand wrapped around the still-steaming paper cup of coffee. It was just a cupcake, he reasoned, but since no one was looking now, he closed his eyes and slowly slid his tongue through the cream on top. There was no longer any point in rushing; the damage to the morning had been done, and he would have to run all the way back home to change his clothes, since the coffee stain on his shirt had dried—the girl was right, the shirt was definitely done for—and his pants were probably completely ruined in the back. Even if he managed to grab a taxi in this rain, it would still take at least an hour to get home and then to the office.

He tried not to think about the office, lit too brightly and drained of color, so sterile the air tasted like Styrofoam, but thoughts kept sneaking over him, filling him with—well, not the familiar cold rush and sinking dread he usually felt when he thought of work. Today, the feeling was more like sadness, like blue-black air, like longing, like an empty space. But it didn't reach his bones, and he felt the deepest pit of him begin to fill up, grow verdant and full of sun, solid and real.

He pulled out his phone and started to compose a careful text message. He would take his time today, for once. And he would be very late to work.

∞

"Are you going to watch him all morning like the big ol' creepy homo you are?" 'Trice asked as she chopped walnuts on the table near the door. "Or are you going to go out there and claim your pride of place as the genius who gave him a mouth-orgasm?"

Jules turned away from the crack in the swinging door where he'd been hovering for nearly ten minutes, watching the dripping man with the coffee-stained shirt licking and nibbling with abandon at the cupcake he'd sent out. "First of all, 'Trice, that is a disgusting way to describe it. Secondly, he seems to still be in the middle of whatever enjoyment he's getting, and it would be creepier to interrupt him while he's doing those… things… with his tongue. And finally," he stopped and carefully curled his left hand over hers, tucking her fingers more carefully under the palm of her hand, "you need to remember your knife skills. *You're* the creepy homo, wielding that knife like a serial killer. I'm a very sweet homo."

'Trice stopped chopping and looked at him, fist on her jutting hip, knife cocked up and glinting dangerously.

"Watch it," she said, "or this creepy homo might just snap and use this knife on something other than *these* nuts."

"Nice. Very nice. A nut joke. How original of you." Jules turned his back on her. Through the crack, he watched the man pop the last bite of cupcake into his mouth and run his thumb slowly over his bottom lip. Jules knew this was a sweep for crumbs, simply pragmatic, but he saw the movement in slow motion, as more of a caress, as the man's thumb pulled his own lips apart ever so slightly, and when it reached the corner of his mouth, the thumb dipped in and he sucked it gently. The tendons of his throat tightened and relaxed when he finally swallowed. Jules let out a low sigh.

"He *is* very pretty," 'Trice said.

"Stop it. I just like watching people enjoy what I make. And it's a recipe experiment. I'm doing research," he whispered, eyes still glued to the crack in the door. "I'm really not being creepy."

"Uh huh," 'Trice said in a monotone.

Jules knew he *was*, of course, being creepy, watching a man who clearly thought he was alone, a very pretty man who'd now gone loose and pliant with pleasure, a man who seemed to be licking his own hand clean like a cat. *Good god*, Jules thought, *there should never be napkins anywhere. Ever.*

He also knew he was telling the truth: He really did like watching people enjoy what he baked. Always in secret, to make sure nothing was amped up for his benefit, he watched, thrilling at the little licks and hums and shivers of delight brought on by something he had made. Too often when people praised him, it hurt—the words glittered like fireworks and diamonds, too bright to be real, so bright that they lit up all his flaws and made him feel shabby and sorry to fall so short of the praise. But this was a secret kind of praise, watching the pleasure he helped bring about: quieter, like fire-glow, like warm hands, like love.

He'd never have believed it of himself when he was younger, struggling so hard always to be *seen* and to be *heard,* but what he wanted most of all now was to put himself entirely into something made all the more beautiful because it would not last and to give it to someone else to be completely devoured, to be smelled and tasted and felt, to become a part of that body. He could put all his tenderness and love there, and it would, quite literally, *feed* another person.

"Go out there," 'Trice said. She pointed the knife at him. "Just go ask him for his number already, Stalker Barbie."

"No."

"Chef Jules James Burns, you are a yellow-bellied chicken. And a baby. You're a chicken-baby."

"It's too soon."

'Trice rolled her eyes, even though she knew he couldn't see her. "It's been more than a year. It's not too soon. It appears to be exactly the right time," she said, nodding toward the outer room.

Jules waved her off and turned back to the door. "Sixteen months. And I get to say how soon is too soon."

Let us halt this story to say, because neither Jules nor 'Trice will mention it, that Jules had once been in love.

The man's name had been Andy. He was a freelance writer and a rabid fan of Jules's baking. He had a job tending bar, a nice apartment on Jane Street and a gray-and-brown-spotted dachshund also called Andy. Lest you think that evidence of some flaw—narcissism or stupidity or lack of imagination—you should know that Andy (the man) had, because of his big soft spot for anything little or broken or both, adopted Andy (the dachshund) at a rather ripe age, when he'd already been answering to that name for many years and, well, you know what they say about teaching an old dog new tricks. Andy (the man) wasn't going to change his own name, either, since that would be patently ridiculous, and he'd had the name even longer than the dog. So the two, man and dachshund, shared space and shared names and eventually came to share Jules, who loved them both fiercely and protectively and gloriously for four years.

How they had met is not important—perhaps that story will be told here in due course. Suffice it to say that they did meet and they fell rapidly in love, and, after eight months of loving him, Jules moved into the little apartment on Jane Street with Andy and Andy, and the three of them began to make a home. Six months later, Jules married Andy (the man) and promised also to have and hold Andy (the dachshund) for the rest of *his* life, too.

It is also not important what the man was like, what it was in Andy that made Jules love him so quickly and completely. Because Andy is gone now, knocked off the road by a city bus, laid in a hospital bed and allowed to rest for days in what Jules desperately told himself over and over was just a peaceful sleep, while his crushed bones and purple bruises and glass scrapes and poor broken body valiantly tried to heal. And eventually, sixteen months ago by Jules's count, he was laid with somber hands in a gray wooden casket and put where Jules could never touch him or look on him or whisper to him again.

"How much chopped walnut do we need?"

Jules jumped and looked at 'Trice as though she'd just appeared from nowhere.

"I'm sorry? Oh. I don't even know yet. I'm experimenting again. That should do it, though," he said absently, glancing at the pile of mangled nutmeats she'd amassed. "Let's toast them first."

"Light or dark?"

"Whichever," he said casually, rummaging on the metal shelves for… he wasn't sure what.

'Trice gave him a lingering, incredulous glance before sweeping the nuts onto a baking sheet and turning toward the ovens. "I'll just char them, then, if it's all the same to you. I'm brainstorming names. Ashy Nut Muffins? Burny Cakes? Charcoal Lumpies?"

Jules was sure she kept going, but he'd tuned her out, turning instead to the crack in the door. But the man had already left, and the shop was empty and quiet.

He poked his head out to check the table where the man had been sitting. He hoped for a brief moment the man had... what? Forgotten his wallet? Left a business card with his number and a note for the brilliant pastry chef? Dropped a glass slipper under his chair? He was being ridiculous.

"You are so far gone, Daddy-O," 'Trice mumbled as she swept past him, heading back out through the door to take her usual place at the counter. Jules ventured out to stand near the man's table.

"He didn't leave anything," 'Trice said, looking right through him. "Give it up."

"I... " Jules sat down.

"I've got your number, Charlie." 'Trice pointed and aimed her fingers like a gun, narrowing her eyes to a focused squint, but did not fire.

The man had politely cleaned up after himself at the table, and nothing—not even a smudge or crumb—was left of him there. All the trash had been cleared away; the table had been wiped clean. Nothing lingered, not even the ring of condensation from his coffee cup.

'Trice made an exploding noise and fired her finger-gun straight at Jules. "Told you," she said, and winked. "But he'll definitely be back."

The stool's velvet cushion bore a faint, damp imprint where the man had been sitting, the only evidence he'd existed at all.

Two

"Stray Gay returns," 'Trice whispered, landing a rough smack on Jules's rear end as she passed him on her way into the kitchen. "I told you so, you lucky horndog!"

"Boss here!" he shouted, shifting away from her reach. "With a knife! Kitchen safety rules! What did we say?"

'Trice stopped and rolled her eyes back, reciting, "No smacking or pinching or sneaking up on anyone holding a knife."

"Especially... ?"

"Especially if it's Chef Jules holding the knife, because Chef Jules has fragile sensibilities," 'Trice finished.

"Fragile sensibilities, that's right. Let that be a lesson to you," Jules said. "Otherwise, no sneaking treats while I pretend to look the other way. Wait. What did I just say? What are you doing?"

'Trice was barreling toward the cookies that were still cooling on their metal racks.

"I'm getting a cookie for Stray Gay," she said, grabbing one, then turned and rushed out of the kitchen in a huff of cloves and patchouli.

"Who is—" Jules said to her back and then gave up. When 'Trice was on a mission, reason was useless. Jules turned back to his chopping—a block of dark chocolate—and managed to concentrate for another six whole seconds before he dropped the knife, wiped his already-clean hands on his still-clean apron and positioned himself at his spy spot at the door.

Jules had always been particular about his person, but years in the kitchen had made him obsessively neat. His chef's jacket was crisp and white and perfectly fitted at his shoulders and cinched at his waist by the tightly wound ties of his apron. He was so pale-skinned that, but for the faded freckles scattered across the backs of his hands, it was hard to tell where his white coat stopped and his arms began. His closely cropped, nearly white hair was tucked tightly into a white handkerchief; his faded gray eyes were barely marked by pale lashes. The only challenge to the strict colorlessness of his person was a red-and vermillion-striped pocket square, which fluttered from the breast pocket of his coat like a flame rising from his chest.

He peered through the kitchen door. In the shop, 'Trice was leaning over the counter, chatting amiably with... someone Jules couldn't see, because that morning, on a joyous whim, he'd bought a bright armful of sunflowers and plunked them in a vase atop the display case to brighten the shop. And, apparently, to block his own view when spying on 'Trice and... someone.

"This requires something smooth and milky," she was saying. "I refuse to give it to you with black coffee. You're having a cappuccino with this. For dunking." Without waiting for a reply, she turned toward the espresso machine and busied herself with pulling a shot.

"There you go, Cupcake," she said, whirling toward the counter and sliding a ceramic mug at the invisible person behind the flowers. "Dark chocolate chunk cookie with orange and candied ginger. Fresh from the oven and a little hot and melty, so be careful. Best to dunk in a brilliantly done—if I do say so myself—cappuccino. With *nutmeg,* not cinnamon. Trust me here. Now get on that!"

Jules heard laughter: masculine, generous, soft as melting butter. "You're the boss!"

He strained at the door crack, watching the empty space to the side of the counter and waiting for the man to move into it. Instead, he heard a lilting, happy cry.

The man laughed. "What *is* that?"

"It's a pig!" 'Trice said, shooting a pointed look at the door behind which Jules stood. She raised her voice dramatically. "It's one of the many reasons I am invaluable to this operation. I am an *artiste*. And," she leaned across the counter to—*what? What did she do? Did she actually* poke *the customer?* "That is definitely *not* a comment on you for eating a cookie. It's just a picture. A brilliant, genius, masterpiece of a picture."

"You're definitely a genius!" The man laughed again. "Not many artists work in milk foam and coffee!"

"Thank you," she sang, and Jules barely had time to leap out of the way before she came charging back into the kitchen.

"I hope you heard that, *Jefe!*" 'Trice honked his nose and brushed past him, taking up the knife he'd abandoned and resuming the chopping where he'd left off. They were like those old couples who finish each other's sentences. "Stray Gay adores me."

Jules gave her a puzzled look, then turned back to peer into the shop front.

It had been almost a week since that rainy day when Irene had dragged the man into the shop, and Jules had convinced himself he probably wouldn't ever see him again, yet there he was, in a gray three-piece suit and a narrow gray tie, tucked into the corner table near the plate glass window. His legs were crossed neatly at the ankles; his brown hair was cropped close at the temples and growing a little long and wild at the crown of his head. He looked peaceful; a sweet smile lingered as he dunked a large piece of cookie into his coffee and slowly brought it to his mouth to suck the milk. His free hand snaked to his collar; one finger wormed into the tie to loosen the knot. He tipped his head back when the tie fell loose so the lump of his Adam's apple rose and fell along the tanned, taut column of his throat and he let out a barely audible groan of pleasure as the cookie broke apart in his fingers and crumbled into his open mouth.

An involuntary echo of the man's groan slid out of Jules's mouth. His hand came up to touch his own throat, where he could feel sudden freedom from the knot of a slim gray tie that hadn't ever been there. On the back of his tongue, he tasted the bitter and sweet of chocolate and orange; and he was overwhelmed by a calm that was earthy, grounded and deep. Jules didn't care if 'Trice was watching him or laughing—he could hear her gentle, rolling chuckle behind him; didn't care that he was mirroring the man, moving his tongue against the roof of his mouth and sucking softly; didn't care where he was or what day of the week it was or how much of himself he was forgetting. He could feel the spiced heat of espresso he had not swallowed spreading into his belly. He could feel himself grow more certain and solid and sure, as if roots were pushing out through the soles of his feet and curling into the earth below the floorboards.

"It's nothing," he said aloud, filling suddenly with regret, because his voice split the moment, and the feelings went wisping away, up in smoke. And just like that it was lost, his bright, fantastic hallucination.

Teddy was no hedonist. At least, he hadn't thought so. But perched as he was on a velvet cushion in the tiny, empty bakery, letting his tongue melt the chocolate and butter and milk and coffee into a decadent warm cream peppered by the occasional burn of ginger, he swiped the corners of his lips with his fingertips, licked them with no hint of his usual self-consciousness and began to reconsider.

Light streamed in through the large front window, filtering through the hanging glass beads overhead and splattering the room with softly shaking spots of color. It was like sitting in the middle of a slow, silent disco, he thought. It was an absolute pity he couldn't linger, was merely stopping in for ten minutes while shuttling between two appointments, even though the bakery didn't quite fall between them. Even though, he admitted silently, the bakery was fifteen blocks out of the way.

That rainy afternoon after his run-in with Irene and his first visit to Buttermilk, Teddy had returned home, changed out of his ruined clothes and started back to the office on foot. He'd taken his trench coat and umbrella, since he'd been given a second chance to prepare for the day, but he hadn't needed them after all. Changed and dry and combed and ready, he'd burst out of the glass doors of his apartment building and into a completely different day: rainless and warm, with the mist slowly burning off the streets in the new sun. He'd ambled to work, stopping to run his fingers through dewy lilacs bursting from plastic tubs in front of a florist.

All day in the cold, green light of his cubicle, he'd burned with a radiating heat that reached out from the center of him and seemed to curl into the cracks between the walls of his cubicle and the next. He'd droned through phone calls and curried columns of numbers and threaded his fingers through the hair at the nape of his neck in concentration, just as he always did, but his mind was floating elsewhere, and bright little beads of colored light twinkled behind his eyelids every time he closed his eyes. He'd bought a spray of orange tulips on the way in and had secretly dropped one on each desk in his section, then hid at his own desk and smiled every time he heard a faint gasp of delight float over the cubicle walls.

The sickly gray-green lights still buzzed above him, and he still felt tired from sitting all day and doing what seemed like nothing. It was very small, the change, almost unnoticeable. But somewhere between his getting knocked down that morning and his leisurely stroll to work that afternoon, something had shifted three degrees to the left, and he felt inside him a new thing opening and shooting out, could almost see the spring-green shoots stretch into tendrils that snaked out from his body and wound themselves lovingly around everything—the rushed and sighing office assistants, the tall vase of calla lilies on the reception desk, the children playing wildly in the park, the people crammed and swaying on the buses, the loose flap of shop awnings in the breeze, the breeze itself wafting like a sigh down the avenues—all of the noise and life and movement in the world was pulled into him, gently, and he felt himself expanding to hold it and extending farther out and, even though he had no window and was shut close inside the gray fabric walls of his tiny portion of the office, that no longer made any difference at all.

He'd left that evening feeling light and open and—inexplicably—joyous.

He'd returned the next morning to find an email that had been sent to him—sent to everyone—asking company members to refrain from leaving anonymous gifts such as flowers for fellow employees. The note explained, with reasoned language, that some employees might be allergic to such things and other employees may feel threatened by anonymous gifts. The note also explained that morale in the department would be better if the workday were kept predictable and free of surprises that might disturb others, no matter how well-intentioned such surprises may have been.

He'd returned the morning after that to find his desk just as he'd left it, except for a neat, square sticky note on the seat of his chair that read simply, in looping red script, "Thank you."

❧

There is no such thing as magic. There is no such thing as fate, or kismet, or destiny. Anyone with reasonable sensibilities will tell you this. And yet, once in a great while, there occurs a kind of practical happenstance that looks very much to the untrained eye like the simple magic of fate.

In Jules's life, this had happened exactly twice. The first time occurred not long ago, on a dreary day when the rain banged in fistfuls against the plate glass window, and all morning the shop had been empty of people, and, even so, he and 'Trice had turned on the velvet lamps to chase out the dimness. He had heard the door bells shimmer and seen Irene coming in with a man on her arm and he'd ducked quickly into the kitchen—Irene terrified him, loud as she was, and broad-mouthed, and never completely present—to watch as she'd dragged the poor man, confused and pitiful as a wet puppy, to the counter to replace his coffee.

The second time occurred on the occasion of the man's second visit to the bakery. He came alone this time, smiled and ate a cookie and closed his eyes in pleasure like a cat. He did not stay long, but Jules felt in his mouth and his belly and his knees when the man smiled. Actually, the second time occurred upon his leaving.

After the front door had slapped closed with a jangle of bells, after the man was entirely gone, Jules crept from the kitchen to inspect the place where he had been sitting. Once again, the man had cleaned the area so well that not a trace of him remained.

"I can't decide if you're adorable or pathetic," 'Trice said, watching him from behind the counter.

"Adorable, then," Jules mumbled, peering at the table as if it might suddenly yield something it had been hiding.

"Pathetic it is, then. Until you actually *do* something about this."

She tossed a paper cup at him. It cuffed him lightly on the shoulder and went rolling under the table.

"Stray Gay doesn't even know you *exist*," 'Trice harped. "To him, you're just an invisible elf baking delicious, invisible cookies in your invisible hollow tree."

"The cookies aren't invisible," Jules said under his breath. "He knows about the cookies."

On his knees, going after the cup, he saw it: a glint of silver on the floor, a ring of keys.

He scooped it up and into his pocket so deftly not even 'Trice would notice, then tossed the cup back at her and, when he flipped back through the swinging kitchen door he called, "Can it!" at her in such a way that neither she nor he was sure if he was referring to binning the cup or stopping the rest of her lecture.

Either way, 'Trice was quiet.

In the safety of his pocket, Jules's fingers curled around his prize. He held the ring of keys like a secret in his hand: warm and sharp, heavy and real.

Three

HE'D LOST HIS KEYS. Apartment, mailbox, bike lock and the strange little key he'd found on the sidewalk one day and decided to keep because it was the key, he'd thought at the time, to something he couldn't even imagine, a reminder of whatever was out there waiting for him that he couldn't yet name. It wasn't a matter of many keys, for sure, but, upon discovering they were missing—which he didn't do until late that evening, upon arriving home, fishing in his pocket while balancing his briefcase and newspaper and a lopsided bag of groceries, then putting everything down and really digging—Teddy had felt as if some important part of him was suddenly gone.

Of course, he'd gotten the doorman to let him into the apartment and had immediately set about his nightly business as a distraction. He'd changed out of his suit and into the T-shirt and pair of ratty sweats in which he liked to sleep, put away all the perishables from the market, leafed pointlessly through the files in his briefcase and polished his dress shoes and left them on the mat just inside his front door, all before allowing himself to lapse into a mild, pacing panic and fruitless mental step-retracing.

Tomorrow, he would have to make time during his lunch hour to carefully retrace his steps and find his key ring. And, just in case, he would also have to call the building super and order new apartment and mailbox keys and buy a new bike lock.

It was no big matter, he reassured himself, but there was nothing he could do about the loss of the mysterious little Hope Key.

❧

You might imagine that these keys, the ones Teddy lost, the ones Jules found, are symbolic in this tale, that the transfer of these keys will unlock something between the two men who've held them. You might even imagine that somehow, by some chance of fate, Teddy's mysterious Hope Key opens Jules's apartment. Certainly it should, you might think, open his heart. You must let go of that silly fantasy, for such magical coincidence will not come to pass here. We who are telling you this story are pragmatists and, more importantly, your own experience should tell you that life almost never unfolds so neatly or symmetrically.

This is something in which Jules firmly believed, that life's coincidences were simply that, and that such coincidences contained no hint of design or rightness or serendipity. Yet he kept the keys in his right-hand pocket and, in quiet moments of his day, allowed his thumb to rub against the warm metal. He imagined that he was polishing a soft groove into the key tops, imagined burnishing the jagged bumps of the keys until they no longer knew the locks for which they'd been cut, but only the shape of his thumb and the constant, slight pressure he exerted upon them, so that, he imagined, when he returned them to their owner—*if* he could part with them—they'd be worn and soft and dully shining, and would fit nothing but his own hand.

Return to me, he found himself singing under his breath as he gently stirred cream into a pot of brown, bubbling sugar at the stove.

Morning light was just beginning to sliver in through the tiny slatted windows on the east wall of the kitchen, and Jules could hear the hum gradually pick up: the city's taxis and rushing bikes and quick-clicking heels on the pavement building to a steady music.

He had always been an early riser, so baker's hours had come quite naturally to him. It was this hour—still gray even in summertime, when the city was slowly cranking into motion, when he felt the solitude and stillness of the dawn hours cracking open and falling away—it was this hour that was his favorite.

Come back to me, come back to me, come back, he sang, investing the song with all his belief. He sang the melody clean out of the words until nothing was left but a soft, breathless chant, an invocation. Jules was not entirely sure to whom he was calling—the image in his head shifted between Andy, whose presence it was his ritual to conjure in the lonely hours of the early morning as he worked, and the soft-spoken, dark-eyed, key-losing customer who'd begun to haunt him.

This morning, he might even have been calling himself, for as his body moved on its own memory, he felt his thinking self fade and blow away like dust. He kneaded butter to a soft spread, then folded and rolled and folded and rolled the dough for the croissants. He set the caramel to cool, creamed butter and sugar by hand, lovingly mixed a dark chocolate cake batter and coiled paper sleeves into a pan for the cupcakes. His hands, his arms, his lower back all worked without his guidance, knowing by heart the movements of stir and stretch and stroke. He closed his eyes. He worked tenderly. He moved like a lover.

Andy was warm and lanky and summery against him. He wrapped his arms, muscled and deep brown, around Jules's waist, dipped his fingertips beneath his waistband and stroked small, teasing circles there. A ghost of breath, a little wet, golden staccato, curled against Jules's throat. His skin remembered touch—no one had touched him like this since Andy—and rose in delighted, skittery gooseflesh between his hipbones and across his belly. He felt Andy's mouth on the back of his neck, a sweet kiss and bite that made his throat close and a warm *ache ache ache* throb inside him.

Jules scraped the cooled caramel into the butter and beat it together, fiercely, by hand, until he was aching and sweating and tears stung the corners of his eyes.

He knew if he stretched his hand back to touch Andy's cheek, it would be gone. The whole of the moment, and of Andy, and even the whole of Jules himself, felt vapor-thin, but Jules's body remembered so clearly in these moments that, if he were careful, if he did not move to touch or look, he could feel Andy for long minutes at a time, long blissful minutes that filled him with a bitter, wanting pang and a ghost-memory on his skin and left him shaking and very hard and too full of his own breath.

"I've lost my mind," Teddy told 'Trice.

"Then you're probably not missing much," she said.

"My keys are missing. I lost them yesterday. I'm going crazy." The bakery was one stop on a long key-finding itinerary he was trying to squeeze into his lunch break, but 'Trice was already pulling him a shot of espresso and rooting for a little curl of lemon peel for the saucer. "And I got the joke, by the way, I'm just not acknowledging it because it wasn't funny."

She laughed. "Oho! The puppy bites back!"

Teddy leveled his best, most serious glare. He came off looking rather pitiful.

"Oh, you are twisted up, honey," 'Trice said. "In that case, on the house." She slid the espresso toward him. "I'm going to go check with the big man to see if he found them. BRB."

Despite himself, Teddy felt the urgency filter out of him as he waited. He'd already made the calls to replace the keys he needed. This was no big loss. Nothing his life couldn't absorb, anyway.

After several loud, metallic crashes, 'Trice returned.

"I'm sorry, Cupcake, nobody has seen those keys. But the boss sent this out for you. He's sympathetic." She turned toward the kitchen and shouted, "I think he's actually feeling *guilty!* I think he *stole* those keys!" She paused. "And baked them inside a pie!"

Another loud crash from the kitchen made her turn back to Teddy, snickering. "That is so fun. Here. Take a break. It's going to work out."

The cupcake she pushed across the counter looked nothing like the dainty yellow one he'd first had. This one was large, a deep brown cake topped with a swirl of pecan-colored frosting, a pearly nugget of caramel and a dollop of soft chocolate nestled together, all of it glistening with little sparkling chunks of… something like stars.

"Salt," 'Trice said. "Trust us. Chocolate cake with salted caramel frosting. You. Will. Die."

"I'm not ready to die," Teddy said, widening his eyes and putting on his most earnest face.

"Get your affairs in order." 'Trice nudged the cupcake more firmly in his direction.

"Thanks," he said to her back as she whisked into the kitchen, leaving him entirely alone in the quiet shop front.

Teddy sat at the little table by the window, the one he now thought of as *his* table. He dipped his finger into the frosting, taking a bit of caramel and chocolate. He licked gingerly, four little licks, then gave up to himself entirely and sucked his whole finger into his mouth. After peeling back the paper wrapper, he bit into the cupcake, which fell apart on his tongue. The frosting was smooth, with a dark, sweet taste, but the little chunks of salt on top bit at him and made his eyes water in the sweetest way. He felt it, the crushing ache in his throat that made swallowing hard, a deep missingness he knew was not about his keys. He tasted bitterness, and wistfulness, and longing, and sugary warmth and desire, and all of it washed inside him like a wave and made the hairs on his arms stand on end. He ate slowly, but without stopping, because he couldn't bear to lose, not even for a moment, the sensation of the soft cake and velvety frosting and poignant salt burn in his mouth. He felt the shiver of fingers trailing slowly up the insides of his thighs, felt the skin at the back of his neck wake to a wet kiss. He felt his stomach turning over, felt his whole body reaching for someone, wanting desperately to be filled. He felt unfillable. He felt hollowness, groaned with it, and the little cake was no match for the space expanding inside him, his depthless, blind, sensate need.

He put his tongue to the palm of his hand and licked off the chocolate, its sweetness cut by the tang of his own sweat. He inhaled deeply; the scent of his own skin mixed with sugar and chocolate ruffed up a hot flush on his belly and thighs. He sucked the skin between his fingers, caught between joyfulness and a desire to weep. His own tongue felt foreign there, as if a stranger's mouth were on him, sucking gently, but nothing was enough.

"Good?" 'Trice asked, leering at him from over the counter.

Teddy couldn't bring himself to feel embarrassed. "Ohhhhh, my god," he groaned, without taking his hand from his mouth.

"You've got a little something there." 'Trice motioned to the back of his hand. Teddy promptly flipped his hand over and lapped at the smudge on his skin. 'Trice snorted.

"Do you think," he said between licks, "I mean—don't you think— can I—I feel like I should meet him."

"Who?" 'Trice asked, though it was clear from her face she knew exactly to whom Teddy referred.

"You know, the brilliant pastry chef who did this. To me. Did *this* to me." He gestured at himself. He felt wanton, disheveled, pleasure-mussed.

"He doesn't do that," 'Trice said, glancing over her shoulder at the kitchen door. "Meet people. He doesn't. He stays in there," she raised her voice to a shout, "even though I keep telling him to come out here and meet his adoring public! But he won't listen to *me!*"

"I'm going to go back there. I have to meet him."

"I wouldn't do that if I were you," 'Trice said. "Not if you ever want another free cupcake in this town again."

There was a clatter from the kitchen. Teddy moved to rise, but sat back down quickly, reddening. He pretended to think about 'Trice's warning, but she couldn't have stopped him if he'd decided to go, if he'd been able to stand up and walk, if he hadn't been embarrassingly—and this fact had swept upon him, a little shock, since he'd been so overcome and warm and tingly from the cupcake—he hadn't noticed that he was embarrassingly, incredibly, insistently hard.

'Trice leered at him. As if she knew. Teddy went even redder.

"It's okay," she whispered. "He has a blog. Google it."

∽

Pastry-Whipped: Adventures in Sugar by a Dedicated Crumpet Strumpet
by Chef Jules Burns of Buttermilk Bakery
March 25: Coming Out as a Pastry Puff, or, Baking with Lust

A recipe will only get you so far. A recipe tells you how much, and how long and how hard. But even these are, of course, matters that must vary from situation to situation, person to person, desire to desire. Certain days call for harder and longer—it's often a question of barometric pressure, mine or that of the atmosphere—or mood, again, mine or that of the atmosphere.

I don't bake with recipes anymore. I write them down, of course, some approximation of what I do, so that if I am made bedridden by a police horse or tuberculosis (it has always been my dream to die a lingering, dramatic death like the great Victorian heroine I am in my head), my assistant can achieve something close to what Buttermilk customers have come to expect. And many people will tell you that baking—unlike cooking, which is to baking as milk is to crème brûlée—is a science, is about measures and calculations and exactitude. To them I say, You need to loosen up. *Actually, what I mean is,* You probably need to get laid.

Some basic understanding of kitchen science will, of course, get you far in your passionate improvisations. Knowing the stages through which sugar passes as it heats, understanding what happens to an egg when you beat it, figuring out the difference between baking powder and baking soda, this kind of basic knowledge will help you, in the same way that a painter must understand how paint behaves, how color changes as it dries, how... I don't know, since I'm not a painter, but I'm sure there are some very specific things painters must know in order to make art. The art, however, comes from passion. One needs to be adventurous, to be in touch with one's ingredients, to feel textures and tastes intuitively, to anticipate needs, like a lover. One needs a healthy dose of lust.

You can taste that. I believe you can taste everything—tenderness, love, sex, desire, anger, bitterness, passion—that goes into the creation of a good thing. A good pastry chef can transmit that. But that means a good chef feels that, too, carries those things around in his body, exposes himself through his baking, nurtures other people with all he is and all he feels. A good pastry chef can't be in the closet, not any of himself. (My assistant 'Trice would say that becoming a pastry chef is a great way of coming out of the closet. Because, she would say, it's really, really gay. Like, we should call this place a gay-kery. That gay. She may be right.)

A good chef, if I do say so myself, is probably really good in bed. Or maybe it's just me.

I had a hard time coming out. I was a milk-skinned, high-voiced teen who spent his time in fashionable hats and large brooches, in a high school full of Neanderthal jocks who took great pleasure in tossing me into dumpsters and creaming me in the face with cold milk (if I was lucky) or fists (if I wasn't). And that was before I came out. Figuring out I was gay meant, to my teenaged mind, a likelihood of losing the love of my friends and family (I didn't) and spending my teen years alone and pining for beefy Indiana-style straight boys who were just a little scared of me (I did). But come out I did, and then I figured out how to be proud (thanks, Dad), and then I went away to school and figured out how to fall in love (rapidly, deeply), and what made me happy (baking, kissing, trying on clothes, in that order), and what I liked to do with the men I fell in love with when things progressed past tentative hand-holding (a subject for an entirely different blog). And because I had to work so hard at it, and because I had to do so much thinking and exploring and soul-searching to get there, and because there weren't so many stories out there telling me what I should do or like or want or be because I wasn't like most of the people about whom stories were written (straight), I figured out how to understand myself and my desires, my lovers and their desires, in a way my straight friends never dared do. I figured out passion, in all parts of my life. And now I often think to myself, thank god I'm gay!

This week, I've been drawn to salt caramel, to its combination of sweetness and richness and wincing bite. I like to pair it with a sexy, espresso-laced chocolate, a little bitter, a little dirty. Butter and earth. Cake and cream. (Like my last relationship: innocent and sweet paired with rich and dirty. I'll let you guess which one was me.)

It's worth it to make your own caramel from scratch, and especially so using the really good stuff. If you can get fresh, organic cream and real butter from a local farmer, well, you know what I'd say about that. (I'd say do it.) Don't stir the sugar while it's caramelizing; you don't want to mix in the crystals that cling to the pot sides. Instead, just watch. Food porn. Sugar burlesque.

I actually get turned on watching caramel form. Is that TMI?

If you don't use up all the fresh caramel by spreading it onto your lover's belly (and elsewhere, like I would), then you've got enough to make this glorious salted caramel frosting. If you wind up licking it all out of the warm pot, you're out of luck and probably have to start over again. As for the pot-licking, I don't mean that as a dirty metaphor, but 'Trice would take it that way, and I've learned that I can't really control that, so take it as you will—I do have to say that I've done the pot-licking thing more than once, and generally have to resist even tasting the caramel now when I make it, because that is a really slippery slope. And again, I can hear 'Trice snorting at me. If you run out of caramel before you've made the frosting due to some miscalculation of your licking capacity, you can instead come to see us at Buttermilk and try a salted caramel and chocolate cupcake here.

Though you may want to eat it in privacy.

Unless you like it when people watch.

Which is the subject of a blog for another day.

❧

Instead of searching for his lost keys, which he figured were long gone by now anyway, Teddy headed back to his office and spent the afternoon reading through the old posts on Jules's blog and falling, perhaps, though he'd resist admitting it so soon, rather deeply in love (well, at least deeply in shy adoration) with a certain talented and witty pastry chef whom he'd never met. He composed and erased dozens of comments, all of which looked stupid when they were typed in black and white (*I totally had sex with that cupcake today.* No. *You're brilliant and brave and funny. Can I meet you?* No. *I bet you were the sweet and dirty one. Is that an option?* Absolutely not.), learning only that he had, for all these years, relied upon the expressiveness and sincerity of his wide eyes to achieve the perfect mix of flirty and charming upon which he'd always depended, and those qualities definitely did *not* translate into print.

ANONYMOUS: *Does your axiom also mean that someone who is really good in bed will also be a really good pastry chef? I am going to try one of your brilliant recipes and find out.*

He settled on this—just suggestive enough, with a wide margin of deniability and an earnest compliment, he thought, without going too far.

He spent the final hour of his workday fretting that the comment was, after all, trying too hard, quite stupid and otherwise extremely transparent and, on the side, making a list of the ingredients he would need to try the lemon and olive oil chiffon cake, the flavors of which he still couldn't get out of his head and which, since it was the first thing he'd tasted at Buttermilk, seemed the most fitting place to start his own trials.

When, that evening, he failed spectacularly (a soft peak was completely beyond his reach, especially since he was only working with a fork and a cereal bowl, and folding was for gentler souls than he, and eggs were really meant for scrambling anyway), he returned to the blog and posted, without allowing himself to second-guess or edit:

ANONYMOUS: *Epic fail. Unless that was a recipe for hockey pucks. Otherwise, I have empirical proof that only one half of your axiom holds true.*

He felt stupid and giddy, even though his comments were anonymous. But he kept his laptop open, kept refreshing the page and jumped so frantically when Jules replied to his comment an hour later that he nearly knocked over the table.

BBCHEF: *Either way I read your comment about the axiom, you still come out good in bed. Impressive, and probably the best anyone would hope for. Start with cookies, Grasshopper. Nobody gets good overnight.*

Four

Jules Burns's user picture was a fruit tart.

And perhaps Teddy *had* spent most of his Friday night on his laptop, scouring the blog—and the rest of the Internet—for information, or pictures or some hint of Jules Burns. Perhaps he had. And perhaps, as a result of reading the entire blog twice through (and finding nothing else of use on the Internet), he had begun to find this little fact meaningful. And rather funny. And one more bit of evidence in favor of his sneaking suspicion that Jules Burns was not only a brilliant pastry chef, but must also be the wonderful, delicious, flamingly man-loving, piercingly beautiful answer to Teddy's every dream.

A *fruit* tart. A fruit *tart*. A He-Is-Actually-a-Genius tart.

Teddy looked at the clock and ran a hand over his cheek, which was prickling already with the early start of scruff. In two more hours, he knew, the sun would rise. Teddy thought very seriously for three minutes about pulling a hat over his unslept mess of hair and riding his bike to the bakery to catch Jules on his way in. He'd pull up just as Jules was struggling to roll the heavy metal gate up and out of the window's way, and Teddy would jump off his bike and help, and Jules would be grateful, and Teddy would be dashing, and Jules would invite him inside to help make the… something… that required the both of them to put their hands into it at the same time, though Teddy could not decide if it would be doughy or creamy. Either way, Jules would press himself to Teddy's back and wrap his arms around him to show him how to do the squishing, with his breath hot and soft on the little hairs on the back of Teddy's neck, and he would whisper, *like this, do it this way, your arms are almost too strong for this.* And Teddy, his hands dripping with cream or dough, would turn around in the circle of Jules's arms and tilt his head and whisper that strong arms were very good for certain things and then he'd lift Jules gently onto the counter and kiss him.

Except. Except that every time Teddy got to this moment in the fantasy of turning around and whispering and softening his mouth (and he'd gotten here at least six times already), he'd want to look deep into Jules's eyes—and he'd discover that Jules's head was a giant fruit tart, a detail he'd somehow failed to notice in all the moments leading up to this ridiculous, horrifying climax.

That settled it, Teddy thought. He was going to meet Jules Burns.

The bakery was different on a Saturday. There were strollers, and people wearing tracksuits, and a general hubbub to which Teddy was definitely not accustomed. Behind the counter, someone had set up portable speakers to play bass-heavy pop music, and a very blond boy, crammed into denim booty shorts, was wiggling his hips to the music in what Teddy thought was a too-self-conscious way, tossing pastries from the case into brown paper bags and thrusting them at the distracted customers. The whole thing, Teddy thought sadly, was decidedly un-magical. But he'd come on a mission, so he waited in line behind a woman in pink velour pants, whose expensive-looking stroller contained a monstrously oversized baby who looked far too old to be strapped into the apparatus. The baby was wet with something viscous. He looked sticky and unpleasant. Teddy kept his distance.

When the customers ahead of him had cleared out and it was finally his turn, he realized that he'd never chosen his own order at Buttermilk.

"Where's 'Trice?" he asked the kid behind the counter, trying not to sound desperate.

"She doesn't work on Saturdays. That's always me," he said, thrusting his hand coquettishly at Teddy. "Avon. What do you want?" He gestured at the pastry case like a game show hostess, cocking one thin, pale eyebrow in Teddy's direction.

"Oh," Teddy said. "Well. What's good today?"

Avon put his hands on the counter and leaned forward. "All of it's always good, as far as I know. I don't eat any of it. These hips won't stand for it." He ran his hands down his sides, shimmying. Teddy tried not to roll his eyes at the kid, who was making him dizzy. He never seemed to stop moving.

"Coffee, please, black," Teddy said, suddenly embarrassed, suddenly unwilling to consume anything Avon might think would damage his hips, about which he'd never previously thought twice. "To stay."

"You got it, sir," Avon said, grabbing a mug and turning his back.

"And," Teddy said, reconsidering, and feeling stupid again, "one of those." He pointed at a jar of chocolate biscotti and held his hand in place until Avon glanced over his shoulder to see. Biscotti seemed like a relatively safe choice, hip-wise.

Avon nodded and finished spilling coffee into his mug, then tossed one of the cookies onto a plate, shoved both things across the counter, carelessly smacked some keys on the cash register and announced the total. Teddy gave him the money (which felt a little sordid, Teddy realized, since he'd never paid for anything here), dropped a bit in the tip jar and took his usual table, which, since most of the traffic in the bakery was takeout, was still empty.

He sat for almost an hour, gathering his nerve and nursing his coffee to no avail. Everything here was off today; without 'Trice around he felt as if he were in freefall. By the end of the hour, the bakery had mostly emptied, with only the occasional customer rushing in with a pitiful shiver of the door's silver bells. The space had finally started to feel warm and velvety-safe again. Avon kept to himself, folding scraps of paper into cranes and lining them up on the counter, pouring numerous free shots from the espresso machine and downing each one in a single, pleasureless gulp while glancing warily at the kitchen door like a hunted dog.

Teddy had given up and was wiping down his table with a folded napkin when it happened.

❧

Jules always hid in the kitchen on weekends. Saturdays and Sundays were the worst, not only because 'Trice had those days off and he was stuck with Avon, whom he neither liked nor trusted but simply tolerated, but also because the bakery was always full and bustling and loud until midday. And Avon insisted on playing that stupid dance music and swinging around the shop like a crazed monkey, wrecking whatever peaceful, lush vibe Jules had otherwise managed to cultivate. So Jules buried himself in work, whipping up buttercream for the week, filing bills in the back office, counting bricks of butter in the walk-in refrigerator.

By early afternoon, however, enough was enough. Every week it was the same routine, to the clock: At noon, Jules would holler at Avon to turn down the music, smack the kitchen door open and parade out, waving his arms dramatically, mostly because he knew Avon appreciated and best understood that kind of expression, and so it would have its intended effect. Avon would sigh loudly and turn off the speakers. Jules would make himself a cappuccino with two shots, then slink back to the relative peace of the kitchen and leave Avon alone—sullen and quiet—for the next few hours.

You might, if you are listening carefully, think you see this moment coming. Let us tell you up front that, if you are hoping for a first meeting, hoping for Jules to make his diva march out into the shop front and come face to face with Teddy, who has not yet finished mopping the crumbs and condensation from his table, hoping that the two will find each other this way and that the world will drop away and their eyes will meet and they will each *know*, in their bones, the meaning of the moment, well, you are going to be disappointed.

Here is what happened:

"Avon!" Jules started his usual hollering. "*Please* turn off that stuff *now!*"

Jules wiped his hands on the front of his apron and pulled at the strings to re-tie them more tightly over his waist, kicking the kitchen door open a little as he did so. As it swung, as he moved to storm out into what he thought was the empty shop front, he saw him, at his usual place by the window, studiously scrubbing the tabletop with a napkin. He wore a plaid button-down shirt, cotton so softened by age it was practically transparent, and graying jeans and a pair of old once-white tennis shoes, the laces of which had broken and been knotted together many times. The muscles and veins on his forearms stood out in shifting patterns under the skin as he scrubbed. He was focused, looking down, a little flushed, heavy-lashed and so casually beautiful.

Sunlight was pushing its way under the window awning and into the shop, glancing off the polished tabletops and the steel and glass of the bakery case, tossing itself upward and shattering through the colored glass beads. The shop was spattered with light, and that man was sitting in the middle of it, oblivious, with everything about him shining: his wiry hair and his lightly tanned skin flecked with sun, glowing like a beacon, anchored and still and warm and bright.

Jules saw all of this in the second it took the door to swing open; the light was unmoving and his own breath caught, as if time had skidded to a stop so he could see it all and jump back into the kitchen, clamping a hand over his own mouth to stop the noise of surprise. The man looked up, briefly, but it was too late; the door had already swung shut, and Jules, hand still against his mouth, breathed through his nose and watched through the door's crack as the man bent to scribble something on a napkin, then carefully and precisely centered the napkin on the table, gathered his bag onto his shoulder and left the shop.

The moment he'd left, Jules was out the kitchen door and striding past Avon to grab the napkin from the table. Mindlessly, he let his thumb worry the warm keys in his pocket while he looked, a little amused, a little mystified, at the drawing the man had left.

"What is it?" Avon said.

"I can't tell," Jules said and showed the napkin to Avon. "What is it?"

"That's totally a cricket," Avon said.

"Oh," said Jules, more mystified than ever. "A cricket?"

"They're supposed to be good luck?" Avon offered. "Maybe it's a luck thing?" Jules looked unsatisfied, but took the napkin with him when he swept back into the kitchen, entirely forgetting to make his coffee.

"Or maybe it's a praying mantis," Avon called after him. "The lady mantis bites the head off her mate after they do it!"

As he did every weekend, Jules thought very seriously about just how and when and for which reason he should fire Avon.

Teddy's life had been composed of a series of near misses.

There had been, of course, plenty of times when he had, proverbially at least, smacked the ball out of the park—exams, first dates, job interviews. But there was something more poignant and telling and truly *him* about the near miss, something more personal, closer to the bone. Perhaps it was the lack left afterward that felt familiar, so apparent, like a lost tooth; perhaps it was that his life so often fluttered in the raw gap, as if he, like the tip of a tongue, were drawn to that vacant place. It was the unsaid words he swallowed before trying them out—*I love you, too,* he'd almost said once, though he hadn't been sure he'd meant it, and so had closed his mouth and petted the boy's cheek fondly and sadly, and things had, rather rapidly, shaken apart after that. It was the doors he'd closed when he left home—the dream of a painting major he'd abandoned when his father had worn that brow-furrowed look, and the question he'd wanted to ask his mother when he hugged her goodbye for what seemed like the last time, leaving her behind in their camel-colored house—*are you happy here?*—thinking better of it and replacing those words with a kiss to the top of her head and a hard squeeze of her shoulders before he turned and left to start his life in New York. It was the lost keys, the missed train, the missed glance, the chance untaken.

He felt it, always, the grate and tug of too-empty space, the missing thing he couldn't name, the thing that had swept by him without stopping on its way to fill bigger and better lives than his.

That day in the bakery, Teddy knew keenly, had been one of those near misses.

He'd been sitting at his usual table, cleaning up and getting ready to leave, having finally given up the plan to storm the kitchen and meet the chef, when the back door had swung violently open as if to herald the coming of something monumental and then, just as violently, had snapped closed without revealing a thing. He'd felt the strongest sense of presence behind the door, presence that refused to make itself real. He'd felt a kind of slipping-off, a falling-down, an *almost-but-not-quite* that burned him inside as intensely as an unrealized sneeze. He'd known, in that moment, that his life had sustained another near miss. That, had the timing been slightly different, he might have met the man for whom he was looking, or might at the very least have caught a glimpse of him.

Instead, he'd given up to go home, but left a gift, a calling card, the napkin containing the little scribbled doodle of the grasshopper, to say that he'd been there, that it had been *him*. It was a half-step forward into chance. As if Jules might remember and recognize him.

Start with cookies, Grasshopper. Nobody gets good overnight.

He had. Started with cookies, that is. He'd tried them the night following his failed lemon cake. And Jules had been right—these were more successful, though half of them had darkened too much on the bottom and tasted a bit like soot; but Teddy had managed to mix the dough and dollop it onto the cookie sheet and felt, all in all, fairly accomplished when the oven spat out something that closely resembled a batch of cookies. Nothing so heartbreakingly tender and melty and sexy as the cookie Jules had made, he thought. He experienced no rush of blood, no overwhelming flood of desire and longing and decadence overtook him when he bit, with considerable difficulty, into the hard little nugget once it had cooled. At least the cookies were recognizable as food. Hard, burned, sorry food, but food nonetheless. It had been a start; he gave himself that much.

He had, he thought, started *something*.

Pastry-Whipped: Adventures in Sugar by a Dedicated Crumpet Strumpet
by Chef Jules Burns of Buttermilk Bakery
March 29: As Long as He Kneads Me

I've been unfaithful. I've strayed. I've done things I never thought I'd do. I've temporarily flown the pastry coop. And boy, are my arms tired.

I've been baking bread, which is quite outside the realm of my pastry training—usually, one spends a lot of time thinking about how to keep everything tender, how not to develop the gluten. But I've been antsy lately. I've been kneady. I've been longing for a firmer touch, longing to roll against something alive and resilient and fleshy and warm, to press against a little resistance, to watch it rise and grow under my hand. It is spring, after all.

Bread baking is a special art. It's all about give and take, about receptivity and being attuned to the needs of another living being. You are, after all, working with a living thing (yeast), nurturing it and encouraging it to grow. Good kneading is essential to good bread—by kneading the dough, you're gently stretching the fibers, developing the gluten, bringing forth that texture of only the most terrific loaves, equal parts chewy and tender. There is nothing like the feeling of a good kneading session: It works out the muscles across your back and all through your arms, right down to your wrists. If you do it right, it even makes your thighs and glutes ache, which I can only assume means they're getting prettier and stronger as you work. You must be energetic, but in a languid, fluid way. You must be strong, but in a manner that yields, that entices and encourages rather than forces.

A good session with your dough will leave you sweaty, a little sore and spent.

When I first started dating (which was not until college, years later than most of my peers, mostly because I seemed to be the only gay teenager in all of Indiana), I had to learn to seduce. I'd waited so long for someone to want me that, when the chance finally came, I jumped in with both feet and a frightening amount of desperate enthusiasm and need, and wound up scaring off more than one initially interested suitor. The problem, I finally figured out, was that I was focusing entirely on myself. Once I let go of that, once I began to trust that my suitor would do that for me, I was free to focus on him *and his needs. Instead of desperately worrying whether a man would kiss me, and then, once he* did, whether he would kiss me again, I began instead to notice the subtle ways in which his body pulled toward me or pushed me away, depending upon where I let my hand or mouth stray. More pressure or less, a touch here, a lick there, a small sound I might let escape into his ear—I could learn the effects of these things on his body, I could map his sweet spots by his whimpers, chart his desires and know him better than he might know himself. And in this way, I could kiss him into anything.

It was a matter of being receptive, being responsive, but in a very different way from how one usually imagines it. Responsiveness isn't about you, isn't about your reaction to another body, isn't really about what you do at all. It's about being completely tuned in to that other body, its possibilities and its desires, and giving yourself over to it entirely.

It's like that with kneading bread. It's not about what I may do—not about, in the end, a kneading technique or a formula for rising times. Instead, it's about being aware of the dough as a separate, living being, knowing what it wants and what it might ask of me next.

Now my kitchens, both at home and at Buttermilk, are filled with fresh bread, dozens of beautiful, golden loaves, crusty on the outside, tender inside (as am I, I can assure you), and in the sheer volume of what I've produced, I am confronted by the evidence of the passionate single-mindedness with which I've recently approached my spring friskiness. I suppose a healthier and less carb-laden alternative would be to channel all of this energy into a new beau, but not a soul has been knocking down my door, so I'm left with the task of finding a use for all this glorious, yeasty, chewy bread.

I've made quite a bit of French toast for friends, and chocolate bread (fry a thick slice of good bread in some butter, melting a handful of bittersweet chocolate into the bread's pores as you do—you'll thank me once your knees stop shaking), and my assistant 'Trice and I have eaten more than our share of simple, warm slabs of bread slathered in good butter this week. But I've settled on bread pudding as the place to put most of it. It's a simple enough dish on the surface, whose flavors can be *made quite complex and layered by pairing it with the right sauce. It's unpretentious. It's honest. It's got substance.*

So this week, I'm playing around with bread puddings of all kinds. And I'm still baking bread. Because it's still spring, and I'm still feeling strong and energetic and, well, just a bit frisky. So, bread it is. At least until the right fellow starts knocking on my door. Maybe you know him. He's unpretentious, and honest and he's got substance. Simple on the outside, but complex underneath. And just a little saucy.

ANONYMOUS: *Grasshopper here. I tried the cookies… success! Or, at least, not hockey pucks! I was even able to eat a few of the less burned ones! You are my baking Jedi master. (I know I'm mixing my cultural references. Go with it.) And since I'm unpretentious and complex and honest and very willing, I'm going to be your best student ever. I'm ready for my next assignment. Bread baking? You make it sound really hot. (This is me being a little saucy.)*

Andy's chin was whiskery and warm against Jules's bare knee. He had drifted into his evening nap in his usual place, with Jules's left hand scrubbing idly at the back of his neck. Though Jules had not been wild about a dog when he'd first met Andy, he'd grown to love these quiet times at night, just the two of them on the couch, with Andy's head growing heavier against him as he drowsed and the little humid puffs of breath slowing and deepening. He loved the little whimpers and kicks that indicated Andy must be dreaming, though of what Jules couldn't imagine, since Andy had never chased a rabbit or swum in a stream or run in a field and, at this point, he was kind of a codger and preferred a nap on the couch over most any other activity except eating. But Jules loved the little body near him, its warmth and weight and need; he loved the already-knowing between them, the routine of their lives together, the expectation each had built around the other. Evenings with Andy were peaceful and lamplit and private.

But this was knocking him sideways a bit. Though his laptop burned against the tops of his thighs, he neither wanted to shut it off (because he could not stop rereading the comment) nor move it (because he would disturb Andy), so he simply let it burn there. He had to reply. The little backflips his stomach was doing told him that. But he'd already made several false starts, all of which ended in erasure, and he just couldn't think. So he dove.

BBChef: *Not bread, young Grasshopper. Eagerness is endearing, but you're moving a bit too fast, and that will ruin your reputation. Didn't your mother warn you about moving too fast? The recipe for Sticky Date Bread Pudding is a good start. It's hard to go wrong, it uses simple ingredients, and you can get your hands dirty in some very delicious ways. Try the recipe I posted, with the bourbon sauce. Use a good bourbon. Taste it first, to be sure. Taste it again to be really sure. At least, that's what I do. One needs to be very sure before diving in. I like a man who's very sure. Or, at least, a man who's very drunk. (I've never had a student before, but I'm picking up the gauntlet you've thrown. I think I have a matching gauntlet somewhere. Gauntlets must be worn as a set, or they are ridiculous. Otherwise, I'll have to wear oven mitts, and those are decidedly less fashionable.)*

He, Grasshopper, must have been sitting by his computer, too, because a few minutes later, he replied.

Anonymous: *Sticky Date? Really? There are so many things I could say to that, but I'm restraining myself and leaving right now to get bread and a bunch of the other stuff, which, being your humble student, I do not have on hand in my kitchen the way I imagine you probably do. I have salami and a half-eaten container of Chinese takeout and probably a very old jar of mustard. The yellow kind. But I can't imagine even you, with your magic baking skills, could do much with that combination. If I knew where you lived, I'd come relieve you of some of your sex-bread. (Did I really just type that out loud? I apologize. Sort of. But, because I am honest and unpretentious, I'll admit that I'm also sort of serious. Your bread sounds amazing.) I do, however, have a good bourbon on hand, which I've tested before, but will test again, just to be both very sure and very drunk. Because you asked. But I notice that you simply assume I'm a man... how daring and saucy of you. Oh, and the fashionableness of the oven mitts depends on what you are wearing with them, of course. But I won't ask, "What are you wearing?" because I am a gentleman and this is a public forum.*

BBCHEF: *I did assume you were a man. I apologize. But the contents of your kitchen as you've listed them indicate you are either a man or a four-year-old with a drinking problem. Maybe it was just wishful thinking. At least, I hope you are not a four-year-old alcoholic. Besides, you just called yourself a gentleman. And for your information, I am wearing nothing but a pair of boxers, oven mitts and a very sleepy dachshund. Which is what I wear at the bakery, too.*

ANONYMOUS: *Oh, Cruella, no wonder everything at your bakery tastes so amazing, if that's your uniform. Do you allow kitchen visits? I'd like to see this.*

BBCHEF: *The dachshund is very much alive, although the dedication with which he's approached the project of sleep would lead one to assume otherwise. So you don't get to call me Cruella. At least, not for that. Wait. You've been to my bakery?*

ANONYMOUS: *Frequently. I'm your biggest flan.*

BBCHEF: *You stole that joke.*

ANONYMOUS: *I want to take you into custardy.*

BBCHEF: *Right. Cute. You're a hack. Go buy your bread and get cooking.*

ANONYMOUS: *I thought I was cooking.*

BBCHEF: *Very funny. Go.*

Five

IN THIS WORLD JULES BURNS valued five things beyond all else. First was his father, Ray, whom he loved more than any person who'd ever lived, whose ability to see clean through him was knife-sharp and whose reaction to Jules's decision to leave college in his junior year (because, as he told Ray, he felt as if he were broken into disparate pieces, as if he were located only in his head, with a ridiculous and passive body dangling below it, and he missed doing things with his hands, missed the scents and the textures and the tastes of the real world, missed making something solid. Nobody, it seemed, in college was *real* in that way. Everything was performance, was distance. When he reached out, in his loneliest or happiest moments, there was nothing to touch, and he felt, as a result, dried up and gone, papery as an old leaf, easily crumbled into nothing) was to sigh and say, *Okay, kid, what is it that's really going to make you happy?* Jules had cried, as much in relief at his father's acceptance as in grief at the thought of finally giving up everything by which he'd defined himself for so many years, and Ray had simply whispered into the phone, *hey, hey, now,* and somehow in that moment all had begun to feel mended.

Ray was the first. The second was the rest of his family, Annette and Nathan and Zack, who cared for his father and cared for him, who hugged him like wild bears when they saw him on the holidays and gave him gifts that were at once entirely wrong for him (Nathan's gifts of overly musky cologne, Annette's rococo faux gold floral centerpiece, Zack's mix-tapes of heavy metal or boy band pop) and yet so painstakingly chosen and laden with the intensity of their wishes for him that he could do nothing but love the gifts and their givers with unreasonable joy.

The third was Andy the dachshund: who was small and always shivering or snoring; who needed him completely and without question; who, despite his great age, romped to the door and bounced in circles every time Jules came through it at the end of his long day; whose bark was hoarse and high-pitched and mousy and frightened absolutely no one; on whose collar Jules had hung a small silver locket with a picture of Andy the man tucked inside; and whose name, each time Jules called him for a meal or a scolding or a walk, pushed up an aching lump in the back of Jules's throat that he knew was a memory, a hard, compact lump that would take hours to melt away, no matter how much Jules stroked the soft fur of Andy's muzzle and whispered and whispered into his neck.

The fourth and fifth were memories: the dimmed and softly polished image of his grandmother and the still-stark, steel-sharp thought of Andy.

There were exactly five things which Jules valued beyond all else, and these were they, and in the quiet interstices of his day, he brought them out, careful treasures, and held them up to the light like glittering things, and let them do their work on him, making him feel loved and loving, and twisted with not-enough, and empty, and so full of the world that he would start, every time, quietly to cry.

In that hour without conversation, still on his couch, Andy still snoring against his thigh, his laptop still burning there as he waited for the notes from Grasshopper to begin again (*go buy your bread and get cooking*, he'd written, without considering the long emptiness that might ensue), he was surprised to find that he could not make his thoughts stick for long to any of those five favorite things.

Instead, he thought about how his insides had begun—in a way that felt both gradual and sudden, sea-change and earthquake—to feel like springtime, awake and open and full of an about-to-bloomness. He thought about the fact that when ice melted, the water it became went running past its own former containment, took up more space in the world, *moved itself*. He thought about hands: Andy's long-fingered, muscled, brown hands spread across his hips, yes, but other hands, too, hands that were olive and nimble and well-manicured and small and square; and though he didn't know whose hands they were (and, though he felt rather stupid admitting it, he allowed himself alternately to imagine they were the hands of the fumbling, gentle-looking man in his bakery and the sure, suave hands of Grasshopper himself, and sometimes other hands, stranger hands, unclaimed hands, hands wandering across his pale skin because they wanted to map him by feel, simply and beautifully to locate him in the world through their touch—and *oh*, how he missed being touched), he wanted to fold his own hands inside them and feel warm. He thought that maybe he had begun, in little ways, to thaw.

BBCHEF: *I imagine that at the moment you are still on your trek for bread and almonds, but just in case you read this in time, I forgot to mention that you should buy real, unprocessed Medjool dates and pit and chop them yourself. There is a difference. And if you can appreciate dates, you'll discover that nothing compares to Medjool—so much meatier and mildly sweeter and more meltingly tender. And don't forget to take the pits out before you chop them, or you're in for a horrible experience. And maybe even some danger.*

He tried to stop himself from writing first, tried to ask himself to wait with some dignity, as if he didn't care, as if he weren't bent over his laptop, wild-eyed as a lunatic, refreshing the screen and chanting under his breath something that sounded an awful lot like *come on, come on, Grasshopper, come back.* And when he felt his reserve failing, he had, at least, tried to sound as if he were speaking as a chef, as if his investment was in ensuring that the food was as glorious as it could be.

It was clear to Jules, however, that maintaining this version of himself—a little cool, in control, professional and decidedly *not* desperate—was not in the cards.

Moments later, when Grasshopper replied (as if he were lurking there, too, waiting for Jules to speak first; as if the two were waging a game of double-dare and Jules had simply folded first), *cool* and *in control* seemed to sail permanently beyond his reach.

GRASSHOPPER: *We are psychically connected. Because standing in the market, faced with the choice between a plastic tub of pitted, chopped dates or a bin of pick-your-own whole Medjool dates, I was sorely tempted by the tub, then thought to myself that if you were standing next to me, as my own official Date Guy for the evening, you might have literally smacked the back of my head if I'd even looked in the plastic tub's direction. So I did what I thought you'd not-so-gently encourage me to do and bought the fresher, whole Medjools.*

BBCHEF: *You did the right thing. I really would have smacked you. And "Date Guy"? Really? (Nice screen name, by the way. Don't think I didn't notice that.)*

GRASSHOPPER: *Date Guy, sure. Because you strike me as an expert, and I am an innocent. I'm young and fresh-faced and I want to learn all about this big, new World of Dates. And I imagine you would corrupt me with your extensive Date Experience and impart to me your vast Date Knowledge, and we would have a stormy, passionate affair during which we did unspeakably sexy things with date paste and built monuments to our love out of date pits and baked a lot of scones or something. And then one day, you'd meet a younger, fresher-faced fellow who didn't know anything about dates, and you'd leave me for him, and the two of you would abscond to Medjool together, leaving me alone. And dateless.*

BBCHEF: *That's quite a story. And I don't think Medjool is actually a place.*

GRASSHOPPER: *I was thinking Medjool was a verb. And I'm not speaking to you. I'm still angry about the absconding and the Medjooling. You're going to have to make this up to me. I was really hurt.*

BBCHEF: *How can I make this up to you, this wrong I did in your weird imagination?*

GRASSHOPPER: *Make up for leaving me for a younger, fresher cream puff? I can think of some things you can do. Sticky dates, for instance. ;)*

BBCHEF: *Did you just virtually wink at me? That is so virtually tacky.*

GRASSHOPPER: *Well, I am tacky. Because of your dates. I'm pitting and chopping the dates and typing one-handed so I don't get my keyboard sticky, too. But I'm very, very sticky right now.*

BBCHEF: *No comment. There's enough comment in your comment for the both of us.*

GRASSHOPPER: *It seems inevitable. I've been following your instructions and somehow ended up all dirty. And I might have tested quite a bit of the bourbon this evening. Just to be sure. But you told me to do that, too.*

BBCHEF: *So your sticky drunkenness is my responsibility?*

GRASSHOPPER: *Absolutely. Every time I get sticky and drunk, I say to myself, "This is all the fault of that amazing, deliciously sexy pastry chef I've never met. But would like to. Meet, that is." That's what I say. Did I just say that out loud?*

BBCHEF: *I think you did type that, yes. Deliciously sexy?*

GRASSHOPPER: *I imagine so. I've eaten your cupcakes on at least two occasions. Your cupcakes are deliciously sexy. They achieved things. For me.*

BBCHEF: *Then it appears we already know each other very well. I don't let just any man eat my cupcakes.*

GRASSHOPPER: *You run a bakery. I hardly believe that. But since I've currently got a privilege you don't afford to other men, if I come to the bakery tomorrow, will you come out to meet me?*

BBCHEF: *How will I know it's you and not just some crazed interloper?*

GRASSHOPPER: *I'll be the one wearing the red carnation.*

BBCHEF: *Carnations are so high school prom, Grasshopper. You'll have to do better than that.*

GRASSHOPPER: *I'll be the one with the red rose in my teeth? Do you tango?*

GRASSHOPPER: *I'll be the one carrying the fluffy red puppy?*

GRASSHOPPER: *I'll be the superfine one? (Get it? It's a sugar joke.)*

BBCHEF: *Stop now, you monster, before you destroy Tokyo.*

GRASSHOPPER: *But I was just getting to the part about the sticky buns.*

BBCHEF: *Exactly.*

GRASSHOPPER: *I'm putting this in the oven now. But this isn't over. You haven't heard the last of me yet. I'm going to be in your bakery every day until I get to meet you.*

BBCHEF: *You've crossed the line from Confident and Forward and into Slightly Frightening.*

GRASSHOPPER: *I'll be the one with the sticky buns.*

BBCHEF: *You just couldn't stop yourself, could you?*

GRASSHOPPER: *No. No, I could not. I'm licking the date mush off my fingers and I've lost all self-control.*

BBCHEF: *Put. The bourbon. Down.*

"I *saw* you," 'Trice said, tossing a paper cup at Jules's back as he pulled himself a double shot.

"Saw me what?" Jules said.

"Gettin' your *flirt* on," 'Trice crooned, and Jules went red, though he had no idea to what she could be referring. He'd spent most of his weekend in the back of the bakery or curled up on his couch with Andy. He'd not even ventured to the market, opting instead for cobbling together his evening meals from the motley collection of dried grains and beans he always kept on hand and the measly, wilting vegetables left in his refrigerator. The world seemed, that weekend, just a little too overbearingly present.

"Online," she added in response to his puzzled look.

"I wasn't—" he tried to say, but 'Trice threw another cup in his direction.

"Don't you *even* try to tell me you weren't trying to flirt, Mister I-Don't-Let-Just-Anyone-Eat-My-Cupcakes. Really smooth, BB."

"Stop wasting cups," he said, because he didn't know what else to say. 'Trice saw him, as she usually did, with complete clarity. "I can't believe you still read the blog and all the comments."

"I need a source of ammunition, since you won't let me use the cups," she said, shrugging.

Teddy carried the foil-wrapped hunk gingerly in front of him like a ring-bearer, imperial and full of importance, when he pushed his way into the bakery—now quiet, now dim, now empty of crowds, now *home* again, he thought—and met 'Trice at the counter.

"Lady, am I glad to see you," he said, without the least bit of irony. "Weekends here? Let's just say I wasn't in Kansas anymore."

'Trice snorted and turned toward the espresso machine, already starting something on his behalf. "Oh, Dorothy, I take it you met Avon, who lacks a brain, and the members of the stroller brigade, who all lack hearts."

"It seemed more like everyone in here lacked a soul," Teddy said seriously. He nodded his thanks when 'Trice slid him a fresh demitasse of espresso. She bent toward the pastry case, humming a bit.

"Oh, thank you, but nothing right now, please," Teddy said, straightening the front of his suit jacket with a tug of both hands. "I'm really just running in to drop this off for Jules." 'Trice cocked her head and looked at him with one eyebrow raised. Teddy stammered. "Chef Burns. Chef Jules. For Pastry Chef Jules Burns. Whatever you call him, okay? I used his recipe, and he gave me a bunch of advice, and I actually didn't burn it, and I'm a little proud that it tastes like food, so I thought I would share some with him."

"Ohhhhhh," 'Trice sang, slowly standing up from behind the pastry case and raising her penciled eyebrows. The symmetrical piercings there glinted in the light like snake eyes. "So. A gift from the Grasshopper, eh?" Teddy reddened and averted his eyes, then picked up the espresso and downed it in one nervous gulp. "Can I have some, too, or is this meant only for His Royal Majesty Pastry Chef Jules James Burns, Boy Genius?"

"Of course you should taste it," Teddy said, but it barely came out a choked whisper. "Thanks for the coffee," he rasped. He stuffed a handful of bills into her tip jar and was out the door before 'Trice could grab his wrist and drag him into the kitchen herself.

"If I on-ly had the noive," 'Trice sang under her breath and smiled.

"Gift for the Cowardly Lion," 'Trice called when she burst into the kitchen and tossed a foil packet in Jules's direction.

"What?" he asked, mid-stir. 'Trice was often confusing, but seldom was she completely mystifying. He laid down his wooden spoon and wiped his hands on his apron before beginning to peel back the foil.

"Your insect devotee dropped this off for you just now," she said. "He was equal parts nervous and proud. He said he made it with your help."

Jules finished peeling back the foil; inside was a sizeable chunk of bread pudding—yellow, with golden-brown patches on the top, almost perfect-looking in his book—and a little paper cup filled with what he could only assume was bourbon sauce. "Grasshopper?" Jules asked her, forgetting to be embarrassed for once. "Was here?"

'Trice nodded, snickering a bit. "Can I taste some of that? Grasshopper has nice hands, so I bet he bakes real nice, too."

"You can have some, yeah. I'm just going to steam it in the oven for a few minutes to reawaken it." Jules put the hunk of bread pudding into a pan and bookended it with ramekins of water. He covered the whole thing with foil and slid it into the hot oven, then stood, very carefully modulating his voice. "So, nice hands, huh? What does he look like?"

'Trice looked at him in surprise, before something seemed to click. "You weren't spying for once?" she asked. "You're growing up, little guy!" She tousled his hair, jumped back to avoid the swat she knew was coming and breezed out to the front of the shop. "I'll make us some coffee to go with that!" she shouted. On her way out, Jules swore he heard her whistling the chorus to "If I Only Had a Brain."

Clearly, she wasn't about to answer him about Grasshopper. She seemed, in point of fact, to be having entirely too much fun teasing him about it.

'Trice returned with two demitasse cups of espresso decorated with curls of lemon peel and set them on the steel countertop between them.

"Ready?" she asked, raising her eyebrows at Jules and grabbing a fork. "We'll do it on the count of three. Let's see if he's worthy of you or just a lowly insect."

"I don't—" Jules started to protest, but 'Trice pushed a fork at him and cut him off, loudly counting down.

"One!" she hollered, holding up a finger on her free hand. The other hand, holding the fork, hovered over the dessert. Jules sighed and took up his own fork and waited.

"Two!" she yelled. Jules rolled his eyes and motioned with his fork for her to get on with it.

"Two-point-five!" she said slowly, waggling her fork. "Will he be worthy of the great Chef Burns? Does he have the chops to deserve your cupcakes? Does he, in fact, have the choppers?"

"'Trice, I *will* fire you for this," Jules warned, leaning heavily on the counter.

"You absolutely will not," she shot back, but sighed and rolled her eyes again. "Okay, you big baby. Three. *Three! Taste!*"

The two of them sank their forks into the pudding simultaneously. When they clinked against each other, Jules eyed her again with irritation and held his still. 'Trice pulled her fork out, held it high, and said, "Here's to you, BB!" With that, she popped the bite into her mouth and made an exaggerated face of delight. "Mmmmmm, good! Chops galore! He can eat my cupcakes any time!" When Jules glared at her, she said, "Taste it, you big chicken-baby. It's not poisoned, if you're worried about that. I have learned to detect Iocane powder."

Just before he could answer, the bells on the shop's front door jangled. 'Trice hollered, "That's my cue!" and was off, leaving the kitchen door flapping in her wake and Jules holding a drippy bite of the pudding on his fork.

It was, for Jules, one of those moments that slows down so completely that the dust motes floating in the air seem to freeze and turn into little stars in the sunlight, the sound washes away to background ocean noise and the breath slides out slowly, like a silk ribbon dropping off a package. It was one of *those* moments for Jules. He held the fork near his mouth and watched one glistening, amber drop of bourbon sauce slip and fall, watched it round itself into a perfect ball as it went, watched it splat down onto the top of the pudding, sending little spatters onto the counter and the back of his hand.

It shouldn't matter this much, Jules thought and shook his head. He slipped the bite of pudding into his mouth, deliberately unceremonious.

It tasted entirely different from his own version of the recipe. It was heartier, heavier (*the bread,* he thought), and smoky (*the bourbon*), with the faintest hint of orange (*improvising!* Jules thought and blushed just to picture this man tasting and imagining and playing as he went). It was a little rough, a little dry and certainly not very subtle, but it was, he thought, sliding his tongue against the thick, eggy bread—bread this man's fingers had ripped and pressed—absolutely sexy.

He took one more bite and held it gently in his mouth, pressing with his tongue until the smoky syrup drizzled down the back of his throat, and then, from the walk-in fridge, he pulled milk, eggs and butter. Because he wanted to answer this, to make something that might hit the same notes, or make a harmony, something that would float above the husky roughness in a playful duet, something sweet and light and floral and beautiful.

❧

Employees should refrain from displaying photographs, memorabilia, artwork or anything else that might be understood as "personal display" on their desks or in their cubicles.

This was the latest in a long list of emails which, lately, came almost daily from the Office of Company Standards, a new entity which had sprung up in recent months, poking itself into the cracks between cubicles and under the bathroom and breakroom doors like a sidewalk weed. It was, Teddy assumed, the latest result of the frequent decrees issued by what he thought must be the very bored, thumb-twiddling band of company heads whom, Teddy remembered, he'd neither met nor seen in person. Their pictures hung in the entryway, a short line of identical-looking tight smiles plastered to the fronts of identical-looking bald heads, all of which poked out of the necks of identical-looking navy blue suit jackets and stiff white collars. The picture frames, identical mahogany wood frames, looked as if they'd been hung with the help of a ruler and a level. On his way down the hallway to the bathroom that afternoon, Teddy had tapped them all slightly sideways with a fingertip. He'd glanced up and down the hallway first to ensure that no one was looking, of course, but he'd still felt a little thrill at the tipping.

For maximum work efficiency, employees should refrain from spending more than forty-five minutes outside the building for lunch. The last fifteen minutes of one's break should be used for resituating oneself at one's desk, so that one can begin working immediately upon the end of one's lunch break.

Gentlemen Employees, please refrain from wearing ties or pocket squares of a color or pattern that might be understood as "distracting" to clients or other employees. Primary colors and pastels are acceptable choices. Shirts and suits, of course, should be of muted and un-patterned fabrics.

Female Employees, please refrain from wearing patterned or colored stockings, as these have proven to be distracting to both clients and employees. Nude, white or black stockings are acceptable if they have no obvious pattern.

Teddy had, on several occasions since the receipt of that email, daydreamed about showing up to work in a skirt and broad-patterned lace stockings, perhaps with a pair of kitten heels to boot, since no prohibition had been made against such stockings for Gentlemen Employees. Of course, he did not do so.

What he did do that afternoon, still a bit rattled by the shot of espresso, 'Trice's rapier stare and his volley at the hallway picture frames, was draw a tiny cupcake on a yellow sticky note and pin it to the wall of his cubicle. It certainly wasn't a photograph, and one would be hard-pressed, he thought, to call it "artwork."

He glanced at it, that tasty little secret, pinned and re-pinned it to the wall, tapped it with his fingers in thought and focused on it like a mandala all afternoon, until he'd memorized the swipes of pen, until, when he closed his eyes, the cupcake danced a jaunty, defiant little dance to the maudlin hum of his computer and the copy machine and the fluorescents overhead.

He drew another cupcake on a sticky note and pressed it to his lapel. Another, he stuck to the left knee of his pants. He stuck two on the computer screen, one on his cheek, one on the pencil cup, one on the stapler (all still carefully placed at right angles), one to the back of his hand. He stuck and stuck, until the whole cubicle fluttered yellow. He was probably on camera, he thought, and removed three from his face, out of dignity.

I quit, he wrote on another sticky note, then scribbled over the words until nothing was left but a ballpoint-blue smudge. He took another note and wrote it again: *I quit.* This one he pinned next to the cupcake. *What do I quit?* he asked himself silently, tapping the cupcake with the tip of his pen, keeping the rhythm of the copier's clank-hum from down the corridor.

What, exactly, do I quit?

He didn't know.

Teddy heard the tinkle of bells before he realized where he was. He didn't remember walking to the bakery after work, hardly felt the weight of his bag on his shoulder, didn't realize he was pushing on the door until he was inside the tiny shop and felt the door shimmer-slam behind him with a huff of air. *It's as if I'm in a trance.* Quickly, he dusted his hand over his suit and face to check that he'd removed the sticky notes and then dropped his briefcase at his usual table.

"I'm back," he said to 'Trice, who'd pushed aside her crossword puzzle and lowered the volume on the radio (jazz, he was surprised to hear, Coltrane; he'd imagined 'Trice's style to be more scream-and-drum) when she saw him come in.

"Long day, you poor puppy! Coffee for sure; I won't even hear you say no." She was already pulling a shot. "Can I talk you into something sweet now? His Royal Chefness was improvising this afternoon after your pudding, you know."

"Yes," he said. "I mean, yes, please, to the coffee."

"Americano," she said. "And this." She was gone and back before he had time to blink, a little plate in her hand. Balanced in its center was the most delicate-looking cream puff, powdered lightly with sugar and topped with a sprinkling of tiny, crystallized lavender flowers.

"It *is* a cream puff, with some sort of lavender-honey cream filling, but once again, it is not a comment on you. Jules made them this afternoon, and he's not selling these—he was just playing around in the kitchen and left the whole batch for me, and if I eat them all, I will literally do a Violet Beauregarde. And then you'd be stuck with Avon behind the counter forever. Or worse, Jules. So eat this. Save me. Save yourself."

Teddy laughed and took the plate and cup in hand. Then he set them back down on the counter and steeled himself with a sigh. "Will you get him to come out here?" he asked her. "I'm dying to hear his evaluation of my bread pudding. He talked me through it. So I'm dying to hear."

'Trice looked at him, face stone-still and completely serious, eyes unwavering, for what seemed like forever.

"I'm dying here."

"Right, okay. Nervous wordplay. You two are made for each other," she said. Then she relented and crossed two of her locks over her lip like a long mustache. "Zee gentleman chef eez not een."

"I'm sorry?"

She dropped her hair and smiled in a way that Teddy thought was meant to be reassuring.

"The guy comes in at four a.m.," she said. "He's out of here by two or three. This isn't the droid you're looking for. Elfis has left the building." Upon seeing the expression on Teddy's face, a look somewhere between squashed pumpkin and fallen soufflé, she softened. "I'm sorry, Cupcake. He'll be back tomorrow, though. Meanwhile, I think he actually made these with you in mind, if it helps." She pushed the cream puff at him for the second time.

He took it and the coffee and settled at his table by the window to watch the flash and flap of commuters in their dark coats crossing and re-crossing the street.

The cream puff was petite—nothing like the oversized, bready and tasteless supermarket variety he remembered his mother bringing home in a plastic clamshell on special occasions. It was tiny and fragrant, with hints of lavender and butter and an airy sweetness, and even a faint note—he bent to sniff a second time—of citrus underneath the flowers. A little of the cream filling—pale yellow, incredibly smooth—oozed from the side of the puff, and he swiped it up with a fingertip and smeared it on the tip of his tongue. *Sweet, floral, light,* he thought, and then it deepened into a satisfyingly fatty bass note of cream as the filling slid down his tongue toward his throat. The pastry itself—here he took a gentle bite, catching the drips of filling on the back of his free hand and surreptitiously licking them off—was also light. It resembled bread, but in a floating way, lightly mocking: a wink, a sly smile, an echo with a difference. It refused to settle into one taste. In this, it was flirtatious, coy, dancing exquisitely between the coolness of cream and the warmth of honey, the earthiness of bread and the baroque glory of flowers.

With one bite, Teddy understood: this was an answer to his earlier gift, a parody, a parry, a partner, *contrapunto*.

He didn't, he understood, need to get into the kitchen to meet the chef. He'd just met him.

PASTRY-WHIPPED: ADVENTURES IN SUGAR BY A DEDICATED
CRUMPET STRUMPET
by Chef Jules Burns of Buttermilk Bakery
April 2: What I Learned from Flowers, by a Lifelong Pansy

Flowers in the kitchen are a wonderful thing. You can't just use any flowers—you need to make sure they're organically grown and non-toxic (the same advice I'd give about anything you choose to put in your mouth… and beyond that, I won't judge you). Not only do flowers add beauty, color and uniqueness to anything you make—I love to top my creamy-orange butternut squash soup with a bright sprinkling of purple pansies, and a sugared rose petal or a pinch of lavender blossoms does wonders on top of a cupcake—but using flowers gives you the opportunity to add incredible scents and flavors, sometimes spicy, sometimes sweet, to what you make. Plus, it's absolutely, over-the-top romantic, and that aspect appeals to me simply on principle.

But you have to be careful with flowers. Flowers can, if not used carefully, with a little cynicism perhaps, become cloying and overwhelming. (Oh, and how I wish someone had told this to my high school self, that glorious hothouse flower that I was, wilting away in the flannel jungle that was Indiana!) The showiness of the blossoms can make us forget that flowers need roots, too. They need their green sturdy parts and the secret parts, those snaky, underground, sinuous sides that we never see. The parts all tangled up with worms. The dirty, unpretty parts, the parts that stay hidden. They need those parts to stay upright, to stay rooted, to stay alive.

Did you know that the roots make up more than half the plant? (I just made that up, but I do base it upon my childhood memory of ripping up my grandmother's garden in an ill-conceived attempt at gift-giving.) I love flowers not only for their sheer aesthetic appeal, their exuberance and celebration of everything fleeting and beautiful, but also because flowers are fighters. They push up in the harshest environments; they spatter the highway berms with joyous color, undeterred by cars or exhaust or tossed-out trash; they persist despite early frosts and late springs, dry seasons and those too wet; they take in all of our pollution and all of our mistakes, and still they open themselves to the world, delicate and showy, in love with their own beauty and reeking of it, ready to be crushed or uprooted or forgotten. (Oh, and how I wish someone had told this to my high school self, that lonely little pansy fighting his way out of the crack that is Indiana!)

I recently had the pleasure of tasting something—bread pudding— someone else baked. I don't often do that. I'm the chef, so I always get to be the one in charge; people rarely want to cook for me. And though it was my own recipe (the one I posted in the last blog, by the way), the dish wasn't really mine. To truly take it in, I had to let go a little bit. I had to put myself in the hands of the baker—to trust—to give up a little of my control, to be open and ready for what he might give me. (Nothing anyone could give me, *I can hear my grandmother saying,* could be as glorious as these flowers, because you picked them yourself, and just for me.)

I'm glad I could let go a bit. I learned from my tasting experience. It was, in a word, wonderful. Smoky, sweet and a bit rough, more petunia than peony. Grounded. Good.

I think you need both, the petunia and the peony, in this life. Or, at least, I do. You need the heartiness of the day to day, the bread and butter, someone to hold on to when everything is crashing down around you. But you also need the light and sweet, the flowers for no reason, the headiness, the play. Each balances out the other, and every living thing needs a bit of both to survive. For me, for my lost teenaged self, for my lost mother and grandmother and for my heart, which I thought I may have lost for good not long ago, for all of these, I'm trying to learn this lesson, to honor my roots, to open up again, to be beautiful and strong and vulnerable at once. All of which I know I must do in order to take in a little of this dazzlingly glorious, bright and warm spring sun.

Six

AT THIS POINT, YOU MAY NOTICE, we have been telling this tale for quite some time, and yet the two men at its center have yet not met. That is no accident.

In life, most things, good *and* bad, are accidental—this is a fact you should always bear in mind. The universe, in its vast and spinning, starry expanse, does not care about you, does not even know that you exist. The universe simply knows its own vastness, its own need to spin, just as you, adjusting your glasses or sipping your afternoon tea or biting the ragged edges of your cuticles, know nothing of the mitochondria that move in you, each one its own little universe churning out pops of energy smaller than pinpricks in your cells, invisible pistons, tiny steampunk organisms that, in their simplicity and in their ignorance of you, give you life.

Life is accidental and you are accidental, and, as we have cautioned before, there is no fate or kismet to effect a cosmic justice and bring together two people who seem so clearly to belong to each other before they have even met. This belonging, you must remember, is simply a wish one projects onto the hapless world, an effect of the story itself, because stories, by their very structure, convince us that there is order and justice and balance, convince us that everything is meant to fit, that no pieces will go missing or be found extraneous, that the plot of our lives will fall, perfectly, along a beautifully drawn arc.

In this life, most things are accidental. But this is a story, you must remember, and so nothing we might tell you in this tale is an accident. It might be a comfort to you, this care, this control that our story affords. But remember, too, the corollary to this comfort: This is a story; nothing here exists.

Teddy does not exist, nor the humming fluorescent office, nor the legal pads and calla lilies and sticky notes and mahogany-framed portraits. Jules, curled on his couch in the low light of evening, Andy breathing rhythmically against his bare thigh, the light-filled sweep of the city outside and the breathless night, every memory Jules holds of anyone that ever held him or cried for him or caused him to cry: They do not exist. The keys (ah, did you think we'd forgotten about the keys?), which he polishes with the pad of his thumb while his eyes go glassy and far away and he appears to be thinking of something beautiful, of some hope, those keys do not exist.

Until and unless.

These men, those keys, the evening's sparkling and dusky sweep, none of it exists until we tell it, call it up in words, and unless those words resonate in you and jar loose a tiny splinter of your belief. And, since we are speaking as honestly and as plainly as we are able, we might say that the condition is, more accurately, quite the opposite. The invisible world will go on spinning without us to narrate it, will spin right on without our belief, but we who are in it, because we are so small and insubstantial, only so many atoms and so much empty space, *we* are the ones who need stories to live. We live—and if we are to be very clear about this, we might say that we *only* live—through stories.

A memory, as you know, is only that. A memory is simply a story.

Jules lived almost entirely, on nights like this, through his memories. Behind his eyes, he clicked a sensory slideshow, everything he knew and must not forget: the little details of his grandmother (the smell of her perfume, the exact shade of her hair, the words she'd say each night before snapping off the bedside lamp and disappearing through the sliver of bright hallway light at the door) and the little details of Andy (his long, wrinkled fingers, their touch always a bit too cool, and the way he'd seem to grow taller and wider and treelike around Jules to steady him against danger and make him feel held and safe and entirely surrounded); the acrid metal-and-sweat smell of the insides of lockers; the smell of the school latrines and the school cafeteria; Andy's cologne, and his hair oil, his mouth like minted coffee and his warm wood-colored skin; his father's smell when he came home from work, sharp and comforting, house paint and sweat.

Jules murmured each of these again into memory, but the litany had become automatic, thin and without feeling, a numb comfort; and though he spoke the memories to himself over and over like a rosary against loss, he felt them slipping one by one and ceasing to exist.

I want something new, Grasshopper had written. *Teach me something.*

The words were only light and air, flashed over the city and into Jules's room like magic, but Jules imagined—and this is another form of belief, another form of storytelling—a man somewhere nearby, his hands hovering over a keyboard, his face lit by screenglow, perhaps biting his lip as he typed, perhaps tapping his foot lightly against the leg of the table at which he sat. Perhaps his sweater was too warm for the night, or his socks had holes in the toes, or he sipped gingerly at a mug of warmed milk dusted with nutmeg while he waited for Jules to respond.

BBCHEF: *The walls have ears, Grasshopper, and then those ears come to work attached to a mouthy, tattooed assistant. I've sent you shopping instructions by private message. You have thirty minutes to complete your mission and get back to me.*

It was, in truth, nothing private or mysterious. He'd sent a short list for the store and instructions for Grasshopper to send him a private message upon his return. While he waited, he sat and thought and remembered. One hand absently stroked the nape of Andy's neck, where the tiny locket at his collar jingled in the soft fur as Jules moved his hand; in the other hand, Jules held the set of keys the handsome man had lost under the bakery table, and his thumb rubbed acrid circles into the shining metal. He felt caught between his own hands; his body hung between moments that had been and had, against his will, begun to fade, and those that were just about to be. The future image was still unclear, but he felt it near him like a body, vibrating with its own possibility.

GRASSHOPPER: *Got everything in one go, and back before my time limit, even though it meant I had to stand in line in front of an old lady who was only buying a roll of toilet paper and not offer to let her go in front of me, which felt really rude, and I think she thought so, too, and probably thought something about "kids today" in her head, because she gave me a pretty dirty look. Do you see what I do to please you? I'm rude to old ladies, just for you. But please note that, as a result, I am on time… no! I'm early! (Where is my reward for that?) Now what, Yoda?*

BBCHEF: *Do not blame your rudeness to old ladies on me; you were probably just waiting for the chance to do something like that, and I was a convenient excuse. Do you kick puppies, too? Because I have a dog and I'm starting to think I should never let you near him. We're making something really fun, very easy and decadent. But it will get messy. Everything fun, easy and decadent is a little bit messy, too, I've found. (Me most of all.) Go put on old clothes. Wash your hands. Do you have an apron?*

GRASSHOPPER: *No apron. And how can I meet your dog before I meet you? I promise not to kick either one of you.*

BBCHEF: *You have a food processor but not an apron? What kind of man are you?*

GRASSHOPPER: *I've never used the food processor. Gift from my mom when I moved out here. For making breadcrumbs for meatballs. Apparently, meatballs were my favorite of the stuff she cooked. She hasn't cooked since I was seven. Our housecleaner cooked dinners for us after Mom went back to work. And anyway, who over the age of seven eats meatballs? So, long story short, I've never used the food processor. But I've pulled it out, and it's sitting on my counter now, staring at me expectantly. What kind of dog is it?*

BBCHEF: *First, a food processor is like any piece of your equipment: There are many amazing things you can do with it. (I did not think that would sound as dirty as it does, I promise.) Second, housecleaner? Cook? Are you a Trump? (If so, perhaps I should be a little more cautious in my affections, since bad hair seems to run in your family.) Third, Vito Corleone. (Eats, I'm sure, meatballs on a regular basis and is well above the age of seven.) Fourth, dump the almonds in there and get it going. This won't take long. Fifth, Andy is a very dignified dachshund.*

GRASSHOPPER: *First, I didn't think that sounded dirty until you said it did. But now it sounds dirty. You did that on purpose. Second, my toupee is way better than his. I'm not a Trump, but my dad is a lawyer and my mom is a financial planner, so I probably come from equally evil genes. The housecleaner, Birdie, hated me with a passion. She used to call me "child," not my name, like it was the worst word she could come up with. She must have been very bitter, because I was a lovely child. But I'm starting to suspect her name might not have actually been Birdie. Maybe that had something to do with it. Third, touché. But—and I hate to break this to you—he is not a real guy, so I'm not sure I should give you points for that. Fourth, they are going. How long? And, wait, going back to two... affections?*

BBChef: *First, there are no accidents, my friend. Second, I suspect that you may not have been as angelic a child as you purport. And "Grasshopper" is a very long name; "child" is probably easier. Third, what?! Then who was that guy with whom I spoke on his daughter's wedding day? Fourth, this is getting ridiculous, and it's about to get really messy and impossible to type. Just call me. It will be easier. And don't make me regret this.*

Jules typed his cell phone number and sent the message quickly, before he could talk himself out of what had to have been, he thought, one of the most rash and stupid ideas he'd ever had.

❧

When the line clicked and the connection was made, when the voice, high and sweet and resonant as a cello on its upper string, said, "Hello," everything inside Teddy dropped two inches and twisted backward. It was not the voice he was expecting. He wasn't sure what he'd expected, but that voice made Jules real and living and warm and very present; it mapped a body through its vibrations, up through a not-too-broad chest, a long throat, a delicate aquiline nose. There was, too, a little laughter in that voice, a note of the ridiculous.

"Hello," Teddy said.

"Grasshopper, I presume," said the voice, and in the pause that followed, he heard it again, a little chuckle under the breath, deeper in the throat, unconscious, perhaps a nervous habit.

"It's me," was all Teddy could say before the breath left him entirely. He swiped at his forehead with the back of his hand and took a deep, shuddering breath. "Is this weird?"

"This is entirely weird," Jules laughed.

"Yeah," Teddy said and tried to let himself laugh, too. It came out a bit strangled, a bit forced, a bit too paltry, with no belly or heart to it. He ground the heel of his right foot down hard against the top of his left, just to feel something solid, to pin himself in place.

"Speakerphone."

"What?"

"Speakerphone. Put me on speaker so you can use your hands. You're going to need both hands, and I won't be held responsible for you mucking up your phone. Speaker."

Teddy set his phone on the counter and switched to the speaker, then stood waiting.

"Hello?" Jules said. "Is this thing on?"

"Sorry," Teddy said. "I'm still here."

"It sounded like you'd suddenly disappeared. I was starting to believe in the rapture," Jules said, and Teddy heard, again, the nervous chuckle.

Their conversation was awkward and full of strange pauses in which there was nothing right to say, and they focused mostly on how awkward and strange it was until Jules told Teddy to dump the almond paste on the counter and start to knead in the sugar.

"I'm doing it, too, along with you," Jules said.

"I'm not sure whether that makes it more or less weird," Teddy admitted, dusting everything in front of him with sugar.

"It's just like giving a back rub," Jules told him. "Roll gently into the dough with the heel of your hand; lean in with your upper body.

Think loving things. Add a little sugar each time—watch for when it's ready for more. Not too much at once."

Several moments passed when all that held their connection was a string of huffed and effortful breaths and the soft thump of dough. Teddy felt Jules pressing and leaning forward into his work, felt the small sweat and ache that had begun to announce itself in Jules's shoulders, felt it when he held his breath as he pushed and then exhaled in a rush as he flipped the dough, felt it all as surely as if Jules's body were there next to him, as if he might reach to the side and, without glancing over, brush the sugar from Teddy's forearm, a gesture which might have been, if real, if the result of many long hours spent in the kitchen together, sweet and familiar and unthinking.

"My grandmother and I used to make this," Jules breathed after a long silence, "when I was little. Mine would always become flowers. She would always make hers into people."

Teddy understood that he needn't reply, that Jules was speaking to him, yes, but speaking more into the empty space in which he stood as a witness, talking a story into the evening around him, and he, Teddy, was lucky to be near, to listen in as the story spun itself out of Jules and into the open, open quiet.

When the dough was finished and Jules had interrupted himself to say, "There, mine's pretty done. I bet yours is done by now, too," Teddy nodded in agreement—and even though he knew Jules couldn't see him, he was sure Jules would sense him nodding through some miniscule change in his breathing or the invisible tension between them slackening just the slightest bit. And he did seem to know, because Jules paused and made a satisfied noise that sounded as if all the spring-coiled readiness had slid from his body. "This taste," Jules sighed, "is like Proust's madeleine."

They spent an hour playing with the dough and molding it into shapes they wouldn't reveal to each other. Teddy felt childish and happy and inept and far too adult all at once as he listened to the rhythmic way Jules breathed and spoke, the way his voice moved in and out of silence, like the advance and retreat of shallow waves that left in their wake little broken treasures on the shore.

Only his fingers moved, fumbling and busy and blind as he listened, his whole self waiting for Jules to tell him the next thing, whatever it might be.

~

PASTRY-WHIPPED: ADVENTURES IN SUGAR BY A DEDICATED CRUMPET STRUMPET
by Chef Jules Burns of Buttermilk Bakery
April 5: Virgin Territory (Deflouring a Tart and Other Fun Things to Do in the Kitchen)

This one? I'm just in it for the title, really. I have no intention of writing about tarts. (Deflouring, however, that's fair; I am going to give you some suggestions for pastry work without flour, so I suppose you can give me points for that part.)

I've been feeling nostalgic lately, thinking a lot about my past; most especially, as the weather warms and it becomes more common to see the raggedy New York sparrows picking through the garbage cans in Jackson Square, I think about people I've loved and lost. (If the boys trolloping around my neighborhood are any indication, I'm living in the hipster tattoo capital of the universe, and boy, do the hipsters love to tattoo birds on themselves; so I've learned, and perhaps you already know, that sparrows symbolize companionship, and that they are also the harbingers of death and the catchers of lost souls. So I really was making a logical leap there, and I'm asking you to trust me with it and follow along for a spell.)

I miss my grandmother. I've lost many people in my life, some to death, some to ill-fated arguments, some to the simple attrition of abandoned intentions, but of all the people I've lost, I miss my grandmother the most. She raised me after my mom left—my mom ran off to join the circus just after I was born, my dad used to tell me, too antsy and too artsy and too tied to constant change to stay in one place and raise a kid. So my grandmother—my dad's mom—took over and helped raise me. She was my One and Only while my dad worked, and she was the most wonderful combination of mother and grandmother (steadfast, stern, but doting and indulgent). But she died when I was ten years old—so, I know, I've lived far more of my life without her than with her, and the memories I have of her are, most likely—or so they tell me—idealized. But my grandmother was, I'm still confident, a uniquely amazing person. She was very smart and knew exactly six hundred and eighty-five stories by heart and played the guitar and liked to spend afternoons with me making secret-saving boxes decorated with sequins and rock salt glitter, or collecting pretty pebbles from the riverbank near our house (which was, I realized later, not so much a river as a concrete pipe into which all the houses' gutters emptied during heavy rain, but my grandmother was a recovered hippie and still a free spirit and entirely undeterred). And on days when it was really pouring outside and it was just the two of us, because my dad worked all day painting rich peoples' houses in tasteful colors named for foods we couldn't ever afford (avocado, mocha, bisque, brandy), my grandmother and I would make deliciously rich marzipan and knead into it several brightly brilliant colors and sit at the kitchen table all afternoon making beautifully clumsy little sculpted treats we'd later think far too precious to ever eat. I did, however, much to my grandmother's light-laughing delight, always consume more marzipan dough than I sculpted. Perhaps this was the point.

The taste of marzipan puts me right back in that kitchen. I'm watching her, bent low over her work at the table, etching a face into the dough with a toothpick, humming softly to herself as if she's entirely forgotten she's not sitting there alone. If I offer to braid her hair, she'll let me, and I like to do it, because her hair is long and softly curling and the same color as mine, but so much more beautiful, and I like to slither it between my fingers like a ribbon and put little kisses on the nape of her neck and listen to her hum as she works. I am six years old. My marzipan treats are always flowers, which are among the few things my stubby little fingers can accomplish with the dough, but my grandmother always makes people. This is, in part, why we can never eat them when they dry; she names them (Jack Inbox, or Sam's son Delyle, or the twins, Pat 'n' Pending), and tells me such incredible stories about their lives that I lavish upon them all my hope and love and belief.

The night my poor, uninitiated father, exhausted and hungry and really in no mood, came home from painting the entire interior of City Hall and, quite innocently bit the head off of Jimmy Headdress—a hat-maker who'd gone crazy from mercury exposure and learned to play, instead, a wicked electric guitar—I subsequently terrified and surprised that gentle man with the heat of my anger and hysteria and was inconsolable all evening until finally, late in the night, I cried myself to sleep.

I miss my grandmother, but I know very well that mostly what I have left of her to miss are stories I've told myself so many times they're only words; all the sense-memory has faded and gone, like the last scent of her perfume from her button box, saved like a treasure under my bed for all those years. I miss her more fiercely, sometimes, because I know that things fade. Over time, I have slowly forgotten so much of her it's painful to recognize, even though I know I couldn't have grown up and gone on with my life had I not done so. Everyone has to let go of their past in this way, whether one loses it to death or simply the washing forward of time, but it is so much harder to let go when it's mixed up in mourning.

I didn't intend this to get maudlin, though perhaps I should have seen it coming when I got out the almonds and orange flower water. Marzipan will always remind me of my grandmother, and it will always make me a little sad.

But recently, I taught a friend to make marzipan and, though it was sad for me, the experience was touched with something else, too. He listened while I talked about my mother running off, and my grandmother, who left me, when she died, her entire collection of cookbooks and spices and copper pots and too many sweet-and-bitter memories of her. And after I'd talked for quite a while, it seemed I'd run out of words, as though I was, for the moment at least, finished telling the story. And we worked for a while in near-silence, which was punctuated only by the occasional chuckle or frustrated sigh, the clatter of a knife or the scrape of a chair on the wooden floor, and then, eventually, we began to talk about new things: how we both hate Central Park because it's too ambitious and not nearly wild enough; how we were both tormented and adored in high school in equal measure; how each of us learned to cook by helping someone else in the kitchen (his mother, my grandmother) as small boys during the long hours our fathers were away at work (and how this turned me towards cooking and turned him resolutely away from it).

I won't tell you all our stories here—some are hidden in the marzipan (my sculptures, this time, were people and playful bugs and model cars and fruits of all varieties). I will tell you that it was one of the loveliest stretches of time I've spent playing with food since those rainy afternoons with my grandmother. And what was loveliest, perhaps, was the fact that I was able, in the same moment, both to remember her and to let her go a little bit. And the marzipan began to take on new flavors for me, too—bittersweet longing, yes, but also newness (which is a bright citrus) and joy and silliness. And this time, I added pistachios to the almonds, which cut the hint of bitterness with its richness and sweet warmth.

I realized, as I played with new tastes and stories and shapes and a few old ones, too, in my grandmother's memory (I couldn't resist making a little mad-hatter guitarist and took great satisfaction in attaching— firmly—his head), that the memory of my grandmother didn't fade when I shared the marzipan with someone new. In fact, the memory grew stronger. I could almost smell her perfume, a spicy note lingering under the sweetness of orange flower. And her memory became a part of this new connection, part of this sweet and awkward evening we shared, a permanent part of the emerging story of my new friendship.

He came, as he had last time, carrying a small parcel, and laid it carefully on the counter in front of 'Trice.

"I know he doesn't ever come out here," Teddy said, "and I know I'm not allowed to go back there. But would you take this to the back for me? I brought it for him to try, since he helped me again."

'Trice peeked. "What is that?"

"That is my attempt at a marzipan calla lily."

She looked at him steadily. "Listen, Grasshopper, I know you're probably not an expert here, but that," she pointed, "is most definitely a vagina. I would know."

"Um," said Teddy, which was the only response he could muster.

"Perfect for him," 'Trice said, turning so quickly the beads in her hair clacked against each other with a plastic slap. "BRB."

She was gone through the kitchen door so fast that Teddy didn't have time to call after her, to remind her to take the marzipan. He sighed and re-wrapped the foil, carefully, then precisely aligned the package first with the edge of the cash register, then with the container of straws by the tip jar and finally with the counter's edge, and waited.

"Urgent bathroom break!" 'Trice said. "There's a customer, but this couldn't wait. You take it."

Jules turned from peeling apples to scowl at her. "You're joking."

"Nope," she said. "Bladder the size of a peanut. Very bad for all of us if I stay out there. Probably a health code violation. Very potentially soggy situation." She slapped her hands on his shoulders, pressing and rubbing hard over his heart. "You can handle this. Up and at 'em! You can do it if you try! Climb every mountain! Follow every rainbow! Ain't no mountain high enough! Go get 'em, Tiger!"

"In the time it took you to pep talk me," he said, "you could have made a Bundt cake." But 'Trice was already gone, and the plywood door to the bathroom had made the distinctive *pop-clump* sound that meant it had been firmly closed and locked. Jules sighed, tightened the knot of the apron strings around his waist and pushed himself into the shop front.

"What can I get for you?" he asked as he rounded the counter's corner and came face to face with his key-losing, unwitting gentleman caller.

The bump of the moment, in which everything around them stopped breathing, swung the world up beneath them both so hard it jolted the sun-glittering strings of crystals overhead and made them rattle and shake a spray of glitter over everything.

"Oh," said Jules. "May I—"

His voice, he thought, maybe it was his voice, too shrill, too high and girlish and completely ridiculous, because the man looked stricken and stepped back, pulling with him the package that lay on the counter between them, as if he were going to tuck it under his arm like a football and run for an end zone several miles away.

"Would you—" he tried again, but trailed off weakly. He might have tried a third time, since dignity was already out the window, but for the way the man was looking at him, wide-eyed, mistrustful, red-faced. Jules pulled at the knot at his waist, tightening the apron strings more securely. "I'm sorry, I... would you—"

The man shook his head and seemed to put a great amount of effort into dragging his eyes up to Jules's face. Once their eyes met, however, he held a level gaze, bright with humor, and Jules was locked where he stood, looking back. The man smiled and cleared his throat.

"Hello," he said.

Seven

Hello.

To utter this simple word was all Teddy could manage, standing, as he was, as he had waited to be, in front of the man he'd wanted to meet for weeks, the man who always hid in the kitchen, it seemed, when Teddy appeared, whose hands—long-fingered, pale, graceful—had mixed and held and shaped the food he'd eaten. He was taller than Teddy had imagined, and slim, with sharp gray eyes and delicate features. He stood still and very straight under Teddy's gaze, like a dancer, the knot of his apron perfectly centered and tight at his waist and not a spot on his coat, which was brilliantly white and crisp and perfectly fitted. He was balletic and beautiful. But—and Teddy's heart stopped halfway up his throat—

On his left shoulder, like a badge, was a yellow sticky note with Teddy's doodle (an excuse for a grasshopper) and scrawl (*I quit*) in red pen.

Perhaps it was meant, he thought, as a quiet message, a wink, a just-between-you-and-me. Perhaps it was meant to mock him. Perhaps it was a warning. Teddy couldn't read the little sign for meaning, but it took every ounce of courage he had to raise his gaze from that yellow square, look the man in the eyes and whisper that word. The marzipan flower in its foil packet now seemed ridiculous; it had been meant as an announcement, as a revelation, as the gift of his own self, an unfurling, but if Jules already knew who he was, it seemed, instead, superfluous and too crafty. Shabby. He curled his hand over the foil packet.

Jules looked at him for a long, silent moment, his lips pressed together in a thin line, before he inhaled sharply and asked again, "How may I help you?"

"Oh," said Teddy, backing away from the counter another fraction of an inch, hoping his discomfort wasn't too plainly visible. "'Trice—she usually—"

"'Trice," Jules said, his voice heavy and flat. "One minute. I'll be right with you." Teddy's heart sank when Jules turned to push back through the kitchen door. The moment was all cement, cold and rough and impossibly hard. Jules pushed at the door, but it wouldn't move; he shouldered hard at it until Teddy heard a series of muffled thumps from the other side.

"No way, you chicken-baby!" 'Trice hollered. "The kitchen is closed!"

Jules gave the unyielding door one or two more hearty shoves, then slapped the wood once with the flat of his hand and turned, his back stiff, and his face blushing all the way down into his collar, to smile at Teddy.

"I'm sorry about that," he said. "This is embarrassing. She's usually better behaved than this. You're stuck with me, I guess." He shrugged and looked up at Teddy through half-lowered eyelids. "What would you like?"

"Well." Teddy wanted, more than anything, to say nothing, to turn and burst out of the door and onto the street and not stop walking until he got all the way back to his office, or his apartment. Or Peoria. Jules would not even look at him, but cast his glance anywhere else: the pastry case, the plate glass window, the countertop.

"'Trice usually picks for me," Teddy croaked, trying to stop his hand from squeezing the foil packet too tightly.

"Picks," Jules said, as if he were practicing the word, re-pronouncing without a sense of its meaning. As if, Teddy thought, it were the stupidest thing he'd ever heard.

He was about to mutter an apology, turn and dash. There were miles between Grasshopper—clever, clear-eyed and suave—and *him*, awkward in his gaping gray suit, a bit too short and fumblingly un-charming and with his best offering—slightly squashed, lumpy marzipan genitalia—sweating in its foil package. When he was young, he felt nervousness blossom with a sense of immanent joy, as if everything would eventually unknot and fall loose and beautiful at his feet. Teddy didn't know how he'd gotten so twisted away from that, how he'd come to feel so insignificant and just not *himself* anymore, but these were the highly polished, too-tight shoes he was now standing in. Perhaps it was hubris when he was younger, but perhaps he'd lost something powerful when he'd tamed himself out of that, too.

"I—" he said, knowing that he should simply pick something and be gone, something that could be dropped in a bag, but something that spoke, too, of his excellent taste and his true appreciation for Jules's art, a choice that would, in his absence, suggest that he was perhaps a little more interesting, a little more worthwhile than his stammering and his red face and shaking hands might suggest. "I—" he said, and then, "Oh!" because he felt, wrapped around his hips, two very small hands pushing him to the side with tiny-fisted force.

Teddy stepped aside, reddening again when he saw his assailant, who could not have been more than three years old. She had a wide round face, knotted blonde hair tied with a fraying blue ribbon and a pot-bellied, squat body stuffed into—bursting out of—a pair of brown corduroy overalls.

"Cleo, keep your jam-hands off of other people," said the woman behind her. She was a longer, leaner version of the little girl, slightly harried; her own blonde hair was a ratty mess spilling over her sharp shoulders. "Remember the talk we had about respecting other people's space? You should apologize to him." She nodded at Teddy, widening her eyes and smiling, as if she were speaking more to him than to the little girl.

The girl looked up at Teddy with watery brown eyes. She held his gaze, then turned and slapped her hands and chin onto the counter and looked up through her thick bangs at Jules.

"Cleo! Nice ribbon!" Jules said, fingering the blue silk. He looked past Teddy to the harried woman and said, "The cake, I presume?"

She nodded, and he turned to pull a box out of the pastry case, setting it gently on the counter and opening the top so that she could see inside.

"Perfect," said the woman. "Charlie will love this. Charlie loves everything you bake. This is perfect."

"If chocolate doesn't fix forty for him, I don't know what will," Jules laughed.

The woman laughed. "What the hell do you know? What are you, twenty?"

"Thank you, but no, well past that," Jules said, his eyes flickering to Teddy's for a moment. "I'm just cursed with this ridiculous baby face. I still get carded sometimes when I try to buy a drink."

Teddy watched as the little girl's pointer finger, deliberate, outstretched, zoomed toward the top of the cake. Slim milliseconds before it could swoop into the frosting, both her mother and Jules, without looking or stopping their conversation, caught her wrist and pulled it back. She slipped her hand away and promptly stuck her unsweetened finger in her mouth.

"Well, you're lucky." The woman sighed. "So's your boyfriend," she said, giving Jules a significant look, then glancing at Teddy. For no reason Teddy could explain, something inside him expanded, warm and slow, as if he were suddenly filled with honey. Jules, his skin crimson, shook his head and concentrated on tying a gold ribbon around the closed cake box.

"I don't," he said, but didn't finish the sentence. Instead, he rang a total on the register.

Cleo, who had wedged herself against the counter, stretched one dimpled arm up and dropped, one at a time, four dried and slightly grubby kidney beans onto the counter, then beamed up at Jules, who looked amused and mystified in equal parts.

"She's paying," her mother said to Jules. "Cleo, my darling, the cake costs a little more than that. I'm going to give some money, too, so we can buy it together." She dug into her wallet and produced a few bills.

"Four beans? I think," Jules said, "that four beans can buy a lot of things here. What do you think four beans could buy?" He glanced quickly at the woman, who nodded, smiling. Cleo pushed past Teddy and pressed herself against the glass of the pastry case.

"Nose and mouth off!" her mother called, and Cleo stepped back a foot. After a moment, she pointed, excited.

"That guy!"

Teddy could have sworn that Jules went even redder. In the top corner of the case, on a square white plate, sat several perfectly shaped marzipan figures: a little yellow dog, a guitar player in a wide hat, a bear cub. Cleo's finger pressed against the glass, pointing at a small, bright green grasshopper.

"The dog?" Jules asked, picking up a pair of tongs and opening the case.

"No!" Cleo giggled, pointing again. "*That* guy!"

"The baby bear?" He pointed the tongs at the brown figure.

"The green guy!" Cleo shrieked, laughing.

Jules looked a little unsure. He glanced right at Teddy, smiled tightly and took the figure from the case, then wrapped it in bakery tissue.

"The green guy, as it so happens," Jules said to Cleo, "costs exactly four beans."

"Just like the guy on his coat," Cleo's mother said, half to Jules and half to Cleo.

"What?" Jules said. "What?" His free hand touched the spot where Cleo's mother had pointed and he held it there over the note, fingers fluttering, tongs wobbling slightly in his other hand, before he peeled the paper from his coat. He glanced at it, and then quickly crumpled it in his fist. (Teddy felt it as if those fingers were squeezing around his chest, as if they were crumpling up his hope.) Wide-eyed, Jules looked at the kitchen door and then back at Cleo's mother.

"Tell Jules thank you," Cleo's mother said.

Teddy couldn't hear the rest of the exchange, though he watched Cleo smile up at Jules and take the marzipan figure from his hands, then hold it cradled in its tissue nest, as she walked out of the shop. Teddy couldn't hear anything because: upon noticing the grasshopper in the case; upon watching Jules gently lift it, his eyes flitting between Cleo and Teddy; upon hearing Cleo's mother mention the sign on Jules's chest, sound outside his own head had gone all white and clear and empty, and he was left only with a pulsing roar in his ears that he knew, distantly, was the racing rush-bang of his own heart.

"Magic beans," the man said to the counter. It came out sounding like an old-fashioned oath.

"What?" Jules was barely able to whisper. His throat felt full of sand and thorns. It had been, by any estimation, a horribly embarrassing few minutes and, even though the people standing in front of him had probably not understood the full significance of any of it, he still felt like an idiot, blushing and stumbling in front of the mystified looking man.

He crumpled the sticky note more tightly and thought about the thirty-six different ways he might murder 'Trice.

"She paid with magic beans," the man said, clearing his throat and speaking more clearly.

"Right," Jules said. It was strange, the two of them speaking to the counter between them. But Jules's humiliation hung like a wet rag around his shoulders, and he was still reeling from the hard smack of two worlds colliding, of coming face to face with the man he'd secretly watched, and, in the same moment, having the ridiculousness of his flirtation with Grasshopper broadcast like a joke or an embarrassing secret. Jules felt, suddenly, foolish and shallow, *unfaithful*, stringing himself between two men whose names he didn't know, who knew nothing of *him*, scattering his attention on the wind like a handful of wildflower seeds and entirely forgetting himself in the process, forgetting Andy, forgetting everything that had happened to put him here, where he usually stood, stoic, with the hint of sadness he'd wrapped around his shoulders as safe and beautiful and warm as a silk scarf. He could not look up. He pushed a bean toward the man. "Beanstalk?"

The man laughed, loud and sharp, one single sound, then seemed to catch himself and stopped. But it broke something open; the air seemed to thin, and Jules could move, could let his eyes wander up to the man's face. He was smiling, lightly, a small smile, kind, his eyes on his own hands, which were folded loosely around a foil package on the countertop between them.

"I could use a golden egg," the man said quietly and took the bean, then slipped it into the front pocket on his suit.

"Tea," Jules said, and the man's eyes darted up, locking with Jules's for one grinding second, confused again, before they slipped away, focusing again on the counter. "You could use some tea," Jules clarified, "and these." He placed two pieces of shortbread on a plate and pushed the plate toward the man, then turned to draw some hot water for the tea.

"Thanks," the man said to his back. "These are…"

Jules dropped a teabag into the water and turned to face the man again. "Chai-laced shortbread cookies. And chamomile tea. Because Cleo is a sticky tornado. And chamomile is calming. And tea is a surfactant. To help with the jam hands." He glanced at Teddy's hips, at the place where Cleo had gripped him, and then, feeling his face get hotter, tore his eyes away. "Which it won't really do, since chamomile isn't really a tea. But—" he stopped himself at the man's gentle laughter and looked up. "I picked for you. I hope that's okay."

"More than okay," the man said, smiling and a little red. "Thank you."

When he began to dig for his wallet, Jules held his palms firmly on the counter, because they wanted to fly out and grab the man's hand to stop him, to touch him, to hold, for a moment, something that looked to Jules completely warm. He shook his head. "No, please, on the house," he said. "Because I picked."

"Teddy," the man said, holding out his hand. Jules froze, looking at him dumbly, his arms still pinched to his sides, until the man smiled and said, "No jam hands. I swear. Very clean."

∞

Jules, his touch cool and dry and gentle, had taken his hand, lightly but firmly, and introduced himself. While he spoke, Teddy had smiled at him and held his hand carefully as a moth wing in his palm. Then he'd taken the cup of tea and the cookies to his usual table by the window, trying not to glance up too frequently at Jules, who was scrubbing the counter with a rag in one hand, a bottle of spray cleaner poised at the ready in the other, smiling faintly and humming to himself.

It was not often, anymore, that Teddy felt completely unsure. He knew the hour he'd wake in the morning, without an alarm, by the dawn's sunlight slicing through the two-inch crack in the blinds he left open every night. He knew when he'd drink his afternoon coffee, and how weak and acidic it would be from the office coffeemaker; he knew

89

when he'd chat up the secretaries, and what each of them would say, the order of questions and pleasantries and idle talk; he knew when he'd stack up the day's paperwork at the corner of his desk, what the fruit vendor on the corner of his block would shout at him as he passed, where he'd leave his shoes and belt when he walked in the door to his apartment, the exact portions of prepackaged meat and pasta and salad greens he'd dose onto his dinner plate in the fluorescent buzz of his kitchen that night. He knew how each day would start and end, with what it would be filled and what the next day would hold for him.

This, however, here, the bakery, dark and warm and colored rich with silks and velvets, full of sugar and soft light and glinting glass, was the slipping spot, the unschooled element, the grain of sand on the oyster's belly, a little irritation to the rhythm, undoing an hour at a time from that tightly wound spool that kept his days in order. He came here precisely to sit and bask in how it felt *not* to know.

Jules glanced up every few moments as he polished the wood and the glass and the metal of the counter with quick, tiny circles of the cloth. More than once when Teddy glanced at him, their eyes caught, and it was like a stubborn match finally striking, the flare that quick and hot. It occurred to Teddy that *Jules* was perhaps watching *him*, though for what reason, he couldn't figure.

Sitting there, watching Jules from the corner of his eye, he felt like a man on a high wire, barely balanced, still up in the air only by miracle and dumb luck and some strange trick of gravity, which refused to let him down.

⌒◞

Jules had watched the man—*Teddy*—sit and nurse the cup of tea and the two little cookies. He'd busied himself with cleaning, but it was a thin excuse and he knew it, woefully transparent, silly. The counters were, as always, pristine. Several times, Teddy had caught him watching, glancing up as if he suddenly felt Jules's stare, and Jules had looked away pink-faced, quickly but not quickly enough.

Nevertheless, Jules had watched Teddy eat, watched him sigh and gaze out the window to the street and watched him, after he'd finally finished the tea, carefully clean up the table, toss the trash in the can by the door and pack up his small shoulder bag. Before he left, he'd come to Jules's counter, placed his hand on the top of the cash register and tipped his head to the side slightly, smiling a crooked smile. "Nice to finally meet you, Jules," he'd said, and Jules had thought how pleasant, how warm and lovely, his name sounded in that man's mouth. Teddy had lingered, his hand curling over the ornately molded metal top of the cash register, as if there were more he might say, then suddenly rapped the top of the machine twice with finality and said simply, "Thank you," before he turned and went on his way, leaving behind only the thud of the closing door and the clap and clatter of the little bells against the glass.

"You morons!" 'Trice yelled, exploding through the kitchen door. The previously quiet shop front burst into a clamor of movement and noise as 'Trice banged the espresso machine's filter to dump the old grounds, then turned to joggle the lever on the grinder and tamp the coffee into the filter with more force than necessary. Jules stood, watching, as she clanged through the routine of pulling two shots and steaming some milk, then dumping everything—somehow both violently and with great precision—into two mugs, sliding one in his direction and taking a long, not-quite-calming sip from the other.

"What?" he asked guiltily.

She glared at him over the top of her mug, which she refused to lower from her face; her left hand was knotted into the long locks at her shoulder. "You've got to be kidding me," she said. "I practically threw you against him, and you did nothing. He had a gift for you, you know!"

"What?" Jules asked again. "Wait! *I'm* yelling at *you* here, not the other way around! You don't get to yell! Were you *trying* to humiliate me with that cricket note? Were you trying to humiliate *both* of us? Where did you even *get* that? Were you rooting through my drawers?"

"It fell off his stupid sleeve last time he was here, and I kept it!" she yelled, then stopped suddenly. "Wait," she said too quietly, looking at Jules with a mixture of sadness and disbelief.

"No!" Jules slammed his coffee mug down on the counter with a bit more force than he intended. "This isn't your little fantasy to direct, 'Trice. You can't embarrass me like that! You can't lock me out of my own kitchen in my own shop! If I don't want to talk to him, I don't have to! You don't get to *do* that to me!"

He felt himself taking off, felt the runway dropping out from beneath him, felt his arms pinwheel against his will in the air above them. He *hated* the feeling of losing the ground under him.

"Wait," 'Trice said again, more quietly. "How can you be so smart, and still be so *stupid?*" She put her hand on his arm before he could wave it again, before he could yell or throw the coffee into the sink and storm out, before he could fire her or cry or run or do any of the twenty other things he wanted to do.

"That," she said, looking at him with wide eyes, shaking her head softly, "was not a cricket."

Eight

JULES HAD TRIED CALLING the phone number he had for Grasshopper several times, but hung up each time just at the voicemail (*You've reached Teddy Flores*, said the familiar voice, and each time Jules kicked himself—a footless, internal kick, but a kick nonetheless—for his own stupidity. No—*blindness*. No—*willful* blindness. Because, he thought, launching another footless, internal kick, how could he have overlooked something so obvious? Only through willful blindness and his willingness to allow other people—'Trice, sure, but *Avon?*—to interpret the world for him. He'd never done that. He'd always been staunch in his insistence upon understanding the world on his own terms. *Until*, he thought, with another internal kick, *now. Why now?*)

For the third day in a row, Teddy had not made an appearance at the bakery. Jules had waited, had watched through the crack in the kitchen door every time he heard the jingle of the door bells; like some slavering, Pavlovian puppy, he'd been trained to the sound. His head would jerk up, and he'd drop whatever knife or spatula or cookie or tart he happened to be holding and, wiping his hands on his apron front and pulling at the strings, bound to the door to watch. Each time, he was disappointed to see it wasn't Teddy.

Grasshopper hadn't made an appearance online, either. A complete and dusty, pregnant, holding-on kind of silence had settled that made Jules itch, made him groan inside with both dread and anticipation.

"You're being a stalker again," 'Trice whispered over his shoulder. She'd come from out of nowhere and pounced as he sat hunched and miserable at the tiny desk he'd shoved into the back corner of the kitchen and sectioned off with a folding rattan screen from the flea market (a desk meant for bill-paying and recordkeeping, but more recently the site of his cranky brooding and the repository of his clandestine collection of Charming Grasshopper things: the set of keys, a doodled napkin, the foil from the packet of bread pudding—which, yes, he'd carefully scrubbed and folded—and now a crumpled sticky note with the words *I quit* scrawled in red ballpoint). 'Trice gingerly set a cup of coffee on the desk in front of him, then put her hands on either side of it and leaned over him; her long locks were stiff and a little scratchy as they slipped over his shoulders. The beads and shells she'd tied into her hair clanked softly as she shook her head. "Liking him isn't wrong, you know. You're not doing anything wrong," she said quietly.

He gave her a hard look over the top of his reading glasses, one that meant she was still on thin ice, and far too close for his liking, but he knew the look had no real heat.

"You have to leave him a message next time, or it's just plain creepy," she said, a little more lightly.

Obediently, he dialed again, and listened to the whole message this time (Teddy's voice was muted and professional-but-friendly, a little raspy on the tenor notes, a little rattly in the bass), but couldn't bring himself to speak when the beep came and hung up with shaking hands and a sigh.

"Oh, Sugar Cookie, this is bad, isn't it?" 'Trice asked before she stepped back and sat on the edge of the desk. "This isn't like you. What is this?"

Jules looked at her balefully, then dropped his head onto his arms, breathing in the paper and ink mustiness of the desk blotter. "I don't even know!" he wailed, his voice slightly muffled by his own arms. "I don't even know what this is!"

"This," she said, dropping a gentle touch to one of his forearms, then carefully moving her hand to stroke the back of his hair, "this is you waking up after sleeping for a very long time. This is you fumbling around because everything's still a little numb from staying so still. This is you finding your sea legs, sailor. This," she said and her hand was cool and almost motherly on the back of his neck before she took it away, "is a fucked up but very fixable situation."

When Jules looked up, 'Trice was standing at a more reasonable distance, with her head bent low, her face shaded by the swinging ropes of her hair and her hands to herself, cradling his phone.

"What—"

"This is a very fucked up situation, the two of you playing stupid staying-away games like this. You're miserable, and you're off and you're hardly getting things done in here, and I can't stand it anymore. Get some caffeine in you," she motioned to the cup of coffee, the lip of which Jules was tracing with a fingertip, "while I fix this, so you can get back to your normal, bossy, picky, know-it-all, stick-up-the-ass self."

She typed rapidly with her thumbs, made a satisfied noise and tossed the phone onto the desk in front of him before he'd managed to close his gaping mouth with a little squeak.

"I miss that guy," she said, then turned and left the kitchen in a flap of beads and cotton and the stale and cloying smell of clove cigarettes. Jules wasn't sure if she was talking about his normal self or Teddy.

"You are such a cliché," he called halfheartedly after her, knowing she probably didn't hear him and knowing, too, that it was certainly a case of the pot calling the kettle black, and that this very fact was a large part of why they loved each other like family. He picked up his phone and peered at what 'Trice had done.

A text message to Grasshopper—whose name, Jules realized, he must soon either change to "Teddy" or delete from his phone entirely, depending on how things went in the near future (and here he felt himself deliver yet another internal, footless kick): *I'm sorry I was heretofore an idiot. Please, stop by the bakery tomorrow after you are done with work. I'm leaving a gift with 'Trice especially for you.*

"Heretofore?" Jules yelled at the door. "Should we change the name here to Ye Olde Bakeree? What am I, eighty-seven years old?" It was a bit better, he supposed, than "hitherto," but not by much.

Please disregard my careless use of the word "heretofore." I know I am not at a Renaissance Festival, nor in a production of A Midsummer Night's Dream, he typed.

Then he waited, staring at the screen of his phone for several minutes before turning it off, placing it in a desk drawer and deliberately concerning himself with writing checks and filing bills.

He could hear 'Trice clatter about in the front of the shop as she cleaned the counters and unclogged the steamer on the espresso machine, scrubbed the sink and re-parked the stools at their proper tables, though it was far too early in the day to do so. She was, he figured, puttering, bored, avoiding the kitchen and avoiding Jules. She was waiting, too.

The noises were distant and softened by the door between them, reminding him of the clamor of his grandmother's dinner preparations, the smell of pot roast and the flicker and whine of the TV while his father half-dozed in the dimmed living room. If he entered the kitchen, he'd be given plates and silverware to lay out on the table and, if he were lucky, his grandmother would step around the center counter and show him how to fold the napkins into pretty shapes, with her hands cupping his shoulders as he worked under her gaze. He missed that feeling, knowing that she was watching, that she'd carefully, sweetly reach down and fix what he managed to botch, while her voice flitted between under-the-breath melodies and careful instruction, as if none of it mattered very much but all of it was very interesting. He missed the warm kitchen, the cooking-smell, the evening light, the creak of the oven door, the thump of the kitchen towel, which she wore tucked into her waistband like an apron, as she tossed it onto the counter when all the work was done.

He slid open the drawer and stared at his phone, willing himself to shut the drawer again before waking it to check his messages. It had only been twenty minutes. There was nothing.

But I am leaving the gift. That part was accurate. You should come by to pick it up. The gift. 'Trice will have it when you come to get it. If you want.

The minute he sent the note, he thought better of it, but it was too late. Instead, he took the phone, pushed out into the front of the bakery and thrust it at 'Trice.

"Take this," he said. "You're in charge of it now. I can't be trusted."

"What did you do?" she asked, shaking her head, but didn't really seem to expect an answer from him. Instead, she pocketed the phone and went back to polishing the glass on the pastry case.

In fifteen minutes, Jules was back, and when he asked for the phone, she handed it back.

Nothing there.

I really am sorry. If you will ever talk to me again, please come get your treat, he managed to send before 'Trice noticed what he was doing and swiped the phone out of his hands.

"You," she cranked, looking at the screen, "*really* cannot be trusted with this. I will let you know when he responds. Now go bake something."

Jules, grumbling, slumped back into the kitchen. He had to think up a suitable treat to leave for Teddy the next day. He kept himself mostly busy, puttering in the kitchen, flipping through the recipes in his notebook and scrabbling in the large walk-in refrigerator for ingredient ideas. The whole afternoon, he'd manage to last twenty minutes at a time before popping his head out into the shop front, only to have 'Trice yell at him to get back in the kitchen and *work*. "I said I will let you know, you burdensome mule!" she would shout. Another time, "You are boring me with this stupidity!" And finally, "Come out here and *take* this phone from me, if you want it, you scrawny thing! I will break you in half!"

This last time, he knew, she meant business.

⌇

Teddy had, upon the advice of his superego or some such sanctimoniously know-it-all inner voice, stayed away from Buttermilk for several days. If one were to be absolutely accurate, in fact, he'd stayed away from *Jules*—the bakery, the blog, messaging and phone. Finally meeting Jules—his stone-gray eyes the only thing, Teddy remembered, that belied his papery, fragile appearance—had been a terrible mistake. Teddy had been pitifully inept, tongue-tied, ridiculous, and Jules had seemed bothered or angry or both, or perhaps—worse— entirely indifferent to him. Teddy had slunk out of the bakery as quietly as he could after spending what he thought was a face-saving amount of time at a table with some tea and cookies.

Since then, there had been no messages of any kind from Jules. Clearly, Teddy thought, pushing himself where he hadn't been welcome had been a huge miscalculation.

The office was a sickly yellow-green. The sickly yellow-green lights whined and zimmed incessantly overhead. The yellow-green walls, the yellow-green Formica of the front desk and the carpets and the air itself—everything felt limp and damp and nauseating. Even the bright orange bird of paradise blooms at the front desk looked peaked and sharp. The day dragged on, but Teddy refused to let himself wander online, knowing exactly where he'd go if he did and exactly what disasters might result. He held firm; he sighed heavy sighs. He sorted the papers on his desk twice over, sharpened every pencil in the cup and refilled his stapler. He linked the paperclips into one long chain, which he then hid under the desk like contraband because he knew paperclip chains were, without a doubt, a complete waste of office supplies and therefore frowned upon. But the chain made a satisfying clink when it dropped against the metal desk or the plastic floor mat, so he clinked it again and again like a latter-day Jacob Marley, rattling up courage or ire or just a little noise, until several heads popped up over the top of his cubicle walls to glare at him and he dropped the chain into a drawer.

Teddy felt full of caffeine when the world wanted to sleep; he felt all pins and staples and broken glass. He couldn't remember how, before *all that,* he hadn't noticed how *empty* his days were, how filled with the hum and buzz and flurry of absolutely nothing to think about. He bought two little purple plums at the fruit stand at lunch, simply to cheer himself up, and they sat at the back corner of his desk the whole day, carefully aligned side by side against the cubicle wall and staring at him accusingly like giant, bloodshot, angry eyes.

When the clock hung high on the wall near the front desk snapped, finally, to six o'clock, his bag was already packed up, his desk was neatened beyond its usual neatness, and he stood jerkily and hurried to the lobby to catch, he hoped, the last few dwindling rays of sun before it set without him.

The street was a noisy, fuming relief; he leaned heavily against the rusting metal sculpture outside his office building (he'd never really understood its simple, fat lines of red steel hulking their way upward and cranking around each other in thick angles; a creaky monument, he always thought, to the mechanical and the doomed and the desk-bound which never seemed to garner a glance of interest from passersby, but did, at lunchtime and after work, become the hangout for desperately puffing smokers and numerous obliviously shitting pigeons, a depressing sentinel to mark the beginning and end of the day) and pulled out his phone to check his messages.

There were few people in the world from whom Teddy expected to hear on any given day: his mother (who left long, winding messages with no point except, he thought, to ribbon her voice into his day and tie up the distance between them so tightly they both felt her loneliness and ache in the camel-colored house on the manicured lawn in a city he'd left far behind years ago, and the gap in her story that was the shape of his father, always traveling, always leaving her alone to feel more keenly against her back the long press of days, all completely alike, so that sometimes Teddy sent her Gerbera daisies, orange and red and yellow and pink, just for the clashy brightness they might add to her day—*you are*, she'd said in one of these messages, *like a missing limb, and sometimes, sweetheart, I think I can still feel you even though you're gone*); his friend Dan (who called like clockwork once a week on Thursday afternoons to say hello and not much else, filling the space— almost desperately, Teddy thought—between breaths with stories about his two-year-old daughter or the alumni association of which he was president, or the last movie he'd watched on the rare night he and his wife could sneak out to see something without puppets or cartoons and asking, finally, always, how was the job, how was the city, how was he feeling—and Teddy felt, always, at those moments, the pressure to say something that made his days sound bumpier and brighter than they usually were—and then the questions to which Teddy always had to answer no: *No*, he hadn't read the alumni newsletter, *no*, he hadn't seen that show because even off-Broadway tickets were expensive, and *no*, he didn't think much about the old gang anymore, and *no*, and *no*, and *no*); and Maggie (who called herself the World's Worst Fag Hag because she was never around to go to clubs or go shopping or go to brunch since her job as a shoe designer meant she was always somewhere more interesting, like China or Brazil, and it didn't matter that Teddy didn't like to do those things anyway, it was the principle of the thing, she'd say, then revolt him with a story about the latest gustatory abomination she'd tried in the latest tiny, foreign town and then fill the final moments of their conversations with fountains of her raucous, unbridled laughter, which made Teddy smile but feel all the lonelier).

Everything in my life, Teddy thought, *is measured in forms of distance.*

Though there were not many people in the world from whom Teddy expected to hear on any given day, there had recently been Jules, with whom he'd exchanged volumes of messages and with whom he had spoken for two golden hours one evening as he bent over his table and tried to mold marzipan into something that *didn't* look sloppy or amateur. Jules's voice, thin and dreamy with memory, coming from somewhere across the city, across the hiss of the cell phone connection, across buildings and parks and darkening playgrounds, across garbage trucks and alleyways, across scuttling rats and the rickety snap of the subway, across pavement and cobblestone and brick, across the distance of everything unnamed and anonymous and rushed and blank that was New York, had felt so near and so present that Teddy could almost feel him breathing next to him. And Teddy couldn't shake the habit, now, of looking for him.

I'm sorry I was heretofore an idiot. Please, stop by the bakery tomorrow after you are done with work. I'm leaving a gift with 'Trice especially for you.

And after that, a long string of messages, which Teddy read eagerly, his relieved laughter cascading, tinny and joyful, like a shaking string of bells.

I really didn't know it was you.

Both of you, I mean. Grasshopper. You.

I'm not making sense. I apologize for the nonsense texts. I'm texting a lot here, and you're probably ignoring me because it's probably getting creepy.

I can be, very often, a complete dolt.

Because I use words like "heretofore" and "dolt." Please don't judge me. I'm trying to be lighthearted here. :)

I apologize for the emoticon. I don't ever use emoticons. I was going for light-hearted, and landed somewhere around twelve years old. I don't know what got into me there. Probably the spirit of Avon. You met Avon.

One last try and then I'll stop, I promise. If you don't come pick up your gift tomorrow, I'll have to eat it myself, and that would be the saddest picture ever. I hope you'll save me from that.

That was the last of the messages, and Teddy felt torn and aching, relieved and sad at all once, though he couldn't have explained it. He sent a single message, and then forced himself to pocket the phone and not look at it again for the rest of the evening.

I'm sorry for leaving you hanging all day; I wasn't ignoring you. We're not allowed to exchange personal messages during the workday. Company Policy. You have nothing to apologize for, but I'm coming to get that gift tomorrow anyway, because who would turn away your baked goods? Not me, that's who. I promise, I'm coming to save you.

◦◦◦◦

Because this is a story, we can reel quickly through a day which, for Teddy and Jules both, was agonizingly long and uneventful. We can skip ahead to the good part, the part for which we've been hoping, when, at five o'clock, Teddy carefully packed his bag, left the office and walked swiftly those many dark and rainy blocks. It was raining that day, pelting and icy and unrelenting, and Teddy's cheap subway-vendor umbrella, the black and flimsy kind every New Yorker carries on such days knowing full well it won't last more than one or two rains, didn't even last the one but was blown inside out by the fourth block, so that, by the sixth block, he was blistered with ice and wet and cold, balancing his bag over his head to provide any protection—too little and too late as it was—against what seemed to be the universe throwing itself against him and his efforts with all its might. (This was *not* the case; as we have said, the universe did not understand that Teddy existed, being as vast and busy and ignorant as it is, and was simply tossing its storms as it might. But to Teddy, scurrying desperately down the unnaturally dark streets, thinking only of the warm yellow light and tinkling glass of the bakery glowing like a hearth at the end of a long journey, it felt very much as if the universe were specifically pelting *him* with its million tiny, icy hands, shrieking *turn back, don't go, we are entirely against this!*)

Despite the rain, he went, and by the time he arrived at the gold and glass door, he was shivering, blue-lipped and pitiful; his coat was clammy against him and his pants and shirt clung to his skin like, well, like a second, slightly loosening and oozing skin. He pushed his way into the bakery. The sweet-smelling warmth and the tinkling music of the glass overhead and the softly shaking fringe on the lampshades brushing the low light felt much more like home to him than home did, he thought, and fought the start of something sob-like in his throat, which mystified him, because he was happy here. He stood, dripping and waiting, at the counter while 'Trice poured coffee for a woman—perfumed, draped in scarves and shopping bags, her hair swept up neatly in a too-tight chignon—who waited, tapping her long nails against the counter.

"Thank you, darling, see you tomorrow," the woman said and turned and almost slapped straight into Teddy, who may, he admitted to himself, have been standing a bit too close in his eagerness.

"Good god!" she said, jumping back, one hand covering the top of her coffee carefully. "Are you always soaking wet and banging into people, or is it just me?"

It was Irene.

"Irene, leave the poor guy alone," 'Trice called, winking at Teddy and smiling. She turned to the coffee machine and started what Teddy assumed was a coffee for him, because 'Trice always seemed to know without asking exactly what he needed.

"I will *not* leave this man alone," Irene said, huffing in an exaggerated manner that Teddy knew had to be her attempt at flirting with him. "He is clearly determined to sweep me off my feet. And," she poked his chest with a red nail as she gnawed the lid of her coffee cup open, "he has yet to call me."

"I'm sorry." Teddy felt sheepish and lost and a little afraid. He glared over Irene's shoulder to send a look of distress to 'Trice, but her back was still turned. He could swear, however, he saw her shoulders shake. "I—"

"I know, I know," Irene said, patting his arm. "You lost my card. Or you have been very busy with work, which apparently you do on a boat of some kind on the open ocean, you poor, wet puppy. Or you have been out of town on business during monsoon season. In any case, I am sure you have a good reason for disregarding the chemistry between us and discarding me like so much trash."

"Irene, knock it off!" 'Trice hollered, finally turning around. "He's not interested! He's *gay!*"

"He's right here," Teddy mumbled, then reddened considerably when both women turned to look at him as if they had forgotten he was standing there. He looked at his shoes, unpolished and squelching water, and said, "I mean—"

"That," said Irene, fluttering her eyes at him, "is really a waste of a very good man. Isn't it always the way? Call me anyway," she called over her shoulder as she left the bakery in a flurry of perfume and paper bags and the slightly bitter scent of coffee.

"That," said 'Trice to Teddy, "is really a waste of a very good hat. She fills it out, but she doesn't fill it in, if you know what I mean." 'Trice slid a cup of coffee at him and waved away his attempt to pay. "Are you kidding? Since when? Besides, Jojo, how can I charge you for that when you look like somebody ran over you with a submarine and then took all your toys away and kicked your dog?"

Before he could respond, 'Trice held up a finger, then disappeared behind the pastry case to reemerge with a small, white cardboard cake box wrapped with a gold ribbon. She placed it on the counter in front of him.

"It's from You-Know-Who," she said, raising her eyebrows and nodding toward the kitchen. "I think they are I'm Sorry Cookies. Or something like that. He was mumbling."

Scrawled across the top of the box in black marker was a note:

Dear Teddy:

I baked these for you because I am (check one)

X an ignoramus who can't see what's in front of me, even when it's entirely obvious to everyone else
X a dumb bunny incapable of acting like a human being in front of people I like
X really in need of a social life
X very sorry for acting like a total idiot
X a brilliant baker but in all other respects a very flawed doofus who needs 'Trice's help to do even the simplest of things, like talk to a nice guy whom I would like to get to know a little better in the near future

Please forgive me. Yours, Her Royal Majesty Chef Jules James "I'm Sorry" Burns

All the boxes were checked. Teddy looked at 'Trice.

"I did that for him," she said, nodding. "It's what he should have said, anyway. I think he thinks the cookies will say everything for him. Clearly, he's putting too much pressure on the cookies, so I helped."

"Is he here?"

"No, he went home earlier." 'Trice sounded mechanical but widened her eyes and jerked her head, almost imperceptibly, toward the kitchen. "He *definitely* wouldn't stick around to make sure I gave this to you, because *he trusts me and he is not a creepy stalker or anything like that!*" She shouted that last bit, and widened her eyes again at Teddy, then laughed when they both heard a faint thump from behind the kitchen door. "It's too easy," she whispered, then raised her voice to a normal volume again. "I'm afraid you're stuck with me today, *amigo.*"

"Thanks," Teddy said, starting to gather the box and the coffee, his broken umbrella and his bag.

"You might want to sit and have one or two of those with your coffee before you go," 'Trice said. "While you dry off a bit. And, you know, so that I can tell Jules if you liked them or not." She faced him with her back to the kitchen, and widened her eyes at him again. She looked, Teddy thought, as if she might hurt herself if she glared at him any more meaningfully and so, although he would have run back out into the pouring sleet and walked all the way to Long Island rather than stay for another minute in the bakery, where 'Trice and Jules and who-knew-who-else were watching his every move, he sat at his usual table by the window, sighed and started to remove his coat.

"You probably don't want to sit so close to the door," 'Trice said, raising her eyebrows. "You'll probably be warmer if you sit over there, closer to the kitchen." She cleared her throat loudly, ignored the series of dull thumps coming from behind the kitchen door and gestured with her head at a table at the back of the bakery. Teddy gave her his most pitiful look before scooping everything up and switching tables.

He peeled off his coat and hung it over the second stool at the table. He blotted his hair and shirt with a handful of napkins. He wiped down the table, settled himself in his seat and took a long drink of coffee before he could bring himself to glance at the kitchen door and pull open the gold ribbon on the box.

Inside were a dozen little heart-shaped cookies, each oozing red jam and dusted lightly with powdered sugar.

They tasted, he thought, when he lifted one to his lips and bit a tiny piece, casting his eyes tableward and not glancing at the cracked kitchen door, they tasted bright and sharp with sweet, tart fruit soaring over the warm bitterness of pecans. Sugar was the first touch, powdery and light, softly coating his tongue, softly, softly cradling the sharp and the sweet and the bitter so that every taste was left lovingly balanced, still real, but muted and made kinder and more beautiful. They tasted, he thought, so *good*.

༄

PASTRY-WHIPPED: ADVENTURES IN SUGAR BY A DEDICATED
CRUMPET STRUMPET
by Chef Jules Burns of Buttermilk Bakery
April 19: I'm Sorry (The Story of Fruits in the Kitchen)

I seem to be saying that a lot lately, and mostly, I seem to be apologizing for my awkwardness when it comes to dealing with the outside world. I spend so much time shut up in the back of the bakery with my head in the oven (not in a Sylvia Plath way, I assure you) that when it's time to come out, I often don't know how to act like a regular person. At least, this is what 'Trice, my assistant, tells me all the time. I think I'm so odd, I barely even notice my own strangeness anymore.

This week, I'm apologizing to you all for having shirked my online duties and neglected to post something on this blog last week. Whatever did you do for an entire week without my sugar-induced rambling and sanctimonious, butterier-than-thou ingredient snobbery?

If you're reading this, then clearly you survived, for which I am truly grateful. Nevertheless, I'm sorry for my inattention, my neglectfulness, my long silence. As a peace offering this week, I'm giving up my recipe for Linzer tarts. Don't expect me to turn over the recipe for my secret filling, though… I'm not that sorry. I suggest indulging in your favorite jam or compote for the purpose, and visiting Buttermilk if you're curious to see what I put in there.

I've gotten very good at apologies over the years, having often been in the position, due to my awkwardness, my eagerness, my stubbornness or my meanness, to make amends. What I've learned, aside from the value of baked goods on these occasions as a kind of delicious wheel-greaser, is that a good apology is one that simply expresses regret for some bad behavior or lack of insight on my part, and does not ask for forgiveness. A good apology is like a steam valve, letting out some of the pressure, de-escalating the moment, unknotting things. A good apology expects nothing in return. It's a gift, freely given, and it must be freely accepted in order to work.

I've also spent a lot of my time apologizing for things that weren't my fault: for loving boys who could not love me back, who felt my affection as a cut against their own importance and safety; for being the kid who couldn't keep his mother interested enough to stick around past his infancy, or keep his grandmother alive, no matter how many prayers I said or wishes I sent out into the universe, whispering over my grandmother's cold hands in time to the beep of hospital machinery; again, later, for being the man who couldn't save his beloved, who lay sleeping in a hospital bed which might have been the same hospital bed, though it was almost twenty years later and several states away from Indiana, the same rhythmic blips on the same gray plastic machines in the background, the same ache in my bones for what I was unable, being only human, being only me, to do for him.

Lately, I've been regretting the forgetting, as if this little and inevitable easing of my memory were an indication of the hollowness of my previous regrets. I've been regretting, too, thoughts of moving on, of loving someone else. The prospect is terrifying; it seems as much like betrayal as it does like possibility. I find myself feeling sorry for that, too.

I've always imagined myself as fierce, free of the self-loathing tether of regret, honest in the world and true to myself, raw and laid bare by my own hand, because keeping myself safe in the bind of my own secrecy always seemed to me much worse. I realize now, despite that, that I've spent a lot of time harboring regret, and mostly for things I could not undo about myself—most especially, regretting my own fallible humanity. I've spent too much time feeling trapped in that particularly cramped and airless cage. I'm here today, in part, to tell you I am letting all of that go.

The "I'm Sorry Cookies" I'm offering here are Linzer tarts, cut into pretty shapes and dusted with powdered sugar to cover any bumps and imperfections, filled, in your case, with any mushy and sweet thing you choose, and, in my case, with a homemade jam of strawberry, rhubarb and mint. I think these cookies do a good job accompanying an apology—they're mild and friendly, a bit sweet, a bit tart and completely unassuming.

I've already made and delivered a batch of these this week to accompany yet another well-deserved apology, though I decline to provide you with the details of my trespass, and for that, again, I apologize. I expect to make many more before my life is over. Today, however, I'd like to imagine that I've baked myself a batch, too. For all the regret I've carried, for all the battering I've given my poor heart (it is enough, my father used to tell me, that others will do that quite willingly for me; I should not help them in their cause by punishing myself too), I want to apologize, and to forgive and to open the little locked cage of my heart and set free the creature that's been beating itself against the bars for far too long.

This is the gift I'm giving to my own self; this is the blessing; this is the benediction.

For loving someone who might never love you back, I forgive you. For letting go what you no longer wanted, I forgive you, and for the failure you thought it was to do so, I also forgive you. For locking yourself away from the world when you lose what you cannot bear to lose, I forgive you. For remembering, and also for forgetting, I forgive you. For being too much in the world, I forgive you. For not being enough, I forgive you. For wanting and not wanting, for needing and depending, for changing and for never changing, for missing and longing and hoping and failing, for all of this, I forgive you. For never daring to ask for this forgiveness, I forgive you with my entire aching self. For nearly crushing your beautiful, fragile heart in your own fist, I forgive you.

For all of these things I've written here, and for ten thousand more things I will never write down, I offer forgiveness. Let me open my hands, lift up my arms and toss my heart—that little fluttering, bruised bird—up and into the sky. Go where you will. I release you.

Nine

You have been very patient. We have been telling you this tale for a good many chapters now, knowing full well what you expect of this story, knowing full well that from the moment we first introduced the two men about whom this story revolves, from the first glance and the first taste and the first hint of the low-lit magic of the little bakery (clasping around them like a pair of warm hands, pressing them gently together), you have expected them to meet in a hail of sparks, to fall in love against a backdrop of slow fireworks and shimmer and to kiss, to kiss, and to kiss.

You will not, we hope, be disappointed then when we tell you, happily—because this is good news—that in the empty, airless space between chapters, there was such a kiss. There were, in point of fact, many thousands of kisses in that space: soft goodnight kisses on the sweat-sweet foreheads of children; the quick-pecked goodbye kisses of mothers and fathers, of grandmothers, of strange uncles and favorite teachers and best friends; starting-something kisses and dare kisses, curious kisses and ones that were shy, or nervous, or bold, taken ones and given ones and sometimes accidental ones; longer kisses, soul kisses, licking kisses with teeth and tongue and going deeper; first kisses and last kisses; kisses like prayers and kisses like pleas; desperate kisses fumbling their way across newly bared skin in a thousand backseats of a thousand cars parked in a thousand different dark, wooded places. There were so many kisses in that vacuum of time between chapters; the world was filled up with kissing but, we know, there is only one kiss about which you care, only one kiss about which you want to hear.

We had planned to start this part of the tale with Teddy, combed and pressed and ready, waiting by the window in the early morning for the honk of the cab he'd called the night before, suitcase packed tight and trim, a pair of dark, reasonable suits swinging hollow and loose in a garment bag at the door. He felt wound, like a coiled spring, and full of energy that owed nothing to the paper cup of weak bodega coffee he nursed in his free hand.

I'm sorry, he typed into his phone with one thumb, and sent the message to Jules. It was a delicate balancing act.

But it is too late, this moment. We must instead rewind the days to tell you what happened before, what led to this moment, why Teddy is apologizing and for what, and why his bags are packed and he is waiting, not so patiently, for a car to take him away in the damp gray of the too-early morning. And we must, we know, give you, who have been so patiently waiting, that longed-for kiss.

Two days ago, Jules had sent out the cookies for Teddy and hidden in the kitchen, peering out through the tiny crack between door and wall, not entirely trusting what 'Trice might do in his absence given her penchant for meddling in his private life. Teddy had sat at the table nearest the kitchen doors and slowly eaten two of the cookies. A peaceful sweet smile had lit his face as he absently chewed and sipped his coffee; his hands had been folded around the warming cup—nails neatly filed, Jules had noted, knuckles slightly red from the chill—and his eyes had been downcast, the lashes dotted, Jules could see, with rainwater; his cheeks and neck were shining with it, his wet white shirt turned pale pink where it clung to his chest, and oh, it was simply *beautiful*. Once, for one brief moment, Teddy had raised his eyes and glanced through those thick, wet eyelashes at the door, and Jules had known without a doubt that Teddy sensed he was there, watching him. It had sent a sharp, electric thrill into the pit of his stomach, that look.

Teddy had eventually left, with one final, quick glance and bright hint of a smile at the door behind which Jules stood. Jules had forced himself to wait a full forty-five minutes before sending Teddy a text message:

I hope you liked the cookies. 'Trice said you picked them up today.

There followed what seemed to Jules like an interminable silence while he waited, though we who were watching might tell you that it was mere seconds before a reply came: *The cookies were amazing. And glorious. And wonderful. Guess who has two thumbs and might be having cookies for dinner tonight?*

And not four seconds later, another message: *This guy. (You can't see me, but I am pointing to myself with my thumbs right now. This joke is better in person, isn't it?)*

Jules felt full of feathers, but he took three long breaths before he dared reply.

If I hadn't seen you with my own eyes, I would swear that you were five years old.

That's not nice, Teddy typed back. *I might require another batch of cookies to make up for that.*

No more cookies for you, mister. You're all hopped up on sugar. You're going to be up way past your bedtime as it is.

There was a very long pause after Jules sent this message, in the space of which he began to panic, and his stomach began to pull down and away from him in a sickening slide. This pause contained all his past mistakes and stupidity, all the hubris and the stupid chance-taking and inglorious overstepping he'd ever done.

But then a message came from Teddy: *I'm going to be up way past my bedtime tonight anyway.*

Oh, Jules typed. *Busy night tonight, I imagine. I should really let you get to it so you're not up all night.*

Doing whatever it is, he added.

That's going to be keeping you up all night, I mean, he added again.

That sounded pretty suggestive, he typed, and though he told himself to stop, his hands kept him babbling. *But really, I'm just assuming you have work, or maybe a hot date, or that you're drying fruit in the oven, or that you teach some sort of late-night aerobics class at the Chelsea Crunch. Plus maybe you have loads of laundry to do.*

Another long pause occurred, in which Jules succeeded in biting two of his nails to the quick.

I'm going to be up way past my bedtime because I'm not going to be able to stop thinking about a certain heart-stoppingly beautiful, gray-eyed and talented pastry chef I met recently. And "hot date"? What are you, seventy-three?

Seventy-eight, thank you very much. But I follow a very careful grooming and exercise regimen to maintain my youthful glow.

Boyish good looks, Teddy wrote. *That's the cliché, anyway... But you really do have boyish good looks... in the classic sense... I'm sure you've been told hundreds of times.*

After a brief pause, Teddy began typing again: *Aaaaand now I'm blushing furiously. Smooth, Flores, really smooth. You can't see me, but I'm a tomato right now. Again, this would make more sense in person, wouldn't it?*

I feel like you're hinting at something here, Jules wrote.

I might be hinting at something. If I were hinting at something, what would I be hinting at?

At what would you be hinting, do you mean? (Oooh, my grammar hackles.)

At what would I be hinting, then? Teddy's reply came quick as a parry.

You tell me, since you're doing the hinting. However would I know at what you're hinting?

It would be easier to tell you in person, Teddy wrote.

Why, Mr. Flores, you cad! Are you suggesting that you would like to see me in person again?

I might be suggesting that I plan to drop by the bakery tomorrow morning very early before work. And I might be suggesting that it would be very gratifying to be permitted entrance to the kitchen, to see where all the magic happens. And that if you happened to be there in the kitchen, when I was permitted entrance, well, that might be very gratifying, too.

Jules waited too long to respond. He knew that he was taking too long, that the pause had moved well past flirtatious and deeply into weird, or creepy or cruel. His fingers, however, were stiff and shaking and refused to move. This, this conversation in space, was so lovely. They were both so easy without bodies, they *fit* so perfectly and simply and beautifully when they spoke together like this. Jules was clever and quick and bold; he was stone-strong and open and sure. But when they'd finally come face to face, he had been none of those things. He'd been young and shaky and stupid. When they'd finally come face to face, it had been so… *not* lovely. It had been awkward; it had been humiliating, and it had resulted in a days-long silence from Teddy.

For both of us, I mean, Teddy wrote. *Gratifying for all parties concerned.*

I don't mean that in a dirty way. I'm only thinking of your well-being, you know, he added. *Because I'm that kind of guy.*

There was a long and empty moment, into which Jules couldn't put his voice. He had no idea how to reply, how to tell Teddy that he was at once so terrified and so excited that his hands were shaking, and that it was a terrible idea; and that despite that, he could not bring himself to say no, *would not let himself say no this time,* no matter how terrible the idea might seem, because the mere thought of seeing Teddy again filled him with... something like joy.

Hello? Teddy's text broke into his thoughts. *Did I say something wrong? Because if I did, it was not my fault. This other guy just stole my phone and started texting you things I would never, ever say to you. I was going to text a very suave, exactly appropriate response, until this other guy, who came out of nowhere, really did just steal my phone. And then he gave it back. This is me now. Are you still there?*

Sorry. Multitasking, Jules lied. *I would be happy to give you a tour of the kitchen. 'Trice gets there at 8 a.m., so if you don't want her hovering over your tour, you should come earlier than that. I'm not telling you what to do, exactly. Actually, I am begging you: Please come earlier than that, so that we don't have to deal with 'Trice. I will be calmer and happier before she arrives. She makes me into an emotional tornado.*

It's a date, Teddy wrote. *And I actually read that wrong. I thought you wrote that you would be an emotional tomato. And I couldn't figure out what that would look like.*

Then stay until 8:15 and you'll have a very good idea.

I will come whenever you tell me to, and I'll stay as long as you let me. If you put a dog bed on the floor in the corner, I may curl up there and simply bask in the amazingness of you and your baking superpowers.

That sounded less cool than I meant it to sound, Teddy added. *What I meant to say was: It's a date.*

You're making me blush. I'm an emotional tomato now, Jules wrote. *Oh! And you'll need a hat or a scarf to cover your head. Kitchen rules. A demain?*

If that means "it's a date," then absolutely.

Jules did not sleep that night. He spent the hours curled up on the couch with Andy snoring against him, his fingers purling through the silky fur on Andy's neck, scrolling back and forth through the message exchange with Teddy. He tried warm milk and it did no good. He flipped through several back issues of the black-and-white photography magazines he kept on his coffee table mostly for show and read another chapter of the novel through which he was slogging. He sharpened his home knives and took inventory of his dry goods. He polished all his shoes and boots. He refolded his sweaters. He took a bath scented with rosemary and lavender oils and buffed his skin to a glow with the loofah. He did everything it was possible to do in his apartment in the middle of the night, but he did not sleep.

By six o'clock in the morning, it had become clear to Jules that the sun had no intention of rising or shining, warming or brightening or doing anything it might normally do. The morning seemed determined to stay gray and clankingly noisy with the rumble of delivery trucks. He had already set most of the day's pastries to bake and had settled at his desk with a cup of coffee, the crossword puzzle and the relative quiet of the day, feeling warm and hidden and peaceful, when his phone chirped with a message.

I'm outside the bakery, but it looks like nobody is home. The gate is down.

Without thinking, Jules's body moved, as if he were a magnet being pulled or a stone rolling swiftly downhill. He moved with that force, without will, tugging at the apron strings at his waist to tighten them—he felt held that way, comforted, controlled—and then flipping loose the lock on the front door. He pulled the door open and rattled the gate upward. Teddy stood near the curb, with his charcoal gray suit jacket slung over a black wool vest, black trilby tipped back and dark hair shining and pressed in finger waves. He looked up at Jules, slipped his phone into his suit pocket, pushed the hat forward and smiled winningly.

"I didn't know if you were in yet," he said awkwardly. "The gate was down."

Jules beckoned him into the bakery, stepping aside and holding the door as Teddy passed. He smelled, Jules thought, like juniper and gin, something old-fashioned like that, a clean smell, and simple. He brought the gate back down and locked the door.

"I keep it locked up until we open, or customers would be haranguing me for coffee at all hours. This city and its coffee fetish. They don't even care if it's good." He rolled his eyes heavenward and sighed, as if Teddy would understand his frustration. As if he *didn't* sound like a pretentious New York wannabe. He bit his lip. "Would you like some coffee?"

Teddy smiled and graciously accepted the cup Jules offered him a moment later. Jules felt better behind the counter. He felt stable; there was something onto which he could hold. He did; he gripped the counter until his knuckles turned white.

"Thank you again for the cookies," Teddy said politely, holding the mug of coffee just under his nose. Jules couldn't see his mouth. "They were... transcendent."

Jules raised his eyebrows.

"Okay, well, they were extremely good, anyway. And I only have a couple left, because I really did wind up eating them for dinner last night," Teddy said, smiling into the coffee.

"Oh, so you really *are* five years old, then."

"Eight," Teddy said seriously.

"And I'm seventy-eight," Jules sighed. "On the bright side, we could both play Monopoly without a problem."

Teddy gave him a look of confusion—still smiling—and Jules stammered, "Because the box says it's for ages eight to eighty. It used to say that, anyway. Now I think it just says for ages eight and up. Because people live longer than eighty now, usually. And it would be kind of insulting to be told that you're too old for Monopoly. Which,

I learned in college, is a tool of the capitalist hegemony masquerading as a family game anyway, so maybe that wouldn't be so bad. To be too old for it."

Teddy smiled again—he was smiling so *much*, Jules thought—and raised his eyebrows, glancing deliberately at the kitchen door.

"I think, Karl or Che or whoever you are, I was offered a tour of the promised land in there," he said.

"Oh!" Jules rounded the counter to hold open the kitchen door, motioning for Teddy to go in. Teddy moved past him, sliding his hand along the wood of the door as he went.

"It's like walking into the wardrobe," he said. "Or maybe I feel a little like Alice."

"You look more like you're disembarking from a time machine from 1947," Jules said. "But thanks for remembering, or I would have had to make you wear The Hat." He gestured to the grimy Burns and Son Painting Company baseball cap they kept by the door for anyone unlucky enough to enter the kitchen without their own hair covering. *So many heads have been in that hat,* Jules thought. Teddy looked horrified.

"Furthermore, we had this nice door put on the rabbit hole last year to keep the evil queens out. No evil queens, I swear," Jules said. And when Teddy looked at him with an eyebrow raised, he said, "Until eight, at least. Before then it's just me. And I'm not evil."

"Was that a queen joke?" Teddy asked appreciatively, and then stopped abruptly in front of the large stainless steel prep table by the door. "Oh! I hadn't pictured it this way. In my head. Not that I was spending a lot of time picturing it," he said, and Jules could see a scarlet blush creep down Teddy's cheeks and toward his collar. He was starting to sweat, and his voice softened considerably. "Okay, so maybe I was picturing you back here sometimes." Teddy drummed his fingers on the table, smiling to himself, still red, "making those transcendent cupcakes with the caramel or something."

"There's that word again," Jules said. He tried to sound as if he were teasing Teddy, but his voice warbled out high and weak and girlish and whispery, making Teddy look up at him and—*again, he won't stop doing it*—smile.

Jules showed Teddy the ovens, the desk, the dry-stock shelves and the walk-in refrigerator with the blocks of butter and small vats of cream, and then they were standing on either side of the metal prep table by the door again.

"I'm sorry there's not more to see here," Jules said. "It's really just a kitchen. The grand tour took all of five minutes, and that was with me stretching it out with needless explanations."

"You could put me to work," Teddy said and, noting Jules's suddenly widened eyes, he added, "if that's legal, I mean."

Jules had supervised Teddy as he washed his hands—carefully, twice—at the large metal sink. He wrapped an apron around his waist and awkwardly pulled the bib up over Teddy's head. It got stuck, of course it did, because they should have done it the other way 'round; and they both laughed nervously, and Jules stepped back with his hands raised.

"I'll let you do that yourself," he said. "I'm not used to the aprons with the tops. Those are 'Trice's. I was trying to be gallant, not to manhandle you or tie you up." He stopped abruptly at that and looked down, furiously red again. He'd blushed at almost everything he'd said to Teddy that morning—he blushed, it seemed, so easily and so brightly, and it was so becoming on him, so endearing, almost innocent. It made Teddy feel stronger, more in control, like a gentleman pitching woo. He laughed to himself silently and happily at that, adjusting the apron over his suit. He liked the thought of it, the thought of being old-fashioned with Jules. They certainly were blushing enough for it.

120

Jules showed him how to zest fruit and brought him a tall stool to sit on. He kept a respectable distance. He didn't, as Teddy had hoped, curl his hands over Teddy's to teach him how to hold a knife, leaning over him with the dry heat of his chest pressed against Teddy's back, his voice in Teddy's ear. He didn't do any such thing, but cheerfully talked him through the first few tries with the steel table shiny and cold between them.

Teddy set to work earnestly on the pile of lemons Jules put out for him. Across the table, Jules was doing something with a large metal bowl and a parade of ingredients, whisk flashing in his hands. While they worked, they spoke a little, in a conversation woven carefully with long silences in which the only sound was the snick of the knife against lemon skin and the occasional clang of Jules's metal bowl.

Teddy asked about the hat—was it the same Burns? Was Jules the "and Son" on the hat? And Jules talked himself hoarse about his father and his painting business and his stepfamily, about his mother's disappearance and his grandmother's death, about loss and mourning, feeling helpless and feeling lonely and, as he grew older, forgetting, little by little. Teddy talked about his job. He talked about Maggie and Dan. He talked about his father and his mother and the camel-colored house in the suburbs of Indiana. ("Indiana?" Jules gasped while refilling Teddy's coffee. "Me too!") They talked about Indiana and about high school and being gay there versus being gay in New York, being gay at sixteen versus being gay at thirty.

"I think," Teddy sighed, dropping the knife, "I'm finished."

Jules looked up from his work at the pile of skinned lemons in front of Teddy, at the little curls of yellow peel in the bowl, and smiled. "That was quicker than 'Trice usually does it," he said, coming around the table to inspect the work. He stood so close that Teddy could feel the warmth rising from Jules's neck and cheeks. "Of course, 'Trice usually spends half her zesting time on the phone, or running to the front for coffee, or slipping out for smoke breaks."

"It was very Zen," Teddy said, looking at his hands, which he laid flat on the table in front of him.

"You did a nice job," Jules said, reaching in front of Teddy to touch the peels. "There's no white on these at all. I might have to get rid of 'Trice and lock you in here permanently with me."

The moment he said it, Teddy felt it, the suggestion of a thing curling up between them. Jules's body was close as he leaned over the table. Teddy felt the rasp of Jules's cotton coat against the back of his hand, smelled the aroma of lemons rising up clean and floral and sharp between them. Jules stood up straight, suddenly, and was still. Neither of them moved. They breathed, looking down, the both of them.

"I mean," Jules said, "it's nice to have you here." He shook his head, as if deep in a conversation to which Teddy was not privy. "I mean—"

Jules held the knife in his hand, turning it over and over between his fingers. They both looked at it, glinting and clicking against the steel table. They watched Jules's fingers, pale and long and nimble, crawling across the blade.

"Are you planning to stab—" Teddy started, intending to lighten the mood, but Jules had, at the same moment, inhaled sharply through his nose and cast his glance upward, his eyes very pale and very wide and lightly rimmed with pink. "I've been—" Jules started, then stopped.

"This is so stupid," Teddy heard him whisper under his breath. "Just—"

Jules turned and put his hands on either side of Teddy's neck. They felt dry and delicate as moths, papery light. Teddy's heart really did stutter; outside, the euphony of the street really did swell like music. In that moment, with Jules's hands framing Teddy's face, holding him still, holding him to earth, they each closed their eyes, because to look was far too close, and they met, softly, in a kiss.

Teddy lit up like glowing coals flickering with low-burning heat; not a fire but a warmth, not a flame but an ember in the pit of him, as if that heat had been there for a long time but he was just now noticing it.

The kiss was not, by the usual standards, a perfect one. It was a little crooked, a little lopsided and unsteady and perhaps too soft at first, more bewildered than passionate, feathering and light like a calling out, like a question. There was no grand moment, no revelation, no specific thing that drove them, passionately, into their embrace. There was only a kind of melting, a giving up or giving in, and they pressed into each other in relief, their bodies finally meeting in a deep sigh. Jules's lips moved softly against Teddy's, the gentlest touch paced by little licks of his tongue and the tiniest strokes of his fingers against Teddy's neck, at once soothing and beautiful and like pushing a hot wire through every one of Teddy's veins so he felt each of them, burning, distinct, twisting in a network under his skin. It was not, by the standards of most stories, perfect. But it was, by anyone's standards, still a glorious kiss.

When they stopped, and they did stop—after far too brief a time, Teddy thought—Jules looked down between their bodies shyly and said, "I haven't had a kiss in years," and Teddy's hands came up to Jules's waist, unknotted the ties and pulled the apron loose, then let it drop to the floor. It was just a gesture, for it left nothing bare, but Teddy wanted to undo every fastening Jules had, wanted him as loose and opened as he could make him when Teddy kissed him again, this time lightly at the corner of his mouth. Jules's breath left him in a rush; he looked down at the apron pooled over their shoes, then wound his arms loosely around Teddy's neck, knocking his hat off and sending it rolling under the metal shelves by the ovens, and Jules kissed him again, kissed him with more strength, pressing in wet and urgent, with the tips of his canines biting lightly at Teddy's lip.

They kissed this way, back and forth, an exchange of breath and pressure, a quiet, liquid conversation, until they heard the grinding of the front gate and then the door's bells shimmering and 'Trice, who hollered from the front of the store, "Jules! I'm getting coffee!"

And with that, they broke apart. Jules covered his mouth with one hand and smiled shyly while Teddy stooped to find his wayward hat.

∾

We can, at this moment, return to Teddy at the windowsill early the next morning, weak coffee and phone in hand, trench coat slung over his shoulders like a cape. He felt, as we said earlier, wound like a coiled spring, full of energy, a kind of reaching pulse that made him feel stretched and open and awake, even at that early hour.

I'm sorry, he typed into his phone with one thumb, *I hate to leave now when it feels like we've started something. I won't sleep tonight. I might not sleep the whole time. I'll be gone three days, and then, when I get back, can I see you?*

Jules replied almost instantly, *Yes. Dinner? Let's cook.*

And then, a moment later, *My kitchen is better stocked, so you should come here.*

And, just as the cab driver outside leaned on his horn, impatient and too loud on the morning-silent street, *I won't sleep either, Grasshopper.*

Ten

TEDDY BOUGHT A CHOCOLATE CROISSANT and a coffee from one of the fluorescent-and-Formica bakeries at Penn Station, protected them from crush and spill, balanced the package carefully under one arm while lugging his garment bag and pull-along suitcase, and bumped down the platform escalators and finally into a window seat near the front of the train. As it turned out, it hadn't been worth the care: The croissant was leathery and bland; its chocolate was far too sweet; the coffee was watery. Nothing tasted the least bit loving or glorious or alive. It tasted like nothing at all.

By the time the train finally dug its way out from underneath the city and was clacking along the tracks above ground, past fences and power lines and gray morning sky, Teddy had given up on his breakfast and settled with his cheek pressed to the cool glass of the window.

When he finished college, his parents had sent him, as a graduation gift, on a month-long trip to Europe. He'd traveled alone and bought a student rail pass because the train was the most romantic way to go. He'd brought a notebook, a small manual camera and whatever clothing he could fit in a backpack, nothing more. He'd spent days at a time without saying a word, moving alone through the thin crowds, whistling under his breath as he climbed the cobblestoned hills of town after little town. He'd gestured and pointed sheepishly for shopkeepers whose language he didn't understand; he'd learned to read warnings and suggestions in pictures and faces and road signs; he traveled without a guidebook, without GPS, without maps. At night, he had slept in hostels and in the sleeper cars of trains, on thin, under-padded beds, tucked into himself and dreaming while other travelers snored and breathed heavily around him in the dark. During the day, he'd slipped between the living throng in Budapest or Vienna or Prague like a flâneur, he thought proudly, and then like a spirit, and then like air, until the day came when he realized he'd finally slid into the being of nothing.

When Teddy returned to the States, Indiana seemed boisterous, offensive, full of invasions; everything around him was jangling and demanding and exhausting. The cool, humming quiet of his parents' house, the stoic dinners around his family's table, the days and evenings he spent alone, reading or writing or simply staring at the walls in his old bedroom, were a relief. It took a long time for him to speak above a whisper again.

Now, years later, he still felt like an apparition, lost from the cemetery he'd never found, wandering.

He typed a message to Jules on his phone, unsure it would go through once he sent it since his phone's signal reception seemed, like all else near the train tracks, shaky and weak:

Above ground, finally. Arriving in DC around 9. You are probably baking right now, something real and delicious. Had the worst pain au chocolat *of my life. It was a PAIN, oh, chocolate! You would have wept. I miss your pastry.*

Outside the train window were the backs of small houses, A-frames with wood siding painted in pallid, community-accepted hues: white, cream, pale yellow, pale green, pale blue; the grass was pale and the air was pale, and so were the sky and the gray antennas jutting from the rooftops and the rusting swingsets dotting the lawns. Everything was breaking his heart with its blandness; his coffee, and the trees and the gravel, and his own hands, pressed against the glass, were pale and colorless.

***

By the time the train had sighed to a stop, by the time he'd dragged his bags out and up and emerged above ground, blinking like a worm in the low light of the last vestiges of the morning rush, Teddy had received four messages from Jules:

Sorry I missed you; I was, indeed, baking. You are probably "landing" soon now. Hope the ride was nice and nobody ate yogurt near you or spanked a baby or had a loud argument on a cell phone (those things always seem to happen to me on the train). I am weeping for the pain au chocolat. *Who did this? What did chocolate ever do to them? I am also weeping for your bad pun, but only because it was bad, not because it was a pun.*

You miss my pastry? Is that a euphemism?

I'm sending you directions to a good bakery for pain au chocolat, *but go early in the morning—croissants get old fast. Plus I'm sending the names of a few places to go for good food and dessert. Because I want your mouth to redeem itself. That is not a euphemism, either.*

The final message was a short list of bakeries and restaurants, with an assignment: *I want a full report on everything you put in your mouth there (within reason, of course).*

***

While I'm a little disappointed that your wish to redeem my mouth was not a euphemism, I want to thank you for the suggestions. I had dinner and dessert tonight on my own, and I have been redeemed, mouth and all. I can't even remember that horrible chocolate croissant. What croissant?

The message lit up Jules's phone just as he was falling asleep on the couch. It was good to wake up, since he was in a terrible position, pinned in place by Andy snoozing against him, head tilted dangerously forward against his chest, legs curled akimbo, a more innocent version of Rubens' Leda. His cell phone was clutched to his chest; his half-drunk glass of wine sat on the coffee table. He may have, all evening, been waiting.

Grasshopper, I believe I requested a full report, Jules wrote, stretching his neck and trying not to disturb Andy. *This is nothing of the sort.*

I don't even remember what I ate for dinner, came the reply, *because I finished with olive oil ice cream served over some apricots roasted in honey, and that almost literally took my breath away. Oh, god, how do I describe it to you? It was... I can't.*

Start with the ice cream, then. Salty, sweet, bitter, sour? Those are the basics. Like wine tasting. What flavor notes were there? (Remember that flavor is a combination of smell and taste, so go there, too.) Think about adjectives or things to which you can compare the flavor.

During a long pause Jules refilled his glass of wine and turned on the lamps by the couch. It was late, and dark, and the air was too warm, unmoving. It was the kind of night that, were he back in Indiana, might have been filled with the soft noise of crickets.

Sweet, with a little tiny bit of salty in there? Does that work? Maybe buttery, even though that doesn't make sense? Mild and fatty and fruity? Silky? Yes, definitely fruity, and maybe a little floral. And soft, if that makes sense. And green, planty, thick. And there were flakes of sea salt on top of the ice cream. So if you got some of that, it was salty, and a little bitter, creamy and tangy, just perfect.

That sounds, uh, very good, but I'll refrain from commenting on that last taste description, Jules wrote. *Were you trying to make a comparison?*

What? Oh… not like that. I mean. Oh, god. Moving on. Apricots. Were roasted in honey. The honey was really floral, too, if that makes sense, but in a different way from the ice cream, heavier, thicker. Almost overpoweringly sweet. Apricots were fleshy, slippery. They were warm, so the cream melted everywhere.

Um. Yes. Very good description, once again.

I think it's your mind, Teddy wrote, *not my words.*

Nope. It's definitely your words. But good food does that to me anyway. To most people, I think. It's part of why I like to cook.

It may have turned me on a little bit. Not in a bad way.

I wasn't aware there was a bad way.

Touché. I just mean that, had I not had a messenger bag with me, it might have been a bit embarrassing, Teddy wrote. A moment later, he wrote, *I can't believe I just told you that.*

You had a… reaction… to the dessert?

You could say that, yes. Like I used to have reactions to Justin Timberlake.

Is this a common occurrence with you and sweets? Jules wrote. *I should remember this. I own a bakery, after all. (And Justin Timberlake? Really?)*

It's happened once before. I had a brief affair with one of your cupcakes.

Which one?

The salted caramel.

Aha. You like salty sweets. (That still doesn't explain Justin Timberlake.)

Maybe that's it. But I think it's more mystical, Teddy typed. *I've had salty sweets before and not had that… reaction. I may have actually licked the plate tonight. (And I admit that nothing really explains Justin Timberlake.) I feel like I cheated on you,* Teddy added.

With the apricots?

With the ice cream.

Well, we haven't really talked about being exclusive yet, so it's probably not cheating.

Excuse me, then, I should go. I promised that ice cream I would call it in the morning.

∾

PASTRY-WHIPPED: ADVENTURES IN SUGAR BY A DEDICATED
CRUMPET STRUMPET
by Chef Jules Burns of Buttermilk Bakery
April 28: Ars Gratia Crustum, or, Art for Art's Cake

Okay, well, that's not exactly the translation (my language in high school was French, not Latin, and I learned it in Indiana, which means even my French is probably pretty bad), but it's certainly the spirit of the pun (I love me a good pun, oh my goodness), so grant me a little wiggle room here. (Actually, I think the translation is closer to "Art for the sake of cake," which is fine with me, too, because in my book—which I've not, admittedly, yet written—everything is for the sake of cake.)

Doing something just for the beauty of it, just for the pleasure it might bring, is hard for me. And doing it imperfectly? Even harder, though it is often more pleasurable that way. I suspect it's difficult for most of us, judging from the shy excuses and blushing that happens at my pastry counter every day when someone dares to ask for some lark of a sweet (for what in this world is more about sheer pleasure and beauty than eating pastry? And why does this make us sheepish?). But it is absolutely necessary. Fiat panis? *Not good enough. I say—and I wish I had a Marie Antoinette wig for this moment—*fiat crustum.

What can pastry do? It does not nourish; it fills no bodily need. It is entirely about sensory pleasure. We've been told all our lives, most of us, about the evils of sensory pleasure, about the evils of taking such gifts for oneself, which has always struck me as ridiculous, since the world seems so full, in its natural state, of opportunities for delight of this kind. For most of us, the daily demands of living—literally putting bread on the table, or even, perhaps, affording a table on which one might put bread—are pressing enough that we have little left of ourselves to give toward true pleasures. Instead we grab, when we can, the roughest, palest suggestion of happiness, and we make do. But oh, my darling, I remind myself, collige virgo rosas. *And even this (and its English version, "Gather ye rosebuds while ye may") contains a hint of the darkness of that decision: Life is fleeting, life leaves you spent and bare and old and empty, and for* this *reason, take pleasure while you can. What would happen if, instead, we agreed that pleasure should be valuable not because it is fleeting, but because it is always available? What if, instead, I understand that pleasure lies in everything around me, trembling there like a bud on a branch at my hand, mine for the taking, if only I am bold enough to do so?*

I have a friend who is visiting D.C., and I've sent him on a mission to redeem his heart through the most gorgeous food possible. An odd mission, I admit. And who am I, lone and lonely soul, cramped up in the back of my bakery, surrounded by sugar and butter and beautiful things I'll make but never eat—water, water, everywhere, *my mother* used to recite, and not a drop to drink—*to send* him *for redemption? But he took the pardon and the permission (hedonism is, after all, an actual philosophy) and went, and on his first stop, he came upon what sounds like a heavenly olive oil ice cream. Just thinking of it gives me little shivers of vicarious pleasure, so I've spent the afternoon on a recipe to recreate it upon his return, as a gift. It was served over apricots roasted in honey, and given, as everything in life should be,* cum grano salis.

That phrase rings doubly right to me: Take everything, yes, with the smallest grain of doubt, of difference to cut the sweetness, but also, let there be a little salt on your cheek as you do, a little sadness in the joy; let there always be the memory of loss in what you find new and opening in your hands.

Not because you need the one to appreciate the other; those Greeks, with their sweet-bitterness, can stuff it. I would have been perfectly happy to have an entirely wonderful life with no bumps or bruises or missing things, without losing my mother or my grandmother or Andy, without being without. *I don't believe you need the bitter to appreciate the sweet, but I do think the bitterness is there, and will always be there, inevitably so, and to push it away or hide it in a closet is useless. Better to call it into yourself, to take it up and turn it, by your own hand, into something beautiful.* Lux ex tenebris, *as they say, though I know I've mixed my metaphors here.*

Though I seem to be roaming without a destination in this essay, I can see that I've accidentally stumbled, as I often do, upon a theme: the sweet-bitter (as the Greeks actually called it), light and darkness, bread and cake, daily life and pleasure… I'm stringing myself delicately within the dialectic. Delicately, yes: It must be done this way so that I do not tear myself in two, so that I do not rend my heart, that fragile beast, that quiet place from which I try to speak to you, ab imo pectore, *my little voice echoing up from the depths of my chest, too small for the words it wants, too small and too weak and too careful, too tiny, I think often,* cum grano salis, *to be heard through the noise of the world. What can pastry do, after all?*

Nothing and everything, is my answer. I can only offer up to you the tools of pleasure, culled ab imo pectore, cum grano salis, *the work of my aching and joyous heart; but you must take it, must accept from me the pleasure as easily as you do the bitterness, and love and celebrate in yourself the cry of delight as deeply as you've come to love the cry of pain.*

I've poured myself a glass of wine tonight and I'm raising it to you: Ad fundum, *I say. It means both "bottoms up" and "back to basics," a toast to the utmost pleasure and a demand to return to the elemental. I'm calling to you from both sides now, standing as I call, in a fragile and impossible place.* Ab imo pectore.

SWEET

❧

On Saturday evening, Teddy left the wedding—a weepy cousin, a frothy meringue confection of a dress, a limp buffet dinner, a sweaty groom and all his frat brothers drinking and toasting loudly and doing the chicken dance—early and curled into the privacy and quiet of his hotel room. Something about being away from home sent him deep inside himself, to the ghost-place he'd never quite left, from which he watched the outside world and listened and thought his own thoughts and judged (and terribly, he knew, but the judgments seemed well-deserved, at least in the case of the sugar-blown dress and the red-faced, uniformly blond groomsmen swilling and dancing around). He loosened his tie and unbuttoned his waistcoat, kicked off his shoes and flopped back onto the mildewed floral bed with a sigh.

For lunch earlier in the day, he had gone to another of the places on Jules's list and, dining alone, had decided to simply watch the crowds of business lunchers in the restaurant, the bustling of the wait staff and the sky darkening with the threat of spring rain, rather than read or work on a crossword or engage in some other self-soothing activity that might help him shut the world out and shut himself down. He had ordered a bit of everything from the mezze menu, far too much to eat alone, though the plates were small, and the waitress had raised her penciled eyebrows in his direction, but he took it all in tiny bites and persisted in his delight: softly crumbling rolls of falafel paired with a plate of warm pita, puffing and gentled with heat; Brussels sprouts, crispy, salted and scented with coriander; dolmades soaked in olive oil and brine and a hint of puréed prunes or raisins; fat, melting fava beans, stewed with tomato and kale until it all wept tenderly apart in a broth of dill and garlic; cauliflower roasted with capers and sultanas and dark, toasted pine nuts; and, finally, what almost broke his heart in its perfect simplicity, fresh watermelon in chunks, yellow and deep pink and cold and dotted with curls of fresh mint (he'd eaten most of this dish, knowing its beauty was momentary, with the juice running sugar-iced down the silver fork and over the back of his hand, where he unashamedly *licked* it from his own skin before it reached his sleeve cuff). The meal had been glorious and reckless excess. He was still vibrating with the bliss of it; even the paucity of the wedding dinner had failed to dull the memory.

Blissfully vibrating, he attempted three times to write a brief description of the travesty of his cousin's wedding, and then about his lunchtime meal. He failed, settling on listing the foods he'd tried, hoping the list alone might tell all of his joy, and sent it to Jules. *Your blog today,* he added a minute later, *was really beautiful, too.* And then, because his phone stayed silent and he felt as if he were speaking out into the darkness, alone, he wrote, *Is Andy okay?*

Your lunch sounds incredibly sexy, Jules replied after a moment. *The wedding sounds anything but that. But weddings usually are. Anything but that. Sexy, I mean.*

And then: *You read the blog? I can't believe you read that. Though sometimes, as I write, I imagine I'm writing to you. And sometimes I forget that you might read it, or anyone might, and it feels secret and private and quiet and mine. I don't know which I prefer.*

Finally, seconds later: *Andy is great. He's snoozing on my lap as I write. Why do you ask? What has he been telling you? I should never have let him have his own email account.*

You wrote that you lost your grandmother and Andy. I knew about your grandma, but I got worried something happened to Andy.

Teddy endured, then, a very long stretch of silence, during which he held his phone to his chest, waiting. Nothing, and then more nothing, and the seconds stretched out into minutes until he'd begun to worry that he'd said something wrong, that perhaps it had been a mistake to mention Jules's grandmother like that, in the same breath as a *dog*, and perhaps Jules was angry, or sad, or, for some reason he couldn't fathom, disappointed in him. And then, just as he'd bent to breaking, just as he was about to call Jules, his phone rang.

Eleven

THINK OF THE THINGS YOU HAVE LOST: the lone sock, the cheap wristwatch, the album you loved as a child, the one working pair of scissors in the house. Your shopping list, your best idea, your voice and the freedom of leaving your house with nothing, absolutely nothing at all, in your pockets. What is it you have lost now that you believed, once upon a time, you could never lose?

"I was married," Jules said into the phone, "To a man. Named Andy. He died."

On the other end of the phone, Jules could hear Teddy breathing—quietly, shakily, but not holding his breath. And so he talked on, told him about Andy—tall, long-limbed, bright and dear, with skin like polished walnut wood and a smile that was immediate and full of bliss. Andy was smart and quick with words, like Jules, and argued passionately for what he loved; he could just as easily be sharp and cruel as funny or kind; he made people nervous and he made people adore him and he barged into the world entirely without fear or reservation. Jules had loved him fiercely and completely and had mourned him that way, too.

They'd met in a bar. No. In truth, they'd first met at a friend's party but had only shaken hands and engaged in pleasant conversation about Jules's work before they'd each turned their attention to other people. It was not love at first sight. But on second sight, in the stuffed and sweaty bar, Andy had come up, held out his hand and simply said, "Janet." Jules knew this meant that Andy remembered meeting him at Janet's party and was being friendly, so Jules offered to buy Andy a drink, and they'd finished the night kissing in the alcove of a pharmacy on Hudson as drunk kids hobbled past them on the blinkered street and Andy pressed Jules up against the shop window, while behind him rose an impressively high tower of toilet paper on display, mundane and crass and so perfect Jules was never quite sure he hadn't invented it.

Much as he knew it was probably wrong to burden Teddy, Jules could not stop talking, because he was wrapped up and drowning and lost and losing all at once, filled with an ache that was missing Andy and missing Teddy and wanting, somehow, for them to know and like each other and approve. So he spoke on and on about Andy. Andy, who was tone deaf but happily sang at the top of his tuneless lungs every time he knew the song on the radio, even in a friend's kitchen, even in public, who put himself at war with the music, barreling in and taking no prisoners, making Jules cringe and beam in equal measure. Andy, who tunelessly serenaded him with "Happy Birthday" first thing in the morning on every birthday they had together, but sped up the song ridiculously because, he said, it always sounded like a funeral dirge the way most people sang it (and, Jules would add, the way Andy sang it, it sounded like a speedy monk's chant or the peppy hoot-yowling of some wild, hilarious animal). Andy, who fell asleep every night in the same position, on his side, one arm slung around Jules's waist, breathing mint and sleep into his ear. Andy, who spent his mornings in the park trying to coax his old, tired little dachshund into a game of fetch (which the man approached far more enthusiastically than the dog, demonstrating, on hands and knees and to no avail, exactly what could be done with a floppy Frisbee and a mouth and a good attitude), who spent his afternoons bent over his laptop, writing, and his evenings pouring drinks for rich kids from NYU with fake IDs. Who had a gray kitten named Ball that died of ringworm in his lungs three weeks after Andy adopted him and for whom Andy had cried deep, hiccupping cries, like a child, furious and lost and keening, even though he'd known the kitten would die when he took him and had simply wanted to give him a warm and loving place until the end. Andy, who screamed and threw cheese curls at the television when the presidential debates were on; who was against marriage on principle but married Jules because Jules had asked him to, and because he knew it would break both their hearts to say no; who dressed, every Halloween, as a pun he knew he'd have to explain to even their smartest friends; who always came home from the market having forgotten exactly two things from the shopping list (which mystified Jules and made him crazy), but made up for it by doing the laundry; who loved the world grandly and without reserve, and always chose Jules over everything, everything, everything else.

This was the last thing Jules could say, and after this, there was a long silence into which both men breathed shallowly, carefully.

"Wow," Teddy said at last, in a voice that sounded defeated and frightened and sad. "Andy sounds like he was an incredible man. You loved him."

"He was amazing. And a jerk, too, sometimes, I don't mean to leave that part out, a real fucking jerk," Jules said, holding his voice carefully and close so that it did not shake. His throat ached with the effort. "But I loved him."

"Jules," Teddy said, as if the name were its own sentence that held everything. Jules heard him sigh, heard the rustle of him shifting against the hotel bed. "I can't compete with that."

"I know," Jules whispered, because it was true. What Jules wanted to say was *It's not a competition,* but that would just sound empty and pat and, after all, he knew it was—and would always be—a competition.

"I'm sorry," Teddy said. "That's so much."

"I know," Jules said again. He sounded very small to his own ears. "I'm sorry, too."

"We're a couple of very sorry individuals," Teddy said. Jules heard the warm smile struggling through the heaviness in Teddy's voice, but he couldn't do more than give a small, bitter laugh in return. "Distance sucks," Teddy said. "I wish I could hug you or something right now."

"Yeah, me, too," Jules said. "And that sucks, too." He was quaking apart. He was slipping down and pulling open. "I want that, and I don't want to," he whispered. He knew it was completely unclear, but Teddy didn't ask him to explain; Teddy didn't ask for anything at all.

"Do you," Teddy started, and then paused for a long moment before starting again. "Do you—and I'm not backing out, I still really want to, if you do—do you still want to have dinner when I get back to New York? Because I would understand—I would be really sad, but I would understand—if you—"

"I do," Jules said, "please."

There was nothing more either man could say, and so that word hung in the distance between them, an ache and a balm and a question and a pardon for the endless minutes they sat in silence and simply breathed together.

⁂

The train would take him back.

It rocked him rhythmically, its gears and pulleys slam-clacking under his feet until he vibrated with the train and became a piece of it, until he was without thought, until he was a pure mechanical body hurtling powerfully toward a city that seemed like his. Around him was the dull hum of chatter and kids whining and the rustle of newspaper and the whistling of air against the windows and other noise of the world, but he pressed himself against the molded plastic wall, felt the thud of movement pulsing through him and heard nothing but the train rumble and smack as they went. He sat still and was thrown forward; he made no effort, but he sped along.

Beneath him, the train mumbled in perfect meter, *iamb iamb iamb. I am not,* he argued back.

He had a secret: Often, he felt nothing. He did not cling, or wish, or want; there was nothing in him that longed for any other thing in the world. When he left a place, when he closed a door, when he turned his back, he could forget in an instant; it was always easy. He used to think, though he'd never told anyone this secret, that he had a hollow in his heart, a small place nothing outside him could ever touch, a part of him always kept apart.

In his first year of college, Teddy had felt afraid and alone just because he was the only kid in his dorm who was *not* afraid and alone, not sick with longing for home or family or familiarity. He made anywhere, instantly, his lukewarm home. Strangeness was a comfort; at night, he'd wander the untamed streets of the West Village to get himself lost so he could, slowly and by instinct, fumble his way back again. He didn't keep mementos or photographs; he forgot people and places and feelings too easily; nothing stuck. He was affable and pleasant and always smiling; he made every person feel like their own best self, and it made him feel, when he saw himself do this properly, so glossy and good. But Teddy could not imagine what it meant to lose someone and to long for that person hard enough to break his heart.

Stand up straight and look a man in the eye, said his father. *Be reasonable. Know the ground from the sky. Be cautious so you will always be right.*

You are my hope in this world, said his mother, leaning hard against his shoulder. *You are my one beautiful thing. Without you I have nothing left.*

You are the nicest guy, everybody said, *and generous. You never take anything away from anybody else.*

He listed in his head all the people who approved of him. It was a long list. He was not on it.

When he looked at the city melting in sunset, or children playing and screaming wildly with joy, or the lonely old men with their broods of pigeons, or lovers swooning in the park, he felt nothing and he knew, in his heart, this was wrong. When he took a lover, for a day or a week or two, and looked into his face, he could feel nothing in his clench-fisted heart—no stir, no clutch, no leap or ache.

But he'd listened, the night before, to Jules crying softly into the telephoned distance, and his body had pulled him hard from its hollow, as it had when they'd kissed, as it had every time he was near Jules or thought of him or felt, to his surprise, warm and good and right in his place in the little bakery. Everything had flipped; Teddy took and he took, and for once he felt full on what someone else would give him. It was terrifying to want and to receive, to give nothing back in return. (It was dangerous, a building wave, a pinprick in the dam: The more he received, the more desperately hungry he felt, needy and wild, and he couldn't be gentle, couldn't control, couldn't be careful or kind; he would rip and tear and devour everything he wanted and ever dared to love. It was, yes, terrifying to want anything at all.)

Everything around him clacked and rocked and he went along with it; he was part of the hulking machine that held him. His body, the plastic, his heart, the window and every place the train pushed past were a fleeting blur on which his eyes couldn't focus; his feet never touched the ground.

Andy opened his hands like a plea, translucent palms tipped up in the moonlight; he was starlit and shimmering and had coin-silver eyes, but Jules wasn't afraid. *Don't go, don't go,* Andy said, *don't go away from me.* He had a boat, and they were balanced in it, and the boat pitched and the water under them roiled like a bad dream. *You're pretty and pale as the moon,* he said, *you're slowly waning, you're moving away, I'm trying to warn you, it's going to rain.*

When the rain came, it was in fat, unmerciful drops that fell on Jules's chest like punches. They were tears, and Jules said, *this is so cliché, tears and raindrops, I apologize for this, it's like a high school poem, isn't it?* But Andy just laughed and said *I didn't know you in high school* and Jules said *in high school they threw the baby out with the bathwater because you can take the boy out of the locker but you can't take the locker out of the boy.* He wasn't entirely sure what he meant, but Andy seemed to understand perfectly; he just shook his head sadly and said *there will be a test on this, so you must memorize the tables of attraction, which begin like this: One take away one is one take away one is one take away one...* and he repeated the phrase like a skipping record until Jules shook his head and said *that's not attraction, that's subtraction, I've memorized subtraction.* Andy smiled sadly and told him *it's the very same thing,* and then he blinked black and out like a television suddenly unplugged, like a star folding in, completely done and gone.

⌇

"I miss you," Jules said.

In the background, he could hear the clatter of metal on concrete, and shouting and laughter; he heard his father mutter under his breath, something about "Nathan and those younger guys," and "jeez," then heard the bang of a door and sudden quiet. In his head, he saw his father sag onto the concrete front step of the house he was probably painting and rub the sweat from his forehead with two fingers, tipping back the ratty baseball cap and closing his eyes as he did.

"You, too, kid," Ray said. "What's wrong?"

"I just miss you."

"Jules, you're full of horse shit," Ray said. "You never call during baking hours unless something is wrong."

"I'm taking a ten-minute break between batches," he tried, until he heard his father's long and heavy inhalation and jumped ahead of the lecture he knew was coming. "Okay. But it's kind of a bad question."

"Jules," his dad started. "I'm old, and I'm getting older here by the minute. I gave you the sex talk years ago, and then *you* gave *me* the sex talk when you decided I didn't know what I was talking about, even though I probably didn't need to know the details. I haven't recently won the lottery or cured cancer, and if you're going to ask about cholesterol, Dr. Baptiste says I'm doing fine. So whatever else it is, just ask me."

"How long was it before you started thinking about dating again," Jules asked around the lump in his throat, "after Mom left?"

"Oh," Ray said, and Jules heard the static scratch of the phone against his shoulder as he shifted in his chair. "That. I don't know why I didn't see this one coming."

"Dad, I'm serious."

"Are you thinking about starting to date?" Ray asked.

"I wasn't. I didn't think I would. But I met someone and then I wanted to, and he kissed me and I kissed him back, but I feel—how long is okay?—I've been seeing Andy. In dreams. Every night. He begs me not to go away," he finished, and let out in one long sigh all the breath he'd been holding in. He had the locket—Andy's locket—clutched in his left hand; he'd unstrung it from Andy's collar in the middle of the night and slept with it, and then kept it all morning in his pocket, where he could worry it with his fingers. He couldn't let it go.

"The dreams are you, you know, Jules. That's you begging yourself," his dad said.

"That doesn't make sense. It's making me miserable. I feel guilty enough already."

"I think you're right," Ray said. "You do."

"I can't stop feeling that," Jules said weakly.

"Jules," his dad said (Jules saw him press the pads of his fingers to his temples and squint as if he had a headache, as he did when Jules was being especially unreasonable or inscrutable—which was, according to Ray, entirely too often), "put the locket in your desk drawer."

Jules's heart lurched. His father always, always knew, as if he could see him, hundreds of miles away, hiding like a mouse by the ovens. He dropped the locket on the desk and pressed it there with his finger as his father spoke.

"It's a piece of jewelry. It's a memory. You can't cheat on a memory. You can keep it or you can let it go, but it won't change any bit of what you had or the fact that you lost it. You can be happy or you can be miserable, kid, and that's in your hands."

"He's almost the complete opposite of Andy." Saying that out loud made a new wave of guilt roll up like nausea in Jules's stomach. "Andy would probably eat him for breakfast."

"Unless this guy is The Hulk, he would probably only be an appetizer," his dad laughed. "As I recall, Andy's appetite was bigger than Nathan's and Zack's put together."

Jules smiled, then, though he knew exactly what his father was doing. He decided, for once, to let him do it, to let it work. "The flapjacks," he said, and heard his father snort back a laugh.

"The Lumberjack of Jane Street!" Ray yelled imperiously, and sent them both into a ridiculous and childish fit of giggling.

"Pearl Bunyan," Jules whispered and giggled again.

"Johnny Dapperseed."

"Gay-vee Crocket."

They giggled like idiots, and Jules felt free and happy and so close to his dad that his heart squeezed around the moment and he let go of everything else. His dad's hands, wide and paint-streaked and strong, would always hold him up and push him forward. His voice was a tether; his heart was a rocket; he listened with his whole body; Jules loved him like crazy.

Ray was making high, hysterical whooping sounds, and it struck Jules just how much laughing sounded like crying. It was simply, he thought, a matter of context.

❦

PASTRY-WHIPPED: ADVENTURES IN SUGAR BY A DEDICATED
CRUMPET STRUMPET
by Chef Jules Burns of Buttermilk Bakery
April 30: Then Practice Losing Farther, Losing Faster

In case you don't recognize it, I stole that line from Elizabeth Bishop. Or borrowed, perhaps. Or better yet, I've relocated it. Put it here, where it can make another life and mean something new. Stealing, in this case, is a noble act. It's liberation.

Speaking of new meanings, let me tell you a story about two of my favorite people in the entire world: my father, Ray, and my once-upon-a-time love, Andy. When Andy first met my father, he was terrified of the man. This is not surprising: My father, though he's neither tall nor especially brawny, is powerful and frightening and bigger than his body. He can stare you down and he can see through you and he is so entirely self-possessed (he has, as that might mean, hold of his own soul in a way most of us will never manage) that everyone who meets him wants his approval immediately. He is completely, unavoidably, present and solid; next to him, the rest of us look like ghosts. My father, if you'll forgive the pun, matters.

So when Andy came home with me that first Christmas to meet him, he was bone-deep terrified of the man. It didn't help that Andy was, in nearly every way, the complete opposite of my dad; they had nothing in common, at least on the surface. My dad is butch, to put it mildly, an Indiana house painter who likes football and hamburgers and women (usually all at the same time); what could he possibly share with a Black, gay, white-collar Brooklyn native who loved Madonna and silver nail polish?

Pancakes, as it turns out. The world is smaller than we think.

After discovering this fact in an awkward series of question-and-answer sessions with my father, each of which lasted exactly the length of one commercial break during Ice Road Truckers *(my father roots for the accidents because they are exciting and he can talk about appropriate tire pressure and snow chains to anyone who'll listen), Andy got up early on Christmas morning to make my father some special, hearty Christmas morning pancakes. He thought, however, that he'd make them extra-manly, just to show my dad that he could be an excellent son, even if he'd never played touch football and owned nary a rugby shirt or baseball cap and fell asleep before the truckers got to the end of the ice road. Extra-manly, of course, to a gay boy who'd never left New York City, means lumberjacky. And lumberjack, as you probably are thinking, spells flapjacks.*

So Andy, who had many talents but could not count cooking among them, looked up a flapjack recipe online, followed it to the letter and pulled from the oven, proudly and with a very manly flourish, the finished product. And my father, napkin tucked into his shirt collar, fork in hand, looked at the tray of lumpy, oaty stuff and said, his disappointment thick and barely hidden, "Where's the flapjacks?"

I should explain. It was a case of mistaken identity. Though Americans often use the term "flapjack" to refer to what is really a pancake, a British flapjack is something closer to a granola bar or, at the very least, a sugary lump of oats and raisins. I don't know what that man thought the oven would magically do to that stuff in the pan to turn it into what he thought a flapjack should be. Poor Andy. For the next Christmas, my dad got him a pink flannel shirt. My dad could be an unforgiving man.

Of course, my father thought Andy was a more than excellent son, not because he was manly or made Christmas granola lumps, but because he loved me and he loved my father and he tried so hard. And because he wore that damn pink flannel shirt every time—every single time—we saw my dad—wore it like a badge and a scarlet letter all at once. And because he sat through Ice Road Truckers *without complaint, though he couldn't be counted on to stay awake.*

What does all of this have to do with losing—which is where, if you've not lost track already, I began this essay? Everything from this story is gone now: Andy is gone; that Christmas morning is long gone; the flapjacks and the flapjack secret recipe, both quite gone; my father, though he's still technically around, isn't the imposing father-in-law-guard-dog-torturer he once was, and the kid that I was then, madly in love and irritated and untouchable and righteously sure of himself, he's forever gone, too. Even that ridiculous pink flannel shirt has disappeared now to parts unknown, cavorting, I'm sure, with the world's lost socks and loose change in the Land of Lost Things. I've lost, in one way or another, all of that.

This isn't actually quite true. Loss is never whole or complete. Because the word "flapjack" still makes me giggle senselessly, and I still sometimes talk to Andy in my sleep. And love and comfort and safety, family and fond ridicule, mistakes and the room to make them, those are still around. The feeling of being in love; of knowing everything for sure and feeling, at the same time, tipped off balance; of being at once very old and very young; Christmas mornings and first impressions and things that will still be remembered and retold in twenty years, and the feeling that time is slipping away too fast and I can't keep anything long enough, all those things are still around. They just come to me now in different guises, in new shirts, with new meanings, and I have to be wise enough to recognize them when they do.

And, I think, Ice Road Truckers *is still going strong.*

My dad recently told me: You can be happy, or you can be miserable, and the difference is entirely up to you.

Let me, then, be wise and in love with the world enough always to see new meanings in things and always recognize the familiar wonders that come to me in new shirts and new shapes. Let me lose and let me let go and let me still want to hold on; let me feel ancient and new all at once, secure and tipped off my feet; let me be a thief, or a borrower—a relocator, a liberator—of my own joy. Let me be brave enough (write it! Bishop is whispering) to be happy.

∾

I know, Teddy wrote when he'd finally lugged himself home, showered, unpacked and set himself gently down to rest in the quiet of his rooms, *that we're not scheduled for dinner until tomorrow, but could we change plans? It was a long trip, and I'm tired of distance and quiet and I want some conversation and some company. I want to see you. And I know all of this probably makes me sound needy or eager or weird, but I think you've already seen me that way and you haven't run screaming yet. So I'm taking a chance here. Can I see you tonight?*

Twelve

JULES OPENED THE TOP DRAWER of his nightstand and let the silver locket fall in with a soft clink. He'd been carrying it around all day in his pocket, unable to make himself reattach it to Andy's collar, and now that simply seemed inappropriate. So he let the locket go.

His rooms were well kept, always lived-in but beautiful enough that if, by some strange chance, the camera crew for an interior decorating magazine showed up on his doorstep, lost and hungry and desperate, he might take them in, and they'd beg to photograph his place instead of wherever it was they'd been trying to go, simply because it was so stunning—*and on so small a budget!* they would exclaim when he revealed that it was mostly thrifted and scrounged at curbsides. His rooms were beautiful in preparation for the wandering photography crew, yes, and also because when Jules was nervous, he cleaned.

So he lily-gilded to pass the time that night. He mopped the floors and scrubbed the counters, scrubbed even the light-switch plates in every room until they shone; he dusted the stacks of his grandmother's books and records that leaned against the main room's brick wall and pulled the covers so tightly over the top of his bed that—and he really did try it, just to see—he could bounce a quarter on them. He lit the main room with the bright overhead, then with the low-light dimmer and then considered putting out candles, but finally settled on using the little floor lamp with the blue glass shade that made the room feel cool and otherworldly, aquatic and intimate.

He still had twenty minutes before Teddy was due to knock on his door and he'd already redone his hair twice and changed his clothing several times. He'd even bathed Andy and dried him with the hair dryer and a wire brush until he shone and smelled sweet and looked miserable. They were as polished, the two of them, as they might get. So Jules sat (carefully, so as not to rumple his third pair of pants) at the window ledge and stared out at the blank, over-lit sky, at the gray building across the street and its massive tree that never seemed entirely to let go its brown and crumpled leaves, but held them and shook like a rattle in the wind.

"Because I thought it would be rude to be late," said a raised voice below him, testy but still kind, and Jules looked down. It was him, Jules was sure, even from this height and this angle. He was gesturing with one arm and cradling a cell phone against his ear with the other.

"Maggie, please just be nice for another fifteen minutes, then I can go," he whined. "I'm completely nervous and I need to talk to someone who will keep me calm, and you're the next best thing."

Jules smiled to himself. He could, he knew, sit for the next fifteen minutes and watch Teddy, but he wouldn't. He would send a text, so as not to startle him, and he'd let him know it was okay to come in. He took up his phone, but just couldn't make himself duck away from the window. He did, however, hunker down a bit, so that he wasn't so visible. He wasn't, he thought, *that* crazy.

I'm not spying, but is that you out there? he typed into his phone.

A moment later, Teddy looked up and about wildly, and Jules hunched down a bit further against the sill.

"I have to go," Teddy said into the phone in a stage whisper. "I think I've been made." He waited a moment, listening and still scanning the building front for an explanation, then, again into the phone: "You're disgusting. I will not. I'm hanging up now."

When he had hung up the phone, Jules typed, *I'm pretty sure it's you. I'm buzzing you up, so if it's not you and you're a marauder, please be gentle when you maraud. I bruise easily.*

Teddy turned his face upward with the broadest, most open smile, and his eyes seemed to lock, for a moment, on the corner of the window where Jules had thought he was invisibly huddled.

"I'll be gentle," he called up, his eyes scanning. "I'm a gentleman marauder. I'll only take what you say I can have."

Jules smiled again and pocketed his phone. He got up and dusted himself off before heading to the intercom by the door, glancing first out the window one last time to see Teddy, looking down now and turned toward the heavy front door, patient and still, waiting for Jules to let him in.

∞

The apartment was small, with white walls and one of brick, low-lit and warm with the yeasty smell of bread. In it was a soft, rumpled couch slip-covered in natural linen and heaped with pillows of the same shade; there were gauzy curtains and piles of books, a hulking cut-glass mirror leaned against the brick and a faded Oriental rug rested on the scuffed wood floor. A pair of bright yellow rain boots, the high kind, with buckles, was neatly aligned on a mat by the door, and at the table near the tiny kitchen were a pair of the same stools Teddy knew from the bakery, with the same worn and melting velvet cushions. On a garnet-colored pillow by the couch, a sleepy dachshund eyed Teddy with equal parts distrust and interest. A little blue lamp near the table cast the room in its little blue glow, and everything felt underwater-strange and breath-holdingly beautiful.

"I baked some bread already because it takes so much time, but I saved the rest for us to do together," Jules said before Teddy had managed to get his shoes all the way off.

"I wasn't spying on you," Jules added while Teddy was awkwardly bent over and struggling with his shoelaces (he had the feeling that if he simply toed off the shoes as he normally did, he might unfavorably impress Jules, and he didn't want to start the evening on that, so to speak, foot). "I happened to look out and I saw you on the stoop, and I thought it was silly if you were planning to stand there for twenty minutes just so you wouldn't be early." He paused again, watching Teddy struggle with the knotted shoelace he probably hadn't undone in months. *I will*, Teddy thought, *take these shoes off like a human being and a gentleman, even if it kills me.*

"Not that I'm calling you silly," Jules said quickly, when Teddy still hadn't answered (though he'd tried to peep up and smile reassuringly at Jules while he fumbled with the knot). "I'm calling *me* silly. Because it would have been silly to let you stand out there, just waiting for me. Unless—" and Jules's face went a bit paler than it already was, "Did I force you in? Were you doing something important out there?"

Teddy stopped and relinquished his efforts with the lace. "No," he smiled up at Jules. "Nothing important. Just killing time because I was too early. I can be a little compulsive, is all. You caught me." He tried to beam, tried to send all his good and willing thoughts up through his eyes and his smile to Jules, while his fingers, despite his decision to let it go, picked at the knot in his shoe.

"Here," Jules said, and bent down on one knee at Teddy's feet. "Let me, before you injure yourself on this." Teddy watched him curl downward and set to work on the shoe. It made Teddy feel regal and dainty and attended to, near swooning and awkward, helpless and childlike, all at once. Jules's hands were at his feet; his head bent so near Teddy's knee that little wisps of his hair clung with static to the fabric of Teddy's pants. At the back of Jules's neck, where the collar of his shirt gaped open slightly as he bent his head forward, the hair was a lighter blond, though that seemed impossible; it was almost transparent, and very short and soft-looking. Teddy's hand was on its way to rest there gently, fondly, when Jules looked up triumphantly and said, "You're free!" and pulled the shoe from his foot.

"Okay," Teddy stammered and slipped his hand under his own thigh to hold it there. "My hero." He wiggled his bare toes.

"I've made you a reverse Cinderella," Jules said, climbing back to his feet and holding out his hand for Teddy to take, "about which I'm not sure… is that a good thing or a bad thing?"

Teddy put his hand into Jules's and pulled to get up, but felt the sickening slide of his nerves: His palm was wet and a little too slippery, and they missed twice before they got a grip good enough for him to get up.

"Sorry," he said, pulling his hand back and wiping it on his pants. "I'm really nervous for some reason." And then he added, because he couldn't stop his mouth from doing it, "I don't know why I'm so nervous. I've kissed you already." And then, because he really couldn't stop his mouth, he said, "Not that I think it's a done deal, or anything. Not that kissing you before means I think I can just do it any time I want. I just mean—"

"We could get it out of the way now," Jules suggested simply. He leaned forward to cup Teddy's jaw with one hand, while the other wound around Teddy's waist and pulled him in. Teddy's arms dangled at his sides because his aching body felt loose and useless, and he said, under his breath and completely redundantly, "Okay." Jules kissed him softly on the mouth, the briefest kiss, dry and gentle and tentative and sweet, leaving a second delicate kiss at the corner of his lips before he pulled away.

"Very smooth," Teddy said, fanning himself and batting his eyelashes, because Jules was deeply red and staring fixedly at his own bare feet. "First the shoe and now the kiss. Are you hiding a pumpkin and some mice somewhere in here?"

"You're mocking me now."

"No," Teddy said seriously, dipping his head to try to catch Jules's eye. "I'm swooning. For real."

"Yes. Well."

There was, after that, nothing that Teddy could say in response, because Jules hadn't really said anything at all, and it was clear from the way he was watching his own toes grind against the rubbed-raw wood of the floor that he wasn't planning to say anything more. So Teddy, with his stomach twisting and his hands sweating and his throat closing around a lump that felt like hope and fear and happiness, put his hands on Jules's clavicles and said, "You're making me so nervous. I'm a wreck," and pressed his lips to Jules's forehead in a gentle kiss until Jules looked up. And then Teddy kissed him again, on the mouth, a kiss that really counted, with his eyes closed tight and his fingers pressing against the sharp bones of Jules's shoulders.

"I'm terribly nervous here, too, you know," Jules said to the floor when Teddy had stopped kissing him. "I don't really do this."

"Let the hoi polloi get so close? Let one of your many wild admirers kiss you in your kitchen?" Teddy smirked and squeezed Jules's shoulders.

"Date," Jules said quietly and looked Teddy in the eye so suddenly and directly and with such clear gray eyes that Teddy felt his heart squeeze and bang hard in his throat.

"We should start that, then," Teddy said. "Maybe we should get cooking?"

"This is nice," Jules said, touching the lapels of Teddy's gray suit jacket with two gentle fingers. "You should take it off first."

Teddy hung his jacket over the seat of a stool and rolled up the sleeves of his shirt, while Jules poured generous splashes of Pinot into two mason jars. Under Jules's direction, they made a sauce of wild mushrooms, celeriac and leeks to spread across a fluttery, hand-rolled pasta. They roasted squash and beets until they were sweet and caramel-brown. They tossed them with figs into a bowl of bitter greens and a curried almond dressing Jules whisked by hand. They moved quietly around each other in Jules's compact kitchen, each laying a hand lightly on the other's hip or waist and pressing gently to pass. They picked at smoked olives and aged Gouda; they broke the bread open and mopped it through olive oil and coarse salt; they drank the wine.

When they had finished cooking, they ate quietly at the tiny table by the light of the little blue lamp, with their forks chiming dimly against their plates in quiet agreement, as if they had done it that way together, at that little table, for years. The near silence between them was comfortable and rich and sweet, while in the background, Jules's stereo crooned low with the voices of women—Bessie Smith, Nina Simone, Billie Holiday, Sarah Vaughan—who were tough and sad and lost and gone.

So much of the time he had known Teddy, Jules thought, had been spent in conversation; tonight, for hours, there nearly were no words between them. In the kitchen, they'd gestured, pressed and simply *known*, moving around each other in a dance they'd never before performed but understood intimately all the same.

Afterward, they sat on the sloping, sunken couch with Andy between them, drinking the dregs of the wine and peeling peaches into a large bowl. Every few minutes, when he thought Jules wasn't looking, Teddy slipped Andy a small slice of peach peel.

"If you keep doing that," Jules said, "he's going to vomit. And I *will* make you clean it up."

"The peels have all the vitamins," Teddy said, popping a piece into his own mouth.

"He's a very old dog," Jules said dryly. "He doesn't *need* vitamins. He needs not to eat things like shoelaces or pinecones or peach skin."

For a moment, there was only the *snick snick* of their peelers on the fruit, and then Teddy put his peeled peach into the bowl, wiped his hands on the towel in his lap and ran his fingers through the fur at the nape of Andy's neck. "Is he," he began, then stopped.

"He's thirteen," Jules said, without glancing up. "Which is, for a dog like him, *elderly.*" He whispered the word, as if he didn't want Andy to hear it.

"No, I know. I mean, is he named after your... Is he named after Andy?"

"Oh." Jules put his half-peeled peach into the bowl and wiped his hands. He looked at Andy, letting his fingers play in the fur so close to Teddy's hand he could feel the heat of it. He didn't, however, touch Teddy and he couldn't look up. "No. Not exactly. He came with the name. It was a coincidence."

Teddy kept his eyes on Andy, letting his own fingers circle through the fur closer and closer to Jules's until the tip of his finger was barely brushing against the side of Jules's thumb. He kept it there, a light and moving pressure, a quiet contact. "I thought he might be a reminder for you or something," he said.

"He is," Jules said, withdrawing his hand and pulling his knees up to his chest. "He belonged to Andy, and he's what I have left of him." This wasn't, Jules realized, entirely true. The apartment had belonged to Andy before they'd shared it, and everything with which they'd filled the apartment (the slumped, soft couch, the bed, the books and the paintings, the silverware and the good wine glasses and the dishes), all of it had been collected and polished and loved with Andy. He was, he came suddenly to see, surrounded by things Andy had chosen, had lived with and touched. But these things, Jules thought, feeling small and stuck in the thought, belonged to *him,* too; he couldn't entirely free himself of Andy without giving up a large part of his own life.

Teddy had stopped petting Andy and had laid both his hands in his lap, palms up, an unreadable gesture—defeated or willing or broken open, Jules couldn't tell. "But," he said, reaching over to slide his hands against Teddy's palms, "I should have told you this before, on the phone, when we talked about it. There's enough room, Teddy."

Teddy's hands stayed open; they didn't close over Jules's. Jules sighed, trying again. "Most people grow up with two sets of grandparents," he said. "And you can love both grandmothers, even if they are very different, and even if they are both wonderful grandmothers. And when you're visiting one, you don't spend your time with her thinking about how much you miss the other one. It doesn't work that way."

Teddy nodded and he smiled at Jules and squeezed his hands, but his eyes were wet and glossy. "I get it," Teddy whispered. "I'm not trying to be dramatic or needy or think too far ahead or something. It's just… intimidating."

Jules nodded. Gingerly, he picked up Andy and laid him on the pillow on the floor, then turned back and scooted closer to Teddy, until their arms and thighs pressed together. He slipped his hand into Teddy's and laid his cheek against Teddy's chest. "I think I really like you. I think it could be good, too."

❧

They took the bowl of peaches to the kitchen, and together they sliced the fruit into thin wedges, their fingers shining with juice.

"Would it gross you out if I ate one of these out of the bowl?" Teddy asked, holding a slice of peach to his mouth.

Jules rolled his eyes. "No, it wouldn't gross me out. I'm not *that* uptight, thank you." So Teddy slowly sucked the fruit into his mouth with a slick sound. It was meant to be a little obnoxious, a little challenging, Jules knew, but it sent a dazzling shudder through the pit of him as he watched. Teddy smiled at him, a little wickedly.

"Oh, so there you go, then. Would it gross *you* out to feed me one, too?" Jules volleyed, barely stifling the smirk in his voice. "My hands are a mess, and you make it… Look. So. Good." He breathed this out in his best Monroe imitation, holding up his fingers, sticky with peach pulp and sugar, and lowering his eyelids and opening his mouth. Teddy laughed a little under his breath and slowly slipped one of the cool slices along Jules's bottom lip before pushing it onto his tongue with one finger.

"Mmmmm," Jules moaned, closing his lips on Teddy's finger and sucking lightly, running the tip of his tongue along its length, doing his best imitation of a desperate starlet. It was cliché and camp, he thought, and perfect to lighten an evening that had gotten too dark too quickly. "*Soooo* sweet," he mumbled around the finger.

But when he opened his eyes to look at Teddy and share the laugh, he was startled to find the man watching him, hazy and wide-eyed and already reaching for another slice of peach with his free hand. Jules opened his mouth and let the finger go. "Oh," he said, his own sugary, wet hands still held up awkwardly near his cheeks.

Teddy raised his eyebrows. "Would it gross you out if I did this?" he asked, and licked slowly up the back of Jules's slick hand from his wrist to the tip of his forefinger, a long, warm rasp with the flat of his tongue.

"No," Jules said simply, swallowing hard. "Would this gross you out?" He pulled the peach slice from Teddy's fingers and put it on his own tongue, crushing the fruit against the roof of his mouth and letting the juice spill slowly everywhere, down his throat and onto his lips. He kissed Teddy, his mouth open, pushing the sticky pulp onto Teddy's tongue and licking there gently until Teddy made a soft, shuddering sound and put his hands, damp and cool and heavy with the scent of the fruit, on Jules's neck and kissed him back.

After the kiss had finished, they simply stood, looking and breathing and not knowing, their faces shining with sugar and pulp. After the kiss had finished, there was a shift and pull, when the gravity of the moment had slipped off and it was, Jules thought, no longer funny in the least. There was a swelling ache in his throat.

"Our clothes," Jules said under his breath. "The juice is going to stain."

So Teddy wiped his hands on a towel and hauled off his shirt and vest in one motion, then unbuttoned Jules's shirt while Jules held his slick hands up in the air like a helpless surgeon. They pulled at buttons and zippers, pulled at fabric until it all slid away with a rough shush and they stood, finally, with nothing to cover them, bare chest to bare chest, and Jules ran his hands flat down the length of Teddy's body, leaving a thick trail of nectar glistening on his skin. He followed his hands with the slippery tongue of a peach, and then dragged his mouth over the skin that had opened up to him, tracing the path again with open kisses and little knowing licks, his fingers sticking in the sugared spots on Teddy's ribs. Teddy shook beneath his hands, then bent and sucked the sweet spots on Jules's neck where his fingers had left streaks of juice gleaming on the pale skin. Jules kissed him down to the tiled floor and they tangled there with the bowl of peaches placed nearby, digging their hands in and painting the juice and the flesh of the fruit across bellies and thighs, into the tender crook of an elbow, the small pool of a navel and the gentle dip of a clavicle, until the whole kitchen smelled like summer: peach-sweet and sweaty and close.

There is no kind and clean way to say it, no tender words for this: They fucked on the floor, slick with sweat and peach juice, the sugar crystallizing in the warm creases of their bodies, rubbing them raw where skin met skin. They fucked desperately, they fucked with absolute joy, they fucked so that they ached and shivered, so that their breath was too thin and frantic and made them dizzy and almost put them out into blackness. They fucked with loose and furious hands and mouths and tongues and flesh, and there was too much of it and not enough; they fucked with their bare toes scraping against the tile; they fucked and they fucked until they disappeared from the world, until their bodies were the only thing left, until their muscles shook and their bones bent under them and they thought they would break, and still they wanted more; they fucked until they yelled and cried and their throats were sore, and then they fucked silently, shaking and panting and smacking together in the dim blue light, searching with their mouths for air and skin and *oh, just, just, just a little more* until they were able to whisper again, and then they fucked with whispers, sweet and hungry and wailingly sad because they could not make their bodies closer, could not smash them together into one, could not ever wholly undo the distance between them and they felt that completely—they felt it like panic and they felt it like bliss and they felt it again like mourning.

They fucked until they broke and then fucked until they healed. They fucked and came and fucked again, until they burst open like sudden flowers and their fragile bodies shattered down to the bones and lay on the cool tile, heaving and shuddering, until they could make their eyes open again and pull their lips apart and slowly return themselves to the world.

In the earliest hours of the morning, Jules woke before the alarm, overheated and a little sweaty, with one bare leg stretching out from under the blankets in search of cooler air. Teddy was pressed against him, breathing in soft puffs against his shoulder; his arm curled up over Jules's chest and his hand tenderly cradled Jules's jaw, as if he were just about to bend him gently backward and kiss the breath out of him. He had, of course, done so the previous night, over and over, until Jules was so full of happiness he might shatter into a thousand spinning little stars, but this morning Teddy was still and sleeping and his face, in sleep, looked so tenderly beautiful—his eyelids almost translucent, his lips just barely open for his breath—that Jules was afraid to move. He ran a finger lightly down the slope of Teddy's nose and pressed it, gently, to his lips, before dragging himself out from under Teddy's arm and into the gray air of the morning.

He showered and dressed, walked and fed Andy, and left a note and a key for Teddy on the bedside table, then walked the short way to the bakery and let himself inside.

Hours later, when the front gate rumbled and 'Trice hurtled in and straight to the espresso machine ("Jules!" she yelled, as she did every single morning, "I'm making coffee!"), the croissants and muffins, cookies and little pies were cooling on the metal racks near the back of the kitchen and Jules's bag was slung over his shoulder.

"I'm going home early today," he called, sailing as smoothly as he could toward the front door. "Call me with any disasters!"

"Whoa, there, Amelia Airhead!" 'Trice said, pegging him with a paper cup just before he reached the door. "Are you sick? Is there a sample sale that's also on fire? Is it Fleet Week? You got a hot date?"

Jules stopped and sighed, turning slowly on his heel. He had just opened his mouth to retort when she interrupted him, hurling another cup in his direction.

"It *is* a hot date, you dirty old man!" she yelled.

"I can go home early. It doesn't have to be an event."

"Chef Burns finally got laid!" she shrieked, banging through her routine at the espresso machine. "I can totally tell! You got grasshopped!" She flung her arm up in the air; the spoon she was using to strain the milk flipped blops of milk foam all over the counter.

"You know," Jules could feel the heat creeping over his face, even as he worked hard to sound sassy and indignant—"you are *not* psychic and most of the time you *don't* know what you're talking about."

"'Trice knows all and sees all," she said in a deep, floaty voice, crossing her arms over her chest and looking at him through narrowed eyes.

"You're a crazy person who's obsessed with my sex life. It's unhealthy. You need help."

"*You* need help," 'Trice said. "And ooooh, girlfriend *got* some help, didn't he?"

Jules glared at her as she took a long, innocent-eyed drink from her mug. "Lots of help, by the look of you. Second helpings. And thirds and fourths."

"Call me *only* if there's an apocalypse here," Jules said and turned toward the door.

"It's *hard* to get good help these days," she cooed at him, twirling her locks in big loops like lassos. "Don't you find it *hard?*"

"In my experience," he grumbled, "it is incredibly hard to get good help these days. Help these days has a giant, smart-ass mouth."

She laughed, and he felt another paper cup hit him in the back, but he didn't stop to reply.

Teddy woke around seven in a bed that wasn't his. The tree outside the window shook the light into unfamiliar patterns on the blankets. The only noise was the electric hum of the refrigerator and a little quiet snuffling and wheezing he was sure was Andy. By the bed he found a key and a note from Jules promising to return once 'Trice got to work and hoping to catch him before he left for the office.

Teddy found his pants on the kitchen floor and his phone in the pocket. He called in sick, and his voice was hoarse enough from the night before, he might've even sounded believably ill. He cleaned up the night's tossed-off clothing and the slopped bowl of peaches (in which Andy, by the matted and sticky look of him, had been exploring) and put a kettle of water to boil on the stove for coffee.

Jules came home while he was in the shower and poked his head suddenly into the bathroom to say, "It's just me here; don't let me scare you!" Which, as Jules should have known, startled Teddy so much he actually yelped and flattened himself against the tile wall.

"Are you rushing?" Jules said when Teddy met him in the kitchen, towel clutched around his hips. "I finished making the coffee, and there's a travel mug for you just in case you have to run."

"I took the day off, but I can get out of your hair if you have stuff to do today."

In answer, Jules pulled off his top and threw it in the general direction of the couch. He put his hands on his hips and tilted his head, looking at Teddy incredulously.

"Oh, thank god, then," Teddy said, and moved to press himself against Jules. "Because I really would rather be all up in your hair all day, if I can."

Jules grabbed him by the wrists. "Don't you ever touch the hair," he warned. "This is perfect, perfect hair."

Teddy wriggled his hands free and cupped them around Jules's jaw. He held Jules's face still, tilted his head slightly and kissed him. And then he slid both hands into Jules's hair and he laughed and *pulled,* but Jules's eyes went wide and he said *Oh* from his throat and the sound traveled like a shiver down into Teddy's belly, and they moved like a waterfall, tumbling together all at once, wild and messy and full of force.

◦◦◦

All day it was like this, lazy and frantic and silver-slick, dipping into and out of kissing, their bodies falling into fucking and out again, sudden shouts and sudden peace, curling into each other to nap, exhausted, on the bed, and waking again hard and full and aching. They hardly knew the hour. They hardly cared the day.

When it was over and the light had gone out of the sky, they dressed and took Andy out on his leash around the block. They held hands and smiled like idiots, while Andy, oblivious, toddled between them.

After they'd rummaged in the fridge and eaten a slim meal of olives and cheese and leftover bread, after Andy had waddled over to his pillow and put himself to bed, after Jules had pulled the gauzy curtains closed and switched on the little blue lamp, he said, "Do you want to try the pie again?"

Teddy smirked and raised an eyebrow, but Jules said, "Seriously. We have an empty crust," so Teddy agreed and they took an empty bowl to the couch and peeled, again, a pile of slithery peaches, smiling slyly at each other when their eyes met.

They cut them into slices, and Jules mixed them (using a spoon this time) with sugar and lemon, heaped them into the crust and deftly, expertly, twisted a lattice for the top.

"You do that so quickly," Teddy said, watching his hands.

"Lots of practice," Jules laughed, weaving the dough and starting to pinch around the sides.

"It's sexy," Teddy mumbled.

"It's what?" Jules laughed. "You have no standards."

"You have incredibly sexy hands," Teddy said. And Jules laughed again until Teddy held up a sliver of peach and said, "I saved one."

Teddy pressed it into Jules's mouth and kissed him on top of it, and Jules sucked on the fruit and let it slither down while Teddy traced Jules's throat with the tips of his fingers, traced down his chest and his belly, down the front of his pants until Teddy was on his knees, his fingers prying at Jules's waistband, his eyes turned up, wide and glimmering and taking him in.

"Okay," Jules whispered and he let Teddy pull his pants loose and away, let him trace his lips over the hard swell of him, his breath burning and wet, his fingers pushing the fabric down. Teddy opened his mouth and swallowed Jules in, let his tongue rasp and undulate

against him, and it felt warm and tight and hot and Jules held the edge
of the counter with whitening fingers and he breathed down *jesus christ
oh jesus christ*. Teddy's fingers dug at the backs of his thighs and played
over the thin skin of his groin in little strokes, and then Teddy closed his
throat around him, sucked hard, and Jules bucked slowly into his open
mouth—it was so slow and so quiet, as if they were underwater, rocking
in a tide. Jules swayed into him like an anemone, dropped his hands
to Teddy's head and held, and the tightening almost-there pleasure
pulled and pushed and pulled him deeper, and it wasn't desperate this
time; it was a wave building and growing in him, slow and constant
and ever-tightening until he was so high above the earth he couldn't
remember it anymore, and Teddy's hands were petting the muscles at
his hips gently, desperately, wanting, wanting, and so he gave himself
up entirely for him, broke suddenly open and made fists in Teddy's
hair and came in his mouth.

The next day Jules had, in all good faith, intended to stay at the
bakery all day—Teddy had even packed him up a little parcel of bread
and salad and a slice of the peach pie they'd finally managed to bake—
but when he heard the familiar noise of 'Trice slamming into the store
and hollering her usual coffee call, he couldn't make himself stay. Teddy
was probably still curled up in his bed, sleeping and waiting for him,
having called in sick to work again, and Jules could not muster the
patience to keep himself away for so long. So he packed his bag and
slung it over his shoulder, called out to 'Trice and hurtled onto the
street before she could say even one word.

When he had gone, the shop was quiet and still, dusty and beautifully
golden in the morning light, and 'Trice, for her part, was happy for
the peace. She made coffee and pulled out a pencil for the crossword,

tuned the stereo to public radio news and thought again about how much she loved the job that let her do these things every morning.

When she found and unwrapped the parcel of Jules's lunch, forgotten on the counter, she thought it would be criminal to ignore the little unexpected gift, and broke into the peach pie first. With a spoon, she took it in, the tender crust and the melting, flesh-soft fruit, and because she was alone, she closed her eyes and let her tongue turn it over—slippery, spiced, yielding—before swallowing it down.

She felt it slip down the back of her throat like a caress, felt it settle in her stomach and bloom warmly like a slow explosion. Another bite, and she crushed the fruit against the roof of her mouth and sucked it down; it lit her up from the inside out with the bright shimmer of delight, like an unfurling flower. She managed only one more bite, all cloves and sugar and summertime on her tongue, before it caught her and shook her body from the belly up, and her mouth dropped open and she gripped the counter's edge and could only whisper hoarsely the closest name for what it was she felt: *Oh, my good god, oh, my god!*

Thirteen

MOST IMPORTANT MOMENTS ARE QUIET ONES. The tide creeps up
on the beach in little licks, a sly advance and retreat, rocking one
fraction of an inch closer each time, until the sand is swallowed and
everything is water, and all the landmarks have been lapped up and
the ground has shifted and you don't know, anymore, where you might
have been standing.

It was, for Teddy, like this. Kissing Jules turned the ground to sand; it
slid out from beneath him, and all the things he used to locate himself
in the world were suddenly gone.

Weeks passed, and the bright green spring wilted into the soldered
heat of a relentless city summer. Days were spent, it seemed to them,
in different climates, on opposite sides of the world: Jules in the dry
heat of the bakery kitchen (the ovens churning out cakes and smearing
the air into bleary waves until he could see nothing straight and sweat
drew its fingertips down his spine like a bitter lover) and Teddy in the
refrigerated blue silence of his office (where sometimes he pressed his
cheek against the plastic skin of his computer just to feel something
warm and humming and nearly alive). Nights, they crawled into
Jules's bed and lay in the clammy, fan-blown dark, too sweaty to touch

but touching still, palm to hip and temple to shoulder, and sometimes slept and sometimes whispered to each other in the cottony heat.

Andy had become, somehow, Teddy's own (*my dog,* he said often in his head and once to the receptionist at the office, just to test how it felt). The sloping couch was his, the tinny coffee press was his, and the bright umbrellas by the door and the chipped bathtub. "We should fix this floor," he said once, after snagging his foot on an uprooted nail in the parquet for the millionth time, and Jules had looked at him and smiled widely and told him, "We should."

He left his clothes in the pressboard dresser in Jules's bedroom, left his razor and toothbrush on the bathroom sink, left his suits in their filmy dry cleaner bags crowded into Jules's closet, left pieces of himself in every drawer and corner of the apartment on Jane Street until there came a day when Teddy realized he hadn't been back to his own cool, clean apartment in over a week. There was no longer anything there he needed.

❦

"Here," 'Trice said, and tossed a piece of paper in Jules's direction as she passed on her way out to the espresso machine. It fluttered softly down onto the table in front of him like a lost moth.

"What is this?" he asked, flipping it over.

"For you, since you're being such a lesbian," she said, and flipped her way out into the bakery storefront. It was a newspaper coupon for a U-Haul rental.

"Very funny!" he yelled after her and, when there was no response, he burst into the shop front, coupon crumpled in his fist. "Very funny!" he shouted, before noticing the two kids in the corner, hunched over a shared piece of cake. They looked at him and then giggled down at their clinking forks. "Very funny," he hissed into 'Trice's back.

"It is," 'Trice said implacably, turning around. "Did he get you pregnant or something?"

Jules rolled his eyes and tightened the apron at his waist. "Yes," he sighed heavily. "Yes, he has gotten me pregnant. I'm a knocked-up and shamed boy, and that is why he's moving in with me so soon. And yes, I'm aware that it's only been a couple months, and yes, I'm also aware that this means we are big old U-Hauling lesbians in your eyes, and yes, I understand that this means, if I'm to follow your example, that I will have to start dressing like a crazy homeless person with no taste and listening to shitty trash can-screaming music and tattooing every available piece of skin on my body that I haven't pierced already. And I'll probably have to become bitter and start living vicariously by commenting on other peoples' love lives, too, if I'm really going to do it right."

"Well, you have a great start on the bitter part, and what have *you* pierced already?" 'Trice muttered, scribbling something onto her crossword. "And," she said, putting down her pen with a click, "I don't listen to *shitty trash can-screaming music*, whatever that is. And up until a minute ago when you started acting like a jackass, I was going to say I was happy for you. It's about time."

Jules deflated instantly, slumped against the counter and laid his head on 'Trice's shoulder. She took a long drink of her coffee, but didn't shake him off. "You don't think it's ridiculously too soon?" he asked. "Everybody else seems to think we're being crazy about this." He picked up her pen and filled in a box with a little scribbled star.

"Don't *do* that, I've told you!" she hollered, and grabbed the pen out of his hand. "This is *pen,* and it's the *Times,* and you can't mess with that! Besides, who's 'everyone'?"

"I don't know. Avon. My family. My friends. His family and friends. Everyone."

"Everyone is stupid. I thought we'd established that."

The kids in the corner were tittering again, glancing at 'Trice and Jules every few seconds, whispering between glances, with huge smiles stuck to their sappy faces.

"Oh, knock it off!" 'Trice growled in their direction. "He's the most flaming of gaylords, in case you're unable to detect that, and I'm a huge queerball, and never the twain shall meet. I find him incredibly irritating, and decidedly *not* sexy. He's just my pet lesbro, so eat your cake and stop giggling at us like idiots! We're *not on your team!*" The kids looked stunned; they hunched back over their cake and eyeballed 'Trice with careful, quick glances. Jules let his head roll off her tight shoulder and propped himself up with a fist under his chin.

"Nice job, scaring the straight kids. What crawled—" he started, then stopped, because 'Trice had her head in her hands, and she was yanking at the locks near her temples. He tapped the back of her neck with a cool finger. "Kitchen," he said simply and spun on his heel.

When 'Trice slammed into the kitchen, Jules was a little more than scared. She was fiery and growling and she moved with such snappish, jerky precision that it sent her locks whipping around her shoulders with claps of beads. Frowning at him, she dropped her coffee onto the metal table with a slosh and folded her arms sullenly around her middle.

"Stop it," he said. "You look like Medusa right now."

"I'll stone *you*, you little gay bastard," she mumbled, but he could hear only half her heart in it.

"Okay," he risked a hand on her arm. She didn't move to hurt him, which, in his estimation, was the best possible response. "Why are you yelling at kids all of a sudden? You're supposed to be the cool-headed one here."

'Trice leveled a dramatic eye roll in his direction, then bent to scoop up her hair, twisting and tying it into a large knot on the top of her head. A few heavy locks snaked out and flopped onto her shoulder. She sighed.

"I just hate everybody right now. Especially everybody with somebody." She took a strangely delicate sip of her coffee. "I kind of hate you right now, too, you boring straight-gay asshole. You put gay men to shame with this. You're supposed to be going to circuit parties and doing it in bathroom stalls and sniffing poppers or something, not shacking up with every guy you ever sleep with."

"I don't even know how to respond to that, except to ask if we've met before," Jules said. He held out his hand to shake, at which she simply glared. "Hi. I'm Jules Burns, mild-mannered baker and romantically challenged serial monogamist. Chronically lonely soul who's finally found a nice boy and is happy for the first time in more than a year, thanks to a big old yenta named *you.*"

When she didn't react, when she merely sighed heavily and dipped her eyes toward her cup of coffee again, Jules felt brave enough to poke her arm and flip, with one finger, a couple of the fallen locks back over her shoulder with a soft clack.

"Who peed on your parade?" he asked. He knew, when pressed, how to speak her language. At least, he figured he did. It didn't sound as good coming from him, but he was clearly trying.

"I've always felt just fine with my life," 'Trice said, finally looking him in the eye. "Actually, I've always felt kind of superior to everyone else, like I was somehow above the whole compulsory need to couple up and get married and have babies and that whole thing. But then there *you* are trying to be Mrs. Jules Grasshopper, and then my cousin breaks her leg spectacularly and my mom and my aunts are all cooing over the fact that *George* showed up at the hospital just for May-May and *George* is going to take May-May home with him while she heals and isn't it just wonderful that May-May is special enough that she has scored *George* to take care of her when she's sick, and poor 'Trice doesn't have *anybody* and aren't lesbians supposed to mate for life and what is *wrong* with you, 'Trice, that you have nobody and you're going to die alone because nobody will know when you fall down the stairs and break your leg, and your forty-seven spinster cats will eat you alive because you are completely, pitifully alone."

Knowing it was probably a very bad idea, Jules risked a laugh. He skipped backward a couple steps when 'Trice looked up at him coldly. "*That's* what this is about?" he said. 'Trice was stony. She picked up a knife and began to chop mercilessly at the pile of walnuts on the table.

"Yes," she said with a sullen whack of the knife.

"Don't mangle those," Jules said, and 'Trice banged the knife onto the cutting board one more time just to show him. He sighed. "This is *not* like you. First of all, do you even *want* a George? Or a Georgia? Or a whatever?"

"Not really," she said. "George is kind of a tool. He wears Dockers."

"Exactly," Jules said. "You don't even want that. And you're not exactly alone. For as long as I've known you, you've had kind of a harem."

'Trice snorted and scraped at the board with the knife. "They act like I'm sitting by myself in the corner, eating beans out of a can."

"You have better taste than that," Jules said, with a dismissive wave of his hand. "You're alone because you *like* it, aren't you?"

"Yes," she sighed.

"And you know you're not so much *alone* as you are *single*. You have tons of friends. And me, you have me. If you broke your leg, I would find you before your forty-seven cats ate you alive." He crept forward. It was like soothing a feral animal. An animal with a knife. "Besides, your place doesn't even have any stairs."

She rolled her eyes at that, but the knife stayed on the cutting board. Jules snaked one arm around her shoulders and gently pushed the knife with his other hand, so it skittered and spun on the metal countertop.

"Really?" she said with another eye roll.

"Just taking precautions," he said, and pushed the knife a little further away.

"You're an ass," she grumbled, but let her head drop onto his shoulder.

"I know," he whispered into her hair and squeezed her shoulders. "I love you, too."

"Whatever," she said quietly. "Coming from the Princess of the Pocket Square-Wearing Gaylords of Homotopia, that doesn't mean much."

"Yes it does." Jules squeezed again, feeling confident that she'd been sufficiently disarmed, both literally and metaphorically.

"Sigh," she said and then did, poking at the knot of his apron with one finger.

"Sigh," he agreed and poked her belly.

They were, in this way, perfectly suited for each other; and this was an idea to which both of them clung fantastically, happily, fiercely.

In the outer room of the shop, the bells jangled and the front door closed with a shuddering thump, though neither of them could tell whether it was the cake-eating couple finally leaving or new people coming in.

"Besides," he said, "I need you in good shape for moving boxes tomorrow. I need your big, overdeveloped, lesbian bean-eating arms for help."

"Please," she said. "How hard can it be to carry five boxes of sweater vests up one flight of stairs?"

"We need you there, 'Trice," Jules said quietly into her shoulder. "We do."

After the boxes and bags had been carried; after the truck had been loaded and the apartment, clean, white and empty, had been swept and checked twice; after Jules had kissed him sweetly in the doorway and 'Trice had rolled her eyes and wiped the sweat off her forearms with a red bandana; after he'd closed and locked the door on the empty echo, Teddy dropped his keys with the doorman and left the place for good.

He and Jules had talked about finding a new place, one that didn't house the memory of Andy-the-man, but in New York City, giving up the cramped but sunny apartment on Jane Street felt like giving up a little glittering trove of gold, and both men knew it would be ridiculous to let it go. And so, instead, they hauled Jules's sloping couch and sprawling white bed to the curb for whomever was brave enough to take them (Jules had insisted on taping signs to each item that read, in neat block letters, NO BEDBUGS, but Teddy was dubious that anyone would bite before the trash collectors came on Monday) and began the delicate process of cramming Teddy's spare but expensive furniture alongside Jules's shabby, shined-up treasures.

At 'Trice's insistence, they ordered pizza and opened the beer Jules had been keeping cold in the back of the fridge. Squatting amongst the half-opened boxes and piles of crumpled newspaper with which Teddy had packed the breakable things, they toasted, the three of them, the little home.

"A warning," 'Trice said seriously, after pulling the beer bottle from her lips with a wet pop. "He's a real bitch in the mornings."

Teddy laughed when Jules slapped her arm, affronted.

"Don't touch his clothing or his hair unless he gives you permission," she continued, and at this Jules nodded seriously.

"And most important," she nearly whispered, pointing the lip of her beer in Teddy's direction, "we're sharing him now, since I had him first and all. If you break him or damage him—even just a little—I will descend upon you with a wrath you have yet to imagine."

"You can't be serious right now. Get the hell out. Uninvited!" Jules grouched at her, pushing at her thigh with his bare feet.

"I'm *deadly* serious," she said, still eyeballing Teddy sideways and pointing her bottle. "Deadly."

"I don't belong to either one of you, so stop giving him instructions on my care and feeding like I'm a hamster."

"Then stop storing grain in your cheeks, Fluffy," 'Trice laughed and squeezed Jules's jaw. Jules pushed her hand away, and the two descended into a pile of slaps and shrieks and amateur wrestling moves. Teddy watched, still smiling stupidly, and when 'Trice had Jules pinned under her thick thighs, with her bottle resting on his forehead, calmly holding his head still with one large hand; when Jules flailed beneath her, helpless and indignant and shouting at Teddy, "Do something already, goddamn it, she's going to leave a *ring* on my forehead!"; when 'Trice slipped her other hand down over Jules's mouth to muffle his protests and shrugged nonchalantly; when Andy shuffled over to inspect the commotion and then turned his back on Jules's wiggling body and settled himself against *Teddy's* thigh—when all of these things happened while Teddy sat, grinning and avoiding Jules's grasping hands, Teddy felt, for the first time in his entire life, totally and completely present and wanted and *home.*

After they'd finished dinner and the small wrestling match, Teddy busied himself in the bedroom, folding sweaters and piling them carefully in the back of the closet behind the row of Jules's heavy boots. From the kitchen, he could hear Jules and 'Trice clattering about as they chopped watermelon and pitted cherries and tossed them into bright ceramic bowls.

"You're a horrible little man!" he heard 'Trice yell, followed by a series of muffled thumps and laughter. "Horrible!"

Andy snuffled in and flopped by Teddy's knee and immediately dropped into snoring.

"Away with you, she-devil!" Jules screeched from the other room. "Relinquish the spoon!"

"My mother used to spank horrible little people with a spoon just like this," he heard 'Trice scream, followed by a ruckus of metal and wood and glass and water.

"Not so little!" Jules shouted above the thumps. "Right, Teddy?"

Teddy felt both inside and outside of their circle, then; he knew he'd been invited in, and rarely did the two of them play like this in front of anyone else; he knew that this was a gift they were giving him tonight, a welcoming present at the door of his new life. But he also knew he could never join them, and if he ran in there and grabbed a spatula and tried to defend Jules's honor, or tried to help 'Trice paddle Jules with the kitchen implements, they'd both stop dead in their tracks and stare at him blankly, as if he'd run in naked or invited them to help him rob a gas station. It was a beautiful and delicate intimacy between the two of them, one he didn't want to disrupt, but one from which he felt painfully, blindly excluded.

"You, sir," Teddy said to Andy, but didn't finish the thought. Instead, he flipped Andy's silky ears back and forth in his fingers and thought *you'll always be mine,* and wasn't exactly sure to whom he was really talking.

'Trice spent that night on the couch, tipsy-drunk and loudly hollering at them every time she caught Teddy's hand on Jules's hip or saw Jules drop a kiss to Teddy's neck. "You're grossing me out!" she yelled, every single time, in exactly the same tone of voice.

"It's like having a giant baby," Teddy had whispered to Jules, once they were finally shut safely into their own bedroom.

Teddy had slept there so many times before, though never in his own bed, and everything in the apartment had, at one time or another, already been "christened;" but Jules insisted that they'd never had sex in Teddy's bed, and certainly not in *their* bed, in *their* bedroom, which it was now, and so, once 'Trice was snoring loudly and constantly from Teddy's transplanted couch and the bedroom was lit blue-white by the streetlight that shone, despite the curtains, directly across the pillows, they locked the door and christened their too-soft bed and their sheets, their dimming bedroom, their streetlight and their neighborhood and their privacy and their sweltering nighttime. They did it with whispers and heavy breath and sliding and sweat, too quickly in the too-quiet night. Jules's knobby long legs were opalescent and delicate with reflected light, and when they were finished, Teddy wrapped his hands around the backs of Jules's thighs and held him there, still above him, and would not let him come down.

He had packed up his life and come here, and they'd pressed him in until he fit, and nothing, *nothing*, had gotten broken.

❧

PASTRY-WHIPPED: ADVENTURES IN SUGAR BY A DEDICATED
CRUMPET STRUMPET
by Chef Jules Burns of Buttermilk Bakery
*July 7: Box of Chocolates? No. Life Is Like a Soufflé
(A Meditation on Straying, on Coming Home and, at the
Heart of It, on Domestic "Bliss")*

A movie which shall remain nameless (and which, incidentally, was sugarier than anything I have ever baked at Buttermilk) once gave us this treasure: "Life is like a box of chocolates: You never know what you're gonna get." This little bit of "wisdom" never made sense to me—even the cheap drugstore chocolates come with a shape key on the back, so in order to know what you're going to get, all you have to do is turn the box over and look at the pictures. It's not rocket science. It's not even fifth grade math.

The point? It's a stupid saying.

Me, I've always been more partial to documentaries. I've always been partial to just plain old solid chocolate, too. The basics.

I've got news, everyone, and it's not a non sequitur, though it might seem like one, so allow me a bit of slack here for a moment, and I promise to bring it all full circle for you.

Recently, the man I've been seeing (let's call him, in the tradition of great literature, T—) moved in with me, and we are now in the throes of domestic bliss. Which means, in practical terms, lots of cuddling on the couch while watching unwatchable movies, and drowsing on Sundays in bed with the crossword, and cooking dinner together, and indulging in long, cool baths in a too-small tub, and choosing groceries and pillows and plates together and calling them "ours," and waking up every day with less heartache about leaving for work because I know I'm coming home to him. It also means less room in the closet, and having no time to myself, and dealing with his hair in the sheets and the drain, and finding my kitchen rearranged (by, apparently, a crazy person who has never used a kitchen in his life), and fighting over the right kind of toothpaste (because really, who refuses to use gel? who in the world prefers paste? Ridiculous people, and also T—), and discovering that, as cute and loving as he is, T is the world's loudest chewer and swallower (so much so that I actually have to turn the radio up to hear it above the racket—it's NPR, not Stomp, but still… that's some loud chewing, when you drown out Nina Totenberg).

This meant accepting, taking in, yes, but also letting go: To the curb went the couch I've had for years, and the bed where I slept with my former love; to the back of the drawer went photos and reminders and memories. They had to go, so that there would be room for the new ones, but it was still a little scary and painful—a little burn with the sweetness.

Where was I? I've strayed again. Ah, yes, domestic bliss.

And soufflé—that was my original point, that life is most like a soufflé. For our Living Together for One Entire Week Anniversary (there's no good word for that under a thousand syllables—I've looked), I baked T a chile-chocolate soufflé—a light and gritty combination of chocolate and spicy cayenne—and we ate it with our fingers in the candlelight of our new home. Dark, warm chocolate balanced with the bite and slow burn of pepper, a little sweet, a little painful, entirely warm and comforting and real. Airy and weightless as it was, it had nothing of the high drama of summer fruit, or the frothy sweetness of pastel frosting. It was a tribute to the everyday, the imperfect, the fragile and tentative, something that both comforts you and heats you up. (And, incidentally, something which is virtually impossible to chew loudly.)

I suppose I'm writing here about domestic "bliss," not about life, per se. Life can go any way it will, and you just have to hang on until it bucks you off. But bliss is about being happy, and that's something one has to craft for oneself. Bliss isn't about perfection, at least not for me, not since I was a teenager; I learned that hard lesson quite a few times before it eventually stuck. Finding bliss is about learning to be happy, not about avoiding pain or engineering a situation to be exactly what you imagine it should be. Unlike a box of chocolates, bliss is actually unexpected and unpredictable. It has to be. When we get exactly what we dream of, we're usually disappointed; bliss comes as a result of what we never even imagined, a little gift from the universe, which knows our needs better than we do ourselves.

Sometimes I wake up in the middle of the night and just stare at his face—it's beautiful in the streetlight that shines, unrelentingly, through our bedroom window, yes, but it's strange, too. It's different from the face I see in the daytime, when he's gazing at me, when he knows I'm looking. When he sleeps, there's none of the care there, or the control—his face, relaxed and unconsciously open, reveals him in ways I'd never otherwise see. I think I know him better than anyone else on the planet, but I know there are things about him I'll never know. He's my familiar mystery, my uncanny lover, and he never stops surprising me in both beautiful and terrible ways.

I've come to depend on him, to expect that he'll be there tomorrow and the tomorrow after that, but I also know from experience that he might not. That's bliss—like a soufflé, it's warm and delicate and absolutely delicious, but it's fragile, too, tentative, fleeting, and more valuable because it's so easy to topple.

Still, I choose this. Every day, I choose it again, and again, I choose him, I choose the risk and the safety and the imperfect thing this is. I bite, knowing it'll be sweet but will also burn, and it might fall or fail, but still, I make the choice. And every morning I choose it again when I kiss his mouth before I leave, and every night I choose it again when I decide to go home to him and curl around him in the dark. And that, more than any metaphor I can give you, is really what life—and bliss—is: a risky, heartbreaking, again-and-again, wonderful choice.

Fourteen

THE FIRST TIME JULES SAW HIM, it was that almost-happening time of the evening, just before Teddy was due to come home and the low hum of the little apartment would break into conversation and the clatter of dinner forks. In the breath-holding hour before, Jules lay curled under an afghan; a ruffled paperback slipped repeatedly from his sleep-weakened hands. Andy-the-dog snored against his thigh. The evening light poked feebly through the curtains, painting the room a dim blue.

Jules saw him first as a flash of movement down the hallway and for a moment he thought Teddy must have come home. But when he called, there was no answer, just another flash of too-tall movement, and then he was sure he must be snagged in a napping dream, because Andy-the-man suddenly stood, silently, leaning against the wall of windows and looking at him with large, mournful eyes and folded arms.

"Andy?" Jules whispered. The man's arms dropped open and his head fell to the side in a sympathetic nod.

"What—" Jules started, unsure of what he was about to ask, but he stopped when Andy shook his head. Jules's heart banged hard in his throat, and he gulped for breath as if he'd been running, though he lay still on the couch. He could only stare as Andy stared back. He was terrified and sad and elated all at once, so he did not breathe. They held one another with their eyes for what seemed like an hour.

"I thought you—" Jules started to say, and then everything happened in an instant: The front door banged open and Teddy tumbled noisily into the room, dropping his briefcase with a flourish by the umbrella stand, and Jules jumped and whirled toward the noise.

"It's official!" Teddy shouted joyfully, throwing both arms up like a referee. "I'm done!"

"Done?" Jules croaked, but when he turned to look back at where Andy had been standing, he saw nothing. The curtains ruffled lightly in the draft from the open window, but no one was there.

"I quit!" Teddy yelled. "Officially!" He kicked off his shoes and skipped across the kitchen floor, slamming open cupboards and drawers and finally emerging with a bottle of wine, the opener and two glasses. "We are celebrating my newfound freedom. Or irresponsibility and uselessness!" He threw himself down on the couch next to Jules's feet. "However you want to view it."

"Celebrating," Jules said numbly, as Teddy popped the cork from the bottle. He couldn't peel his eyes from the windows. The curtains billowed so lightly, it looked as if the wall were breathing.

"I'm free. I'm completely lost. I'm terrified I did something really stupid. I'm delirious, and anxious, and I'm excited and I'm exhausted," Teddy said, handing him a filled glass. "I'm—I'm not sure what I am now, exactly, but I'm not a CPA at that firm anymore, for sure. And I'm an emotional tomato." He winked at Jules and took a deep drink from his own wine glass. "And I'm pretty sure I'm happy."

Jules smiled brightly and clinked his glass against Teddy's in a toast. "I'm so entirely proud of you," he said and swallowed a gulp. "I think I just saw Andy's ghost."

It was not the last time.

The second time Andy appeared, he stood at the foot of their bed, gently looking at the two men sleeping, until Jules awoke with the strange feeling that he was being watched. He nearly lunged out of the bed when, upon prying his eyes open in the dark, he saw the figure hovering at the foot of the bed.

"No!" he yelled.

"What!" Teddy shouted, sitting up and casting about for the bedside light. "What!"

"I had a dream." Jules soothed Teddy back down into the bedclothes. "I'm sorry. Just a dream."

This time, Andy had not gone away. He stood still, a dark shadow against the pale wall, watching silently as Jules curled deliberately into Teddy's side and squeezed his eyes shut. Jules could feel Andy lingering there, heatless and silent and watching them, as he willed himself back to sleep.

It went this way for weeks: Jules would find Andy lurking silently in the bathroom, holding Jules's hairbrush, or sitting near Andy-the-dog as he snored on the couch, or standing sentinel in the hallway as Jules rushed through his morning routine in the gray hour before dawn. Once, he found Andy pressed in among his suits in the closet. Once, Andy lingered near the records on their shelf as Jules browsed for evening music, nodding when Jules chose the battered old Coltrane.

Teddy never saw him. Until he did.

It was late evening, the remnants of supper were long put away and the wine glasses empty but stained with dregs, and Jules lay dozing against Teddy's side as the television flickered out the news in the dark.

"Shit!" Teddy yelled, standing so suddenly Jules was dumped onto the floor. "Get the hell out!"

He fumbled for something, anything, on the coffee table, and came up brandishing a ceramic coffee mug like a gun.

Andy was standing near the bookshelves by the television, watching them sadly and calmly.

"Get out!' Teddy shouted, aiming the mug at him. "Jules, call the police! Get out!" He flew forward, pinwheeling the arm with the mug frantically, attempting to herd the stranger toward the front door, but before he could reach him, Andy had disappeared.

"Jesus, where did he go?" he shrieked. "Call 911!"

"It's okay," Jules attempted in his most soothing voice. "He's not going to hurt anybody. He's gone."

"You can't be calm!" Teddy yelled, whirling on him. "You can't be calm! Call 911! I'm going to find where he went and get him *out!*" He grabbed an umbrella from the stand by the door and lunged toward the hallway.

Jules could only repeat, "It's okay," stumbling toward Teddy with his arms outstretched.

"Are you crazy? Call 911!"

"I know him," Jules said softly. "That's Andy."

⌒◝⌐

And so it happened again and again like this; when Jules came out of the shower, Andy's reflection peered at him from the steamy mirror, still and serious as a burnished wood figurine in a pink flannel shirt. When Teddy rounded the corner from the hallway into the bedroom, Andy was leaning silently against the dressing table, his long legs crossed gracefully at the ankle. Andy appeared hunched in his seat at the breakfast table, waiting patiently on the twilit couch, peering from behind the books on the shelf, patiently lurking in the dark of a kitchen cupboard.

He did not speak. He gave mournful looks, beckoned to Jules with his open arms and ran loving fingers over the pillows and record albums and battered books, but he never spoke a word. He appeared without warning, startling and stinging as a paper cut, but so frequently that he became a part of the apartment itself, like the creaking of the floorboards on a rainy day, or the low electric hum of the refrigerator—expected, always there, a constant, pleading presence.

Jules, every time Andy appeared, broke a little more deeply. At night, shut tightly alone in the whining fluorescence of the bathroom while Teddy snored in the next room, Jules cried into the mirror. He begged, at these moments, for Andy to appear, to come and cup his shoulders and smile gently against his cheek. But Andy refused to come when he was most achingly wanted; he only appeared as an unexpected shout in the dark, an uninvited guest at the table, an interjection into the peace of the little home.

∞

PASTRY-WHIPPED: ADVENTURES IN SUGAR BY A DEDICATED
CRUMPET STRUMPET
by Chef Jules Burns of Buttermilk Bakery
August 25: There's No Place Like Home

Whenever I'm creating a new recipe, I like to think like a sommelier or a perfumer, and consider how scents or tastes complement or overshadow each other, or how they might simply coexist. In everything I create, I like to imagine a base taste that undergirds all the others (perhaps the bitterness of almonds, or the warmth of whole wheat flour), topped by different notes (a floating floral, or the wince of citrus) that mingle, twist around each other and assert themselves in differing degrees.

My favorite taste to consider—and the one I find most difficult to account for in my recipes—is the taste that lingers long after the bite.

There are those bright, brief tastes that flare up suddenly and are, just as suddenly, gone, easily giving way to fresh sensations as those arise. That kind of taste is all about the pleasure of newness, of variety, that showy flash and gone of the momentary sensation. Then there are those flavors that hang on long past the initial bite, that make themselves motifs, lingering and coloring every new taste.

Those are ghost tastes, the ones you really have to pay attention to, because they're going to haunt everything that comes after.

When I was a child, after my grandmother had died, my father and I saved her pillows, her books, her old clothes—anything that might retain the last, fading remnants of her scent. I used to hide in the closet among her empty dresses, tucking myself under the curtain of plastic dry cleaning bags my father used to keep them safe (yes, I know I was risking my life), press my nose into the fabric and just breathe. *I would slip my too-small feet into her empty shoes, a tiny Dorothy, and try, with my eyes squeezed shut, to take myself back to the home of her embrace. I so missed my heart, I sought her in everything. I desperately wanted to be haunted.*

Even now, I can't love someone, can't lean into his arms for comfort or fall asleep against him on the couch, without smelling my grandmother, the clean scent of hyacinths lingering there between us. My grandmother's scent flavors every embrace, floats underneath the warmth of every friend's or lover's body. I even, sometimes, smell it underneath the paint and sweat on my father's jacket. I wonder if he smells it, too.

When Andy died, it was the same: His smell lingered in our blankets, hid in the folds of my winter scarves and would come over me suddenly when I opened a long-closed drawer or closet door. It hid itself everywhere in my home, waiting to spring on me just as I was beginning to forget what I'd lost.

Sometimes even now, caught in the spinning of my own new life, I sense a whiff of walnuts and mint on the air and Andy is there with me again. And I'm torn. They say you can't go home again, but I'm not so sure Andy is my home anymore. I don't think it's to him I want to return.

I should say it—I should let him go. If I only had the nerve.

I've gotten my childhood wish: I'm a haunted man. What I didn't realize then, when I was small and wishing so hard for my grandmother's ghosted hands to hold me, was that being haunted—being held—is a mixed blessing. It's memory made material, clinging hard and holding me in place, but that holding is both a holding on and a holding back. It's stones in my pocket: More gravity is both a good and a bad thing. One won't get carried off by strong winds, it's true, but this is precisely because one can't be moved at all.

Marcel Proust wrote, in Swann's Way, *about how the taste of madeleines and tea could instantly transport him to his grandmother's kitchen. I think he was on to something: We're most easily haunted by remnants of the past through scent and taste. Tastes and scents are the tornadoes of our emotional lives, instant transportation to the glittering gem city of our memories.*

To this day, I treasure the thin gold cuff my grandmother used to wear on her wrist because her perfume still clings there, warm and floral, cut through with the sourness of the metal underneath. After I hold her bracelet, that smell haunts me all day long, clouding around my hands so that everything I touch, every contact, releases the smell, again and again. It grounds the world for me, painting everything in it with the memory of her. Some nights, I think I can smell him, Andy, in the dark of my tiny apartment, and though he's long been gone, suddenly he's there again with me. I can almost hear his broad laugh. I can almost taste the salt of his skin. It's a bitter taste, a sour note in the cream, a memory that curdles everything around it. But I crave it, even knowing that.

"Haunting" wants to tell a different story than it does: It's not the ghost of the dead person imposing upon the world of the living, but the living person who haunts the world of the dead. Those ghosts don't hold me in place; I'm not bound or weighted or held back. I choose to stay still. My

past does not haunt me—those who have died have surely moved on; they are something new, now, and probably don't even remember the lives they once lived, probably have no memories at all and exist only as motion, hurtling forward into the darkness of new space. I am the one who clings, I am the one who is the stone in the pocket of those spirits desperately trying to float home.

This week I offer up, in Andy's memory, a recipe for madeleines— those sweet, French sponge cookies that so moved Proust. They are the simplest of cookies, at least as far as ingredients go: butter, sugar, eggs, flour and little else. But so much haunts that simple taste. Mine are cut through with a bit of citrus for sparkle and bite. And, as pliant and sweet as they are, they must be served with black tea to make a base note, a little bitterness under the bright and sweet.

When I eat a madeleine, like Proust I'm overcome with memory— for me, it is most specifically the first time I baked these cookies with my grandmother, our cotton aprons drooping in the too hot summer kitchen, my grandmother laughing at the flat, failed and slightly too-brown cookies we'd produced and ruffling my hair as if to say It's okay; failing is fun, too.

Golden, soft, perfect as my grandmother's madeleines usually were, I never loved them as much as I loved that first batch of failed and browned cookies I baked with her.

And they bring back another moment, when I brought a package of madeleines home from a twee French bakery hiding on one of the corners near the home I shared with Andy. He was mystified by the delicate things and laughed at my prissy insistence that we make a good pot of tea and use the nice teacups and saucers, dip the cookies and take tiny bites and try to act like civilized people for once (read: not like the busy, irritated New Yorkers we'd become). It was a very small moment in a very big life I shared with Andy, but I still cling to the memory: that giant man, gamely and delicately holding the little sponge cookie above his steaming cup of Earl Grey, his voice softening as he eased into the quiet meditation of a ritual that was new to us.

This is what it is to be haunted: to stand with one foot in the past and one in the present, always trying to balance oneself between two radically different but simultaneous experiences. It's perpetual culture shock. It's always living with dissonance.

So many people I know spend their entire youths struggling to grow away from their families, from the places and people that made them them. But once one does manage escape, I've learned from experience, one spends one's time trapped in nostalgia for what's irrevocably gone— for what one once fled. It's like what They say: Leaving only makes you miss what you've left; wherever you go, there you are; there's no place like home.

∞

We are certain you expect, by now, this moment, when Jules walks into the apartment to find Teddy perched on the edge of the couch, a few hastily stuffed duffel bags leaning against his legs. The only person who did not see this moment approaching is Jules himself. Torn as he was between looking behind him and keeping his chin up, he didn't see what loomed in front of him.

Softly, Teddy shrugged. "I'm leaving." When Jules started forward, Teddy held up his hand to stop him. "Just for a little while," he said. "I can't live here with Andy. And you can't seem to let him leave yet."

At first, Jules assumed Teddy was talking about the dog, but the long look Teddy gave him, the serious knit of his brow, told him otherwise.

"I've let him go," Jules insisted.

"I read your blog. You haven't."

Jules was stunned into silence and then lunged into action, reaching for the duffel bags before Teddy pushed him away and he was left standing empty-handed and exasperated.

"I don't know what to do," Jules said.

"Neither do I," said Teddy, his voice barely wavering. "But we can't all be here together; one of us has to go. Whenever I get out of the shower, there he is in the mirror. When I make coffee, he pops out from behind the milk in the refrigerator. I feel him staring at us in bed, sometimes; I know he's there, watching me, even if it's too dark to see him. It keeps me awake. I'm never alone with you anymore."

Jules felt the floor seesaw beneath him. He felt as if he were ill or drunk or had missed a step while running down the stairs, and was tumbling down with no hope of stopping himself before the inevitable, painful crash to the ground. There was nothing onto which he could hold, no solidity to grab. He tried to catch Teddy's eye, but Teddy kept his gaze focused resolutely on the edge of the rug.

"So we'll get an exorcist or a priest or something! We can move to a new apartment! We can leave the city!"

"I don't think any of that will work," Teddy said quietly. "I think *you* have to do something. I don't know what it is, but I think *you* have to be the one to do it."

He shrugged, slipped his hands through the straps of the duffel bags at his feet. "Or maybe you don't. Maybe you just need to be alone with him. Maybe this isn't right after all."

"You can't go!' Jules shouted, fear welling up in his throat. "You can't go! And you can't leave me alone!"

Teddy stood, his bags gathered in his hands, and gently kissed Jules's chin. "I can't stay," he said. "And you're not alone. That's the problem."

The roar of what must have been his own blood rushing in his ears was so loud, Jules barely heard Teddy say goodbye, barely heard him promise that he would call the next day, before the door closed behind him for good.

When Teddy had gone, when the apartment had quieted and gone blue-black with early evening, Jules finally moved from his spot on the couch. He took Andy-the-dog for his evening walk, filled his bowl with kibble, and then calmly turned to face the empty apartment and uproot everything: He knocked every book from its shelf, pulled the photographs down from the walls, threw the shoes from his closet and pulled the sheets from the bed until the whole place was chaos, tornadoed, at once too empty and too full.

When it was finished, he looked up to find he'd completely dismantled his quiet little home. He'd broken most of his dishes, the little blue glass lamp was shattered and the curtains barely clung, askew, to the windows. He tripped his way through the rubble to his bed and collapsed onto the bare mattress, too exhausted to undress or find the blankets he'd thrown somewhere, and stared into the empty dark, waiting to fall asleep.

Fifteen

TEDDY SPENT THE FIRST PART of the evening wandering. It felt natural, to cast himself out and walk the blackening city with his bags banging against his hip, to speak to no one and to slip, unnoticed, between the cars and people. He could be almost nothing. He could be barely there.

He bought a bitter cup of coffee from the corner store and sipped at it to keep himself going, despite its unpleasant, burned taste—it became, for him, a test of will. He could endure it, even welcome it, watery and awful as it was.

He walked for what seemed the entire afternoon, all the way uptown, through the park near its edge, where he could still hear the groan and squeal of traffic from the streets beyond the stone wall. He liked balancing on the edge like this, between the deep dark of the trees on one side and the flat, lit-up black of the street on the other. His bags banged cheerlessly against his thigh with every movement, so that he was keenly aware of every step he took: With each slap of the duffel on his hip, he moved farther and farther away from Jules and the warm, blue rooms of the apartment on Jane Street.

When real night started to ease in and the city rhythm seemed to shift to something more frantic and electric, Teddy figured he'd better find a place to be for the night. Too tired to keep walking, too sore to listen to the traffic noise anymore, he called 'Trice.

"Did you have a fight?" 'Trice asked, pulling the bags from his arms and setting them near the door.

The place was a studio, one large room, which 'Trice had sectioned off into tiny quadrants—bedroom, kitchen, living room, office—by hanging ratty-looking tie-dyed blankets from ceiling to floor. The whole room had a provisional, improvised quality. The mismatched furniture (beaten plaid couch, milk crate bookshelves, two wooden chairs draped with blankets and pillows for comfort) and the collection of illegibly scribbled notes decorating the walls, all gave the apartment the atmosphere of a temporary hideout for a half-crazy, unemployed superhero or a whole-crazy, misanthropic conspiracy theorist.

"No, no fight," Teddy said. "I just couldn't stay there."

'Trice gave him a sidelong glance as she pulled a couple of tumblers from the kitchen cupboard and set them on the counter next to a bottle of whiskey.

"That is the worst explanation in the history of explanations," she said.

"I promise, 'Trice, I'll explain everything, I will, but tonight I am really so shot, I just can't. Can we just—" he gestured limply toward the glasses, hoping she would, uncharacteristically, let him off the hook, just this once.

She nodded at him, slopped a little of the brown liquid into each glass and then held hers up and said, "To oblivion and beyond, then," and sucked the whiskey down in one go.

"Thanks," Teddy mumbled, and drank.

Cleaning the apartment exhausted Jules, but he had to keep moving, to keep sweeping up the broken glass and replacing the books on their shelves. If he stayed still, if he stopped for even a moment, Andy-the-man would move from the corner where he lingered, silently watching, sympathetically cup Jules's shoulders in his large hands and shake his head sadly.

Jules righted the curtains on their rod, fluffed the pillows on the couch, refolded blankets and soothed the dog, who followed him around with a focus that was probably more desperation than curiosity. Andy-the-man stood in the corner by the windows and watched him work. With every passing moment, Andy seemed to grow more wooden and solid, while Jules felt his hands slip through the things of the world with watery fluidity.

He knew it was impossible, what he felt happening—that, moment by moment, he was fading, becoming light and air, insubstantial as a memory. Still, he checked twice upon passing the mirror to make sure he was reflected, and found himself there, bruised eyes boring out from his too-pale face, his lips too red, his whole body impossibly present and real.

'Trice wobbled as she held up the half-empty bottle to Teddy. "Another?"

"Too rich for my blood," Teddy sighed, and covered his glass with his hand—which, he noticed, was wobbling too. He squinted at her. "You look like a Rorschach test, all blotchy."

"You don't look so great yourself. Plus, you're being an ass. No more for you," 'Trice said. "We totally ate the worm."

"That's tequila."

"Duh. Figure of speech." 'Trice rolled her eyes. "So, why were you on my doorstep, my darling Stray Gay? Why are you on my couch? Or half on my couch? You're dripping off there like a sea slug."

Teddy shifted a bit, so that his shoulders weren't pressing so hard into the floor, and glared at 'Trice. "Like you even know what a sea slug looks like. Besides, it feels good on my back." And, he didn't add, everything looked a little less horrible upside down.

"Get your feet out of my face and tell me what you're doing here, dripping off my couch and drunk as a…" 'Trice waved her hand in the air. "Drunk as an I-don't-know-what."

Teddy smirked. "Good one. You must be drunk if you're at a loss for words."

"And you must be stalling, if you're giving me lip when you're in such a vulnerable position, little one," 'Trice growled back, jabbing his unprotected belly with a bony finger. "Spill."

Teddy sighed and slid the rest of the way off the couch and onto the floor, where he laid on his back. "I don't think he's over his ex."

"Andy?"

"Yeah. Every time he calls his dog, it's like Andy's there again."

"You know he didn't name the dog after—"

"Yeah, I know." Teddy sighed. "But it doesn't make a difference."

"Well, that's on you, then. But," 'Trice said, and Teddy knew from the furrow of her brow that this would be no platitude, that she would take him seriously. "But, but, but he was completely wrecked when Andy died, I know that. And for months after, it was still always Andy-this, Andy-that."

"Yeah." Teddy sighed again. "I knew that."

"But he hasn't been talking about Andy since he met you."

"Believe me, Andy's still around."

"He's always going to be around," 'Trice said, patting his thigh. "And Jules is terrible with people. He's much better with pastries. He has a very good, longstanding relationship with sugar."

"He belongs there," Teddy said mournfully.

"Andy? True, he will probably always be there."

"I don't—" he started, but quickly bit his mouth shut.

'Trice waited, then gestured and waited again, but Teddy was silent. "Belong there?" she finished for him. He nodded.

"Cookie, belonging is overrated. It's just another obligation. A rolling stone gathers no moss, right?" When Teddy responded with a shaky inhalation, 'Trice changed her tack. "But it probably feels pretty good, anyway."

"It feels pretty good. And now I don't have a job, I don't have a place to live, I don't have Jules. I don't have anything."

Teddy poked absently at the thick weave of the cushion under him, too embarrassed to look at 'Trice. He heard her shift and settle close to his side.

"You've got a couch," 'Trice told him. "And tequila, and this girl." She sloshed the remaining contents of the bottle while pointing to herself and leering slightly.

"I'll take the couch," he said. "But that's whiskey."

"Worm," she mumbled cryptically.

Teddy didn't say anything. 'Trice's face had gone watery; her hair was waving softly like leaves of seaweed. In the dark, she looked pillowed and beckoning, so he fell into her chest and closed his eyes; her dreads clacked gently around his shoulders.

"You're wavy," he slurred into her neck.

"You're drunk," she shot back. But she still hugged him tightly, and it was long minutes until he fell asleep against her shoulder.

⌘

For two weeks, Jules crept around the apartment like a spooked child, refusing to look into the mirrors or open the cabinet doors. Andy was everywhere, and if Jules dared to look up, he'd find him leaning against the shower stall or crouching in the back of the refrigerator or sitting still as stone on the couch in the living room. He was always silent, always waiting, though his mouth gaped uselessly, as if he were trying to speak and couldn't find words. And so, for two weeks, Jules combed his hair and brushed his teeth without a mirror, and fixed his early morning coffee and smoothed his clothes while keeping his eyes trained carefully on his own shoes. His neck began to hurt from looking down.

In the rare moments he managed to drowse, he was quickly awakened by Andy-the-dog's frantic barking at something—or someone—Jules could never see. Exhausted, he lumbered around like a zombie. Once, he could have sworn he heard Andy's tuneless singing from the bathroom; once, it was the gentle brush of Andy's hand at his cheek that woke him. Each time, he would look up wildly to find he could see nothing there at all, not even the dimmest shadow. It seemed as though Andy-the-dog and Andy-the-man were conspiring to keep him awake until he died of exhaustion. His vision swam; his ears rang. His house was too full, yet he felt entirely alone.

"I miss you," he told the ghost one night as he sat on the couch and stared at his knees. Andy-the-man sat beside him, unmoving, his legs awkwardly folded underneath him; he didn't seem to hear. "Sometimes I forget you're gone, and I half expect you to walk in the door from work and kick off your dirty shoes and get mud all over the kitchen floor and leave your umbrella on the wooden bench, even though I've told you a million times that bench is untreated wood and it's going to warp or split if you do that."

Andy tilted his head and looked at Jules balefully.

"You left too soon, and I never got to look you in the eyes when I said goodbye," Jules said. "And you didn't even say goodbye to me. You just slept and slept."

Andy attempted to cover Jules's hand with his own, but it was like trying to hide a rock under bright starlight, and the gleam on Jules's pale skin that was Andy's touch was like a spotlight, and only made his hand look emptier, smaller and more alone. He closed his hand into a fist.

"I miss you, but I think you hanging around is making everything harder," Jules admitted. Andy looked at his knees and nodded.

"I think you have to go," Jules said.

Andy simply smiled sadly and brought his hand up to brush Jules's cheek. Jules let it pass, even though he knew it wasn't much of an answer.

Andy didn't go.

If anything, he clung to the air around Jules. When Jules sat on the couch in the evening to read a novel, with Andy-the-dog flopped sleepily in his lap, the cushion next to him would sink, a tingling-light arm would drop around his shoulders, and Andy-the-man would be curled there at his side. When he pulled back the curtains to let the sunset's orange light into the room, Andy stood sheepishly, revealed suddenly, peeping from behind the drapery. When Jules cooked his dinner, Andy hovered near the salt. When Jules showered, Andy slowly appeared through the bathroom steam. When he slept, Andy kept watch.

His house was full, with Andy there, but too quiet; Teddy's absence stung, like cold water on the gums after getting a tooth knocked out.

Nights were the worst, long and empty without Teddy. The bed was cold, and Jules's suppers were lonely. In the early mornings, as Jules dressed to leave for the bakery, Andy sat on the edge of the bed, shimmering and gray in the predawn light, watching. Jules could see right through him to Teddy's empty side of the bed: the sheets tumbled, the pillows askew, everything slightly grayer through the light of Andy's image.

The morning Jules woke to find Andy-the-man curled against his back in bed, one translucent arm draped across Jules's waist, was the last morning he could endure Andy's strange and silent presence-not-presence and the gap left by Teddy's absence. He sprang up with a shout of fear, frantically brushing the clammy feeling of Andy's not-quite-touch from his arms. But when he looked around, Andy was still there, silently cowering against the head of the bed, staring at him with huge, dark eyes.

Terrified and sad as Jules clearly was, Andy still would not go.

<hr />

"Short stuff! Half-pint! Volkswagen Golf!"

"Golf?" Teddy asked, peering out from behind the newspapers under which he was buried.

"It's a compact car," 'Trice said, roping her locks into a knot on top of her head. "I was doing a thing."

"Brilliant," Teddy said dryly. "You know, I'm not short so much as you are gargantuan, you sky-scraping Godzilla."

"Genius. I've never heard anyone comment on my height before. Plus, very bitter."

"Sequoia," Teddy said. "Empire Snot Building."

'Trice sighed. "Go on, I know you've got more. Get it out of your system, my pipsqueaky pocket-gay."

"Giraffe," he said. "Lesbian Lamppost."

"Done?" 'Trice asked, throwing herself down onto the bench by the door.

"Jerky Green Giant," he said and then sighed. "All done."

"Good. Why are you under all that paper?" 'Trice struggled into a pair of heavy black boots that were a bit ridiculous for the weather.

"Jobs."

She cuffed him lightly on the back of the head as she passed on her way to the front door. "Don't look in the *newspaper,* you dork! What are you, ninety? Is this the Great Depression? Should I leave you a penny to buy a loaf of bread? We're a paperless society in this modern world! I thought you only *looked* like a man of 1922!"

"Not helping." Teddy grumbled and straightened his tie. 'Trice looked pointedly at his outfit and raised her brows. Teddy knew it was silly to dress in his business best to look through the newspaper's want ads in a friend's kitchen, but at least it made him feel a bit more professional than wearing boxers and a sweatshirt.

"In any case, my shiny and tiny friend, I'm off! Good luck with the hunt and get out of my house!" She banged out the door, then, less than a second later, popped her head back inside. "JK, Mister Thing. Stay as long as you want. But don't sit here all day and mope over job listings. Stop by the bakery later, and I'll make you a coffee. Love you!"

She was gone before Teddy could formulate a snappy retort. In her considerable wake, the apartment seemed very still and quiet, and Teddy tossed the papers aside with a deafening rustle. 'Trice was right—he needed to look online; the paper was probably hopelessly outdated. He adjusted his tie, poured himself a fresh cup of coffee and settled at the table with his laptop and a clean pad of paper on which to take notes. He set down two freshly sharpened pencils, aligned them neatly with the side of the paper, opened the laptop, propped his wrists against the edge of the keyboard and stared at the screen.

The problem was that there was *so much* online, and Teddy had no idea what he could—or wanted—to do.

Jules loved the large mixer that sat on the floor near the prep tables, whose bowl was so big that, if he were inclined to do so, he could curl up inside it for a nap. Its low mechanical grind, broken rhythmically by the bump of the beaters knocking against the side of the bowl—it definitely needed to be adjusted soon—lulled him into the first peace he'd had in days.

Bright sunlight filtered into the kitchen through the small windows near the ceiling; it was a rare improvement over the usual view of slush and foot traffic the sidewalk-level windows allowed. He measured butter into the pan on the scale, then dumped it in one big, soft blat into the bowl of the mixer, watching the pale yellow disappear into the dough as the beaters turned. Out in the shop front, he could hear the banging noises of 'Trice entering and starting her day.

"Jules, coffee!" she hollered, before slapping the kitchen door open and barreling in with a cup for him. She sloshed it down on the prep table.

"Oh! 'Trice, I—" he started.

"No way, Jose."

"What? I didn't—"

"Teddy Ruxpin is indeed staying at my place, just so you know he didn't get eaten by a miniature Chihuahua at the park. But that's all you're getting out of me, Mister Sister. You need to call him and talk to him yourself and solve this business on your own."

"I didn't say anything." He fixed his attention on chopping the pile of dried apricots on the prep table.

'Trice took a long, slow sip of her coffee, with her eyes grinding into him from above the rim of the cup. "You were totally going to, I can tell. And no, absolutely not. I might be fat and Black, but do *not* mistake me for Oprah. I do *not* want to hear about your feelings, I do *not* think Tom Cruise is awesome and I did *not* hide a free gift under your chair."

"Fat and..." Jules shook his head and took the coffee she'd offered. They stood, glaring at each other over the rims of their coffee cups, and sipped deliberately. It was a waiting game, one they'd played before. In the background, the mixer clank-hum-clanked. Jules could almost imagine he heard the whistling showdown music of *Gunsmoke.* 'Trice slammed down her cup and sighed.

"Fine. He's looking for work. He's freaked out. He's sad. He's probably still hung over from Monday, but otherwise he's fine. He's sleeping on my couch until he finds a place, or until you two fix your whatever-is-going-on thing. I think he misses you."

"Oh," Jules said. "Okay."

'Trice rolled her sleeves up past her elbows, pulled a bag of lemons out of the walk-in refrigerator and began scrubbing them in the sink and tossing them into a prep bowl.

"Is he—"

"Zesting!" she shouted, banging the bowl noisily against the metal table.

Jules nodded and clamped his mouth closed. When 'Trice made a decision, there was very little that could turn her from her course.

"Right." Jules rearranged the pile of dried apricots. "Chopping."

They worked in near-silence for a good five minutes, the only sounds the splash of water in the metal sink and the crunch of his knife on the plastic cutting board. He had learned, from years of dealing with 'Trice, that the best way to handle her when she was acting like this was to wait. If he fought her, she'd dig in her heels like a mule and pull away from him as hard as she could. If he simply waited, it was likely she'd come around.

He was right. She softened, dropped the lemon she was holding and turned to him.

"He's coming in for coffee later. I don't know when," she said gruffly, turning and heading for the front of the shop. "I'm pretty sure I'll be taking my break then, though."

Early in the afternoon, as Jules was washing his hands ready to leave the kitchen for home, the bells on the front door jingled and, a moment later, 'Trice burst into the kitchen.

"Break!" she shouted at him, running for the back door. "Shop's yours!"

Jules knew, because he knew her, that when he went to the front of the store, he'd find Teddy waiting. He sighed heavily and pushed his way into the front of the shop, nervously pulling his apron strings tighter. But when he arrived at the counter, all he found was Irene.

"Coffee, coffee, coffee, Hot Stuff!" She rapped on the counter with the back of her hand in time with her words.

"Clearly, you've had enough coffee for today," he said dryly, but turned to the espresso machine anyway. *Whatever Lola wants,* he thought.

"Nope, no coffee, just adrenaline today," she said. "The daughter's bringing her fiancé in from Indiana to meet me. I've got an hour of freedom left before I have to start behaving like a good Midwestern mom."

Jules rolled his eyes and decanted hot milk and espresso into a to-go cup. He didn't bother asking for her order anymore. It was always the same.

He glanced up at her as he slid the coffee her way. "Muffin?" he asked.

"Yes, Sweet Buns?" she said, and when he raised an eyebrow, she continued in a lower voice. "Sorry. On edge. No muffin, just the coffee, thanks."

She stuffed a five-dollar bill into the tip jar, scooped the coffee into the crook of her arm and rushed for the door.

"Treat that coffee right," Jules called after her. "It's like a child to me!"

"Yeah!" she called over her shoulder. Jules doubted she'd even heard him. He turned to wipe the back counter near the sink, and the door bells jingled again.

"You accidentally put a five in the tip jar…" he said to Irene, only to turn around and discover it wasn't Irene at all.

"Hi," Teddy said, shifting from foot to foot. "'Trice said to come in now because she was going to give me coffee today. I'm sorry."

"I can give you coffee," said Jules, and turned to wrestle with the filters on the espresso machine. He would not look, but he could, out of the corner of his eye, see Teddy's small, brown hands folded together on the counter's surface, one finger lightly tugging at the edge of a sleeve. His nails were impeccably clean; one shirt cuff was lightly frayed from years of rubbing against a desk; the raveled threads were twisted together to stop the wear. He could smell Teddy's cologne; the fresh piney scent of juniper floated over the bite of alcohol. Teddy cleared his throat.

"Could I also have, please," he started and then paused, unsure.

"Could you have… " Jules prompted gently. The conversation felt delicately balanced, as if he were walking on a tightrope. He wanted to hurl himself across the counter and wrap his arms and legs around Teddy, but held himself steadfastly still.

"I don't know," Teddy shrugged. "I don't know what to ask for."

Jules nodded and slipped a single small cookie onto a little plate for him. "Pine nut cookie," he explained.

"Thanks." Teddy slipped some money onto the counter—it seemed sordid and wrong to him, but it was a way to measure the distance between them. He saw Jules wince at the money, and Teddy wanted so badly to smile. Instead, he pulled the coffee and cookie toward him. He started to turn toward the tables and seemed to reconsider. He turned back. "Are you okay?" he asked Jules.

Jules wanted to slip away, wanted to shrug and slink back to the kitchen, but Teddy's eyes were wide and sincere and just the slightest bit wet, and Jules couldn't look away.

"No," Jules said quietly. "I miss you at home. Home misses you. Andy misses you."

Teddy looked down quickly.

"Andy *the dog* misses you," Jules corrected.

"Ah." Teddy nodded. He clenched his hands. Jules cleared his throat and wiped uselessly at the counter.

When Teddy neither moved nor spoke, Jules added, "I miss you, too. I miss you a lot."

"I miss you, too," Teddy choked, finally looking up. "I hate staying at 'Trice's house."

"*Hey!*" 'Trice shouted from the kitchen. Jules looked at Teddy with widened eyes and motioned toward the front door. He slipped around the counter and tugged Teddy behind him out onto the street.

The midafternoon sun was just starting to glance off the top row of windows of the building across the street, casting the sidewalk in what would have been a romantic glow if it weren't for the pigeons and skittering trash, the grease-choked cars and gum-speckled sidewalk.

"Okay," Jules said, when they were leaning together against a banged-up station wagon parked in front of the bakery. He hesitated and then ran his fingers down the side of Teddy's neck. "Come home, Teddy. We *really* miss you at home, me and Andy."

"Is he gone?" Teddy asked carefully. "Not the dog," he added before Jules could shake his head.

Across the street, two boys were having a noisy argument over something innocuous. Their voices echoed on the narrow street, and Jules hugged himself. The sound of boys yelling, no matter how innocent, would always chill him a bit. Teddy seemed to notice, to start forward, his hand outstretched, and then catch himself, drop his hand and step back. Jules sighed.

"Not yet," Jules said. "I've asked him to go. I don't want him to stay, I really, really don't, I promise. I don't see him as much as before, but he still pops up sometimes."

Teddy looked at his feet, at the gum and candy wrappers and stray cigarette butts, the gutter and the filmy water there.

"I'm not sure he'll ever really be totally gone," Jules added.

"I'm not sure I can ever really be totally there, then," Teddy muttered, his voice wavering.

∽

Jules felt like a squatter in his own home.

The rooms belonged, now, not to him and to Teddy, but to Andy and Andy. When he came home to find Andy-the-man and Andy-the-dog huddled together on the couch, when they both—simultaneously—looked at him, guilty and irritated, as if they'd been caught whispering, as if he were interrupting some private moment they were sharing before he burst in, he felt a piercing loneliness that ground from his bones through his muscles and skin and made every inch of him hurt. He squatted and called the dog to come to him, but Andy-the-dog simply flopped his face down onto the couch cushion and went to sleep, and Andy-the-man wrapped his own transparency around the little dog like a haze and stared smugly at Jules.

Jules left the room and hid in his bed to read by the dim bedside light, because there was no room left for him on the couch, neither physically nor otherwise. He could hear the muffled rustling and whimpering of his dog in sleep from the other room, and was shocked to overhear the low tones of Andy-the-man cooing soothingly at him. (Apparently, to Jules Andy would always appear as a silent film, flickering badly and gaping without sound, but this was not always his condition; it pained Jules to know that others could hear him, as if it were some sort of willful deafness on his part and not insubstantiality or muteness on Andy's which was at fault.)

He avoided Andy-the-man as best he could, which meant relinquishing his living room and kitchen, relinquishing cuddling with his dog, and creeping into each room in his own apartment cautiously, lest he be surprised into confronting Andy's presence. He and Andy lived like a warring couple not on speaking terms: silently slipping past one another, always unpleasantly surprised to enter a room and find the other already in it.

Still, despite the tension that wound tightly around them and cut into his skin like tightly pulled cotton thread; despite the fact that he neither spoke to, nor touched, nor acknowledged the ghost; despite the fact that he desperately wanted his home to himself again, if he could not share it with Teddy, despite all of that, Jules could not make Andy-the-man go.

And so, that evening, when Jules had made himself a lonely dinner (the greens were too bitter, the meat too salty, the beans overcooked, soft and gray as stew), he sat alone at his cramped table in the fading light of sunset and called for Andy-the-man to join him.

It was a long time before he did. Jules had nearly given up, had looked down at his plate to push the food around with his fork, and felt the brush of Andy-the-dog against his leg. He bent to pet him, but Andy avoided his hand, slipped by quickly and settled himself on the garnet-colored cushion across the room. When Jules looked up again, Andy-the-man was gazing at him from the table's second chair.

"Andy," he said, his throat aching with the words. "It's over now. You have to leave. You're not welcome in my home anymore."

Sixteen

JULES WORKED FOR HOURS. He packed up all of Andy's clothes, shoes, record albums and books, left them in boxes by the door and scheduled the Salvation Army to pick them up. In a small plastic box, he saved one shirt (Andy's pink flannel one, which still smelled of him and reminded Jules of his father, too), and every photograph of Andy and scrap of his spike-loopy handwriting he could find. Tenderly, he pressed the plastic lid onto the box and slid it far under the bed, where it could be forgotten but not lost forever.

When he had finished, when every scrap of Andy had been packed safely away or readied for charity, Jules sat at the kitchen table and stared at the apartment. It felt so much more barren than it was.

"You have to leave," he told the empty room.

The sun flickered in through the curtains as it readied itself to set and fell warm across his neck. He felt the tingling of a not-quite-solid hand pass down his spine to rest on his lower back, but he would not look. Instead, he squeezed his eyes shut, covering them with his hands, and shook his head.

"No," he whispered. "I don't love you anymore. I love the memory of you, but I will never love you any more than I do now. You're *not* anymore. Nothing will grow, because there is no more of you for me to love. There is no more to continue. You have to go. Now."

As he whispered, it was as if his chest finally cracked open, and everything came pouring out. He felt his heart flop out of his chest, hot and wet and ugly, and flap in his lap like a dying fish. He felt heat burn his neck and cheeks. He felt so empty and so hungry; he felt cold and he felt as if nothing would ever fill him up again.

And then, in the space of a moment, he felt nothing at all. The tingling at his back was gone, the hunger and the pain in his throat, everything was gone in an instant, as if a heavy coat had suddenly fallen from his back. Andy-the-dog came waddling up to him and dropped his wet jowls against the top of Jules's foot. The sun finally set and took its light with it, leaving the room in deep indigo shadow. He felt his heart press itself back into his chest; felt his chest clasp and seal around it; felt the air slip, light and clean and sweet, into his suddenly loosened lungs.

He felt it as surely as he could feel a lick of bright, hot sun or the soft warmth of a down quilt: Andy was gone, and Jules was finally, completely alone.

Alone, Jules slept. Alone, he woke and showered and dressed, and he dragged himself out onto the gray early morning street and walked to the bakery. In the street-noise quiet, he unlocked the front gate and sent it rattling upward with an effortful shove, pressed open the front door, slipped behind the counter and set the espresso machine humming.

He began his morning preparations in the kitchen, heating the ovens, leaving the butter to rest on the counter, mixing the dough and batter for the day's pies and cakes and muffins. He worked without the radio, listening only to the swish and groan of cars on the street outside the windows, humming to himself, enjoying his solitude.

He made, just for fun, a very light, airy brioche dough touched with the bittersweetness of orange zest. He let it breathe in the heat of the kitchen to rise and decided to drizzle it with dark chocolate when it was done.

After several hours, when most of the work was finished and nothing was left to do but wait for dough to rise, Jules sat at his desk and began to work through the bills and filing that had built up there, since neither he nor 'Trice ever wanted to attend to it. He heard, vaguely, the front door bells jingle as 'Trice burst into the shop, heard the slamming sound of her banging on the espresso machine, heard her yell, as she always did, "Coffee!" Because he knew no work would get done with 'Trice slamming about, he put the papers into the top drawer of his desk.

There, in the corner of the drawer, was the ring of keys he'd found on the floor so long ago: Teddy's keys. He hadn't touched them, or even looked at them, for a long time; now he took them out and held them, warm and sharp, in his fingers. He counted through the keys, tracing their shapes, until he paused at the last one. It was small, slender, gold, with a tiny engraved "JB" on the head, an elegant key, a key he knew well. It was the key to his bakery. Andy had gotten the engraving done as an extravagant, ridiculous surprise when he had first opened the place. How it had come to be on Teddy's key ring was a mystery.

Just as he was turning the ring of keys over and over on his finger, 'Trice kicked open the door with her foot and burst into the kitchen, a cup of coffee in each hand.

"Coffee, I said!" she shouted.

"Thanks," he muttered, and dropped the keys in his lap so quickly, he hoped, she would not see.

'Trice, however, he sometimes forgot, was like a hawk. Or a buzzard. Some bird of prey. She swooped in, plopping the cup in front of him and grabbing at the keys in his lap.

"What are you hiding, *mon petit chou?*" she asked, dancing away before he could grab the keys back.

"Give those back," he grumbled, pretending to write in a ledger and eyeing her without turning his head from his desk. "And, really, *petit chou?*"

"*Petits choux* pastry?" she tried again. "I'm not giving them back until you tell me why you were trying to hide them." She dangled the keys in front of her on one long, teasing finger.

"You should be flogged for your shoddy wordplay. I was not hiding them. Those are *my* keys. Give them back."

"These are *your* keys?" she asked, waving the little metal key fob in his face. Engraved on it in looping script was "TF." "Is your name Tools, not Jules? Have I been saying it wrong all these years?"

"Funny. Give."

"Okay, Tools Fortunecookie, here you go." She smirked and tossed the keys back into his lap.

"Ass!" he yelled, though he wasn't entirely sure if he mightn't be yelling at himself.

"Yes! Lots of it!" she yelled, heading toward the front of the bakery, then stopped. "Speaking of ass, Tools, your piece of it misses you. He's on my couch, bitching and moaning about it all night. Would you fix this so I can get rid of him, please?"

She slipped into the front of the bakery before he could answer. The shop front radio popped to life as soon as the door flapped closed behind her. "And give him his keys back, Tools!" she shouted.

Jules shook his head, laughing. He may be an ass, but 'Trice was… something bigger than an ass. A monolithic ass. A triceratops ass. An avalanche of asses.

There was a scraping noise behind him, and when he turned, he saw that the screen that sheltered his desk from the rest of the kitchen had been pushed aside. There, sitting on the metal prep table by the ovens, was Andy: hollow, flickering, gray, and definitely Andy.

"What is wrong with these?" Jules shouted. "'Trice! You put too much baking soda in these! It's a good thing I decided to taste! They taste like soap!" He tipped the entire batch of muffins into the trash can.

"What are you hollering about now, Necker-Chief?" 'Trice asked, cracking the kitchen door to pop her head in.

"Nice one," Jules grumbled.

"Thank you, I've been working on that one for a while," 'Trice said smugly. She slid through the door and into the kitchen, leaning against the metal prep table and gently patting her hair back under the white scarf from which it was trying to escape.

"It's not nice enough to get you out of the mess you made, though," Jules said sourly. "I had to throw away a whole batch of muffins because you put too much baking soda in them, and the whole thing tastes awful. Apparently, you can't bake while you're mooning over whatever fake-punk boy band you kids are dreaming about lately."

"I didn't bake those, Chief, *you* did." 'Trice widened her eyes and made spooky hands above her head, humming ominously. "Dun-dun-daaaaaaaaah!"

"Oh," he said, mollified. "Sorry. My head's off lately." Jules turned back to the counter, wiping furiously at the stainless steel. It was already very clean; the sunlight gleamed loudly from its surface. Undeterred, Jules scrubbed.

"Then we should taste everything you did today, just in case."

"I guess we probably should. Can you…"

"I'll get it," 'Trice sang as she ran to the front of the store carrying a wide plate. "Back in a flash!"

In less time than it took him to start panicking, 'Trice was back with a plate full of the day's goods. She placed it on the prep table between them and gingerly broke off a small piece of the apricot scone and popped it onto her tongue.

"Oh, no, no, no!" she yelled, and spat the rest of the bite onto the counter in a wet glob.

"Disgusting, 'Trice."

"You said it, mister," she replied, wiping at the mess with a sponge. "Those are no good. Way too salty."

"These taste like actual crap," Jules frowned, spitting out a bite of blueberry muffin.

"I won't ask how you know what that would taste like."

Together, bravely, they sampled each and every thing Jules had baked that morning; salty, soapy, overly sweet or plain as cardboard, each and every one was horribly, irrevocably bad.

"How could this happen?" Jules moaned. "We have to close! We have nothing left!"

"We wouldn't have stayed open much later anyway. It's a miracle nobody complained yet today."

"I'm starting over, just so we have something here," Jules said, frantically tossing a whisk into a bowl and whirling toward the refrigerator for the butter and eggs.

"Whatever you say, Chief," 'Trice muttered as she left the kitchen.

Madly, he beat together the ingredients for his most basic, tried-and-true blueberry muffins. They were bestsellers, and if he had nothing else on hand, they would work. Just as he was finishing mixing the batter, he heard 'Trice shriek from the front of the store.

"Jules!" she screamed. "Now! Here!"

When he burst into the shop front brandishing a chef's knife—just in case of robbery, it was handy to have such things—he found her crouched on top of a stool holding aloft a paper cup, her eyes darting wildly around the counter.

"I saw a mouse!" she whispered.

"What?" Jules stage-whispered back. "Impossible! I clean this place myself every morning!"

"Why do you make me clean it every afternoon before I close, then?" 'Trice glared at him.

"Not important," Jules whispered back. "Where did you see it?"

"There!" She pointed with one shaking finger to the counter near the espresso machine.

Jules bent over the counter and ran his finger along the joint with the wall. There were no holes, no crumbs, nothing that might attract a mouse. "Here?" he asked skeptically. "Over here? What exactly did you see?"

"I saw a shadow, so I looked," she whimpered. 'Trice was a tough girl, laced in tattoos and leather boots and bad attitude; Jules made a mental note that he'd found her Achilles' heel. "And it must have been under that cup, because it moved. I swear to god it moved. It slid across the counter by itself, like three feet."

Jules inspected more carefully, quickly upending the cup and then tossing it into the trash. "There's nothing there now."

"I'm calling the guy," 'Trice said and hurried to the desk in the kitchen.

After she had gone, Jules turned back toward the counter with a disinfecting rag and began furiously to wipe. He pulled all of the equipment, the stacks of cups, the bins of coffee, away from the wall and scrubbed as hard as he could at the still very clean counter.

When he looked up from his work, Andy was standing next to the counter, flickering in the sunlight from the front window. His arms were folded; he leaned against the counter with one transparent hip. Jules jumped back, tossing the rag at the vision before he thought better of it. Andy didn't move from the spot, but he reached down and batted the paper tip cup next to the register across the counter.

"Balls!" Jules shouted without thinking. It was one of 'Trice's favorite expressions. Andy shook his head slowly.

"You were gone!" Jules yelled. "You were gone! I felt it!"

Andy shook his head again and leaned against the espresso machine. The machine hummed and hissed out a jet of steam when he touched it.

"What?" 'Trice yelled from the kitchen.

"You can't be here," Jules whispered harshly at him. "You have to go. I have customers."

"Did you see it again?" 'Trice asked, poking her head out of the kitchen. "Did you yell for me?" She didn't seem too anxious to come out of the kitchen and into the Mouse-Infested Area. She also didn't seem to notice Andy, who was standing not three feet from Jules, flashing with the sunlight.

"Jules! Earth to Chef Jules! Did you call me?" 'Trice waved her hands at his face. "Did you see the mouse again?"

"No," he said, motioning absently over his shoulder toward the kitchen. "Go back. I'll call if I do."

"O… kay," she sang and slinked back into the kitchen. The door flapped shut behind her. When Jules turned back to the counter, Andy was gone.

Andy appeared to him several more times, always at the bakery, always when he was alone and most easily startled.

Early on the morning of the fourth day, Jules sat at his desk, waiting for his doughs to rise. He'd abandoned bowls of half-mixed cake batter—just the dry ingredients, waiting for their eggs and milk—in order to sit at his desk and scribble recipe notes and a quick to-do list for the day. Over his shoulder, the light shifted in dappled yellow-green patterns as the trees outside shook in the wind. The radio tinned out a fuzzy doo-wop tune.

When the light disappeared and shifted to black shadow, he noticed immediately, and glanced up, thinking perhaps 'Trice had, for once, come in quietly and early.

It was Andy, more solid than Jules had seen him in a long while, hunched over the bowls that lay waiting on the counter, his hands stirring above them in small circles.

"Hey!" Jules yelled, though he quickly thought better of it—knew it was ridiculous—and chose instead to lunge toward Andy's figure. By then it was too late; Andy filtered quickly into the shifting sunlight and was gone.

Jules crept to the bowls and peered in: nothing appeared to be amiss. Just in case, he dipped a spoon into one and tasted the contents. Far, far too salty. He tasted the other: bitter.

The batches were ruined, so he dumped them and started again.

He had to throw out two more batches before he realized he could not let the batters leave his sight for one second; the moment he turned his back, they would grow sour, or salty, or bitter or too wet to use.

He dropped into the desk chair in the corner, hid his face in his hands, and cried.

Pastry-Whipped: Adventures in Sugar by a Dedicated
Crumpet Strumpet
by Chef Jules Burns of Buttermilk Bakery
September 8: How to Blend But Not Break

Something's wrong with my mojo. I just can't get it right lately. Baking is, yes, chemistry and know-how, but it's also a little bit about magic, a little bit about being charmed in the kitchen. It's being able to soothe disparate ingredients and flavors into some kind of harmony, something wonderful. It's being able to blend well. Essentially, it's matchmaking. Being good in the kitchen means being a little bit of a yenta.

I need a good yenta in my own life, lately. I'm trying to juggle too many people I love, but they don't blend together right. I need to figure out how to balance things. I need to find the right recipe for a kind of happiness that lets me keep everything.

When I first learned to bake, in a sweltering kitchen with my laid-back grandmother, there were no mistakes. We turned out lumpy, salty, frankly awful cookies and cakes together, but it was fun, and that was entirely the point. It was a way to be together. That's where the blending happened.

During the days, it was just the two of us, and there were plenty of days I gave that woman absolute hell over not being my mother. I don't think she was ever very thrilled about having to deal with a stubborn, angry child when in her golden years. "Haven't I already paid my dues?" she used to cry, waving her hands in the air and looking heavenward in her best exaggerated imitation of Scarlett O'Hara. "I raised one little devil child already! As god is my witness, I should be on a beach in Sarasota!"

Now, I bake largely by myself, in a little kitchen in which the sunlight and sounds of the outside world filter weakly through three tiny street-level windows. In fact, my life has become like this: home life and baking life, personal and public, passion and duty, joy and pain, everything filtered tepidly together but never quite blending, never quite becoming one holistic experience of everything at once. I long to be overwhelmed with everything at once.

Baking has become a profession, and so I take it much more seriously than my grandmother and I did. It's still about blending, of course, it's still about balance, but not just when it comes to ingredients.

When I was a kid, it was me and my dad and my grandmother. Between my dad's guilt and my grandmother's hawk eye, I grew up *expecting quite a bit of attention. I was, for a very long time, the center of my father's world. I never had to learn to compromise with other kids, or outsiders in general; some people might hear that and call me spoiled. I'm not patting myself on the back when I tell you that isn't true. As the only child of a single man, I had to learn to compromise with my dad much more than other kids did. It was just the two of us all the time, so the pressure was on. I could never play one parent off the other, or blame any mess or breakage on a sibling. Balance—just the two of us and our love, like a fulcrum—was delicate and crucial. It was like living my entire life on a tightrope.*

Then my father met a really lovely woman, Annette, and she moved into our house, bringing with her two teenaged sons, one of whom was exactly my age, large, sweaty and football-playing, and my time with my grandmother diminished in favor of time spent with Annette and Zack and Nathan. I had to learn my lessons all over again. Suddenly, there were three times as many showers being taken, three times as many hands grabbing for the television remote, three times as many people with an opinion about what to eat for dinner. All my routines were upended. I had, quickly, to learn about compromise, and I had, very quickly, to learn how to incorporate these new people into my life, to make them my family, to love them as much as I loved my father.

I also became more, well, more myself*, because I became more what my brothers were* not*. That's how I thought of myself: the not-Nathan and the not-Zack. If Nathan was big and gangly, I was delicate and thin. If Zack ate hot dogs straight from the package with the refrigerator door open like a wild monkey, I became a thoughtful, loving cook with a refined palate. If Nathan and Zack dated lots of girls, I… well, you get the picture.*

What I discovered, after many months of frustration and missed showers, was that the key was not to find a way to live as though Annette and her sons weren't there—that was impossible, and even more so after I discovered Nathan's house-quaking snore and penchant for draping wet towels over every surface and Zack's habit of leaving his smelly, gondola-sized sneakers in airless rooms. They both had a presence, my dad would say. I would say, more accurately, that they had a smell. The key was, instead, to find a way to blend my former life with these new additions. Blending meant not silencing any part of the whole, but allowing each individual note to sound and finding a way to make those sounds harmonize.

It took finesse and patience. And lots of air freshener.

Now, I use much the same skill when it comes to baking—I know you could see that one coming. But I also use my baking skill when it comes to people. I like to think of myself as a matchmaker, connecting the right person with just the right pastry, which can—as food tends to do—also connect him to memories of other people and places and experiences. It's such a cliché to say that food brings people together, but I don't mean it in the cliché way (the happy Midwestern family sitting around the dinner table, eating Mom's pot roast); I mean that food connects us to our memories, to our lives, to love.

I remember an old cartoon that was intended to explain the "melting pot" of America. It used as its visual metaphor a big stew pot in which different kinds of people floated together and made a (presumably) delicious stew. But they got it all wrong. That's not what a melting pot is.

The image of the melting pot comes from alchemy: You put all these different metals into the pot, melt them together and they become gold. Unlike the individual ingredients of a stew, which are supposed to retain their carrot-ness or onion-icity, their potato-ish-ness or their celery-nature, the ingredients in a melting pot are supposed to blend and turn into something else entirely. They are supposed to stop being silver and chrome and brass, and become gold.

That seems like a radically different metaphor for blending. To blend, you become something entirely new and stop being the old thing completely. My family was what people call a "blended" family; we struggled hard—and usually failed—to be that melting pot. Zack and

Nathan stayed very, well, Zack and Nathan, and Annette, bless her soul, in her daily struggle to adjust to her sudden life with five men, tried very hard to make me into her girlfriend. It all failed terribly, in my opinion—though everyone seemed happy enough when we were together, Zack and Nathan and I ran screaming in separate directions as soon as we'd finished high school. (Zack went into the military and got stationed overseas; Nathan went to L.A. to audition for movies and works, I think, as a Starbuck's barista. I fled to New York City as rapidly as I could.)

My life now is failed alchemy. In fact, I'm not really convinced I want everything to blend and homogenize and become something entirely new, with no trace of the past. I love my past dearly; it's why I am who I am in the present.

In fact, I know it: I don't want an alchemical miracle; I don't want a melting pot. I want to keep my present as beautiful and perfect and full of love as it can be; I want to keep my past as it is, as it haunts me, my memories pure and real as the smell of fresh-baked bread. I want to live at the fulcrum, which is the point in the center, but also that point which endures the most pressure. Balance, I remember a physical science teacher telling us in high school, is an active state, not a place of rest or stasis. It requires constant effort to maintain. The fulcrum, where I live now, is a careful balancing point between past and future, between rock and hard place, memory and hope.

We would be pleased to have someone of your caliber working at Sturm. Please contact Greta at your earliest convenience to discuss the next steps.

Teddy stared at the humming computer in his lap. Sturm was one of the larger firms to which he'd applied for work, an old behemoth of New York, staid and golden in its reputation in the business world. He'd approached them as a matter of course, never imagining that he'd be chosen to join their ranks. But he'd been offered a position in their accounting department.

It was everything he'd been looking for: a powerful, well-respected company; steady, predictable work; a too-big-to-be-true paycheck; a suit-and-tie tradition of gentility and excellence in everything they did.

He didn't want it.

Jules stood patiently at the metal prep table in the bakery kitchen, waiting. 'Trice had left long ago; the bakery been closed for hours. Every few minutes, he whispered, "Andy!" The sun drifted, orange, through the little ceiling-level windows; outside, cars slushed by in the rapidly deepening dusk.

"Andy, I can't wait much longer," Jules said. "Please, I need to talk to you tonight."

There was a small noise near the sinks, and Jules turned to see Andy there, standing quietly with his arms folded.

"You came," Jules said. Andy nodded solemnly. "I'm glad you came," he added nervously, gesturing awkwardly. Andy didn't move, but tilted his head, listening.

"I need you to stop doing things to what I bake here," Jules said. He was terribly nervous, and Andy's silence, however expected, made it worse. "I need things to taste like they're supposed to, or I'm going to have to close the bakery."

Andy tilted his head the other direction; the expression on his face gave nothing away.

"Look, I miss you a lot, but I have to keep on going, and that means baking and selling what I bake so the store stays afloat, and that means bringing Teddy home and keeping our dog healthy and happy, and letting Teddy and our dog love each other, and generally living a good life without you, much as that hurts."

Andy nodded, but started to flicker.

"No. Don't go, please, yet. I'll make you a deal."

He paused for effect, and Andy rolled his eyes and put his translucent hands on his translucent hips, waiting.

"I'll make you a deal," he repeated, stalling. "You can stay here, and we will talk every day, and I'll keep remembering you and loving you and telling you about everything, as long as you stay here, don't hang out at the apartment, and don't mess with anything—not what I bake, not the customers, not me and not Teddy."

Andy nodded again, and the flickering became more off than on. He spread his hands open, palms up, as if he were offering something, and then he flickered out and was gone.

"Andy?" Jules asked the dark kitchen.

He called again, then again in a whisper, but there was no reply.

"I need to talk to Teddy," Jules told 'Trice the next morning, when she shuffled into the kitchen. He stopped sifting and wiped his hands down the front of his apron, as a way to make clear how desperate he felt: He *never* wiped his hands on his apron. That was for slobs and unprofessional people.

"Tough break, kid," 'Trice said. "I'm neither his nanny nor his booking agent."

"Would you please just tell him for me? He won't pick up his phone. Tell him the apartment's empty now."

"I'm not in the middle of this," she said, washing her hands.

"You look like a wrung-out rag today," Jules said bitterly. "What happened to you?"

"Another half a bottle of tequila, so I *feel* like a rag, un-wrung," she said. "I'm not your go-between, you lovers, but I'll pass on your message, just to make the tequila rampage stop. I'm getting too old to do this. I'm losing my youthful glow."

⟪∞⟫

The next afternoon, 'Trice came barreling into the kitchen, waving a paper cup over her head.

"Emergency!" she yelled, running for the bathroom and slamming herself inside. Jules heard the bolt latch firmly. Through the plywood door, she shouted, "Pee break! You man the front of the store!"

After a brief pause, during which Jules sighed heavily and closed the ledger book in which he'd been scribbling doodles, she shouted again through the door, "When I say *man the store,* I mean that metaphorically, Necker-Chief! Obviously, *manning* anything is a stretch for you! You're more like—"

Jules thunked his pencil onto the desk. "All right! Going! Can it!" he yelled, slamming out the kitchen doors.

Teddy stood at the counter; he waved awkwardly when Jules stepped behind it and looked at him without saying a word.

"Uh, hi," Teddy stammered. "I'm coming in to see you."

"Okay," Jules said. He tried to be cold, he really did, but warmth crept into his voice despite his efforts.

"'Trice said the apartment is empty now," Teddy said and waited. Jules simply looked at him, so he stammered again. "I mean, 'Trice told me you told her to tell me you needed to talk, and that the apartment is empty now, and I'm pretty sure I know what that means, but I thought I would come in to talk, since you said you wanted to." He petered out helplessly and shrugged. "If you want."

Jules tried his best, but he couldn't sustain an icy manner—Teddy had only left because the situation with Andy had become impossible.

There wasn't much reason to be cold aside from pride, which, Jules decided, was overrated compared to sex anyway.

"The apartment's empty," he confirmed. "Tea? Scone?"

"Well," Teddy said. "It's not like I have to rush to work anymore, is it? Yeah, please, tea."

Jules steeped him a cup of chamomile tea with a little lavender in it and handed him a pretty little scone with currants and orange zest.

"Fruity," Teddy said, lifting an eyebrow.

"If the shoe fits," 'Trice shouted from the kitchen.

"We're not going to be able to talk privately here," Jules whispered.

"No, it's okay, I'm not listening!" 'Trice yelled from the kitchen. Jules heard a worrisome clanging of pots. "I've got better things to do than listen to the gossip of Siegfried and his gayest tiger, anyway!" 'Trice made a whip-cracking sound, and Teddy's eyes widened in Jules's direction.

"I'm *the gay tiger?*" he mouthed at Jules. Jules shook his head.

"I'm the flaming circus performer who wears sequined jumpsuits," he whispered. "Wanna trade?"

Jules followed Teddy to the table by the front window and slid onto the stool across from him as he dunked his scone.

"Will you please come home now?" Jules whispered. "It's all clear, and it's not like we can talk here, with the human satellite dish homing in on our every word. She's judging. I can feel it."

"Home," Teddy said, smiling at his scone.

"Please come home," Jules said again. He pushed a set of keys across the table at Teddy.

"Those are my lost keys!" Teddy exclaimed. He grabbed the set of keys from the table, though he had neither the apartment nor the bike lock to which they belonged. Still, the Hope Key glinted from the ring like a winking eye.

"Then it's a sign for sure," Jules said. "I added the apartment key, too."

That afternoon, Teddy shoved his clothes, his razor, his comb and his toothbrush into the bag he'd brought to 'Trice's house. Just as quickly, she removed the items. Each time he repacked, she unpacked just as quickly.

"I can do this for hours, Tweedledee," she said, tossing a balled-up pair of socks onto the couch behind them.

Teddy turned to grab the socks and put them back into the bag. "I am healthier and happier than you and have more stamina," he said. "Besides, 'Tweedledee,' seriously? Does that make Jules Tweedledum?"

"It would fit, but he's totally the evil Queen of Hearts," she said, grabbing the socks again. "That ridiculous yappy dog is Tweedledum. And you may *not* move back in with the Queen yet. You guys haven't even talked! This is horrible idea number one!"

"I'm going back so we *can* talk," Teddy said. "I'm just anticipating that I'll be staying. Besides, you should be dying to get me off your couch."

"Touché, but not really. Because, though you may not be used to it, I actually *care* what happens to you."

She pulled a stack of pants out of the bag and tossed them unceremoniously onto the floor. "Besides, if the Queen is miserable, so will I be. So will be all the peasants in the land." She paused a moment, then added, "The land is the bakery."

"I *know*," Teddy said. "I just think you're wrong."

"Croissants never lie," she said seriously.

According to the rules of every story ever written, this is the point at which everything wraps together neatly for a *happily ever after,* and all the untied strings magically fade into a tawny swell of sunset and music. Teddy must walk into the bakery and find Jules, and they will fall together with gratitude and joy. Andy-the-man will cease to be, will dissipate faster than memory. 'Trice has served her purpose; her story need not continue at all, unless she is made to meet the woman of her dreams and, finally, settle down into domestic bliss.

But this is not to be that perfectly symmetrical story; there will be no neat wrapping up, no fairy tale sunset into which everyone might ride. We warned you at the beginning of this story. 'Trice will stay, though she might be difficult at times; Andy-the-man will not disappear for our lovers; there will be no fade out into sunset and bliss.

Because you have been reading this story all this time, though, you will demand that it end the way it should. We will do our best to give you that much, without falling too deeply into the cliché of senseless happiness. We will do our best for symmetry, too, and for the gentle miracles that love might be enough to bring about.

Teddy left 'Trice's apartment with his bags once again slung over his shoulder and banging his hip with every step. He moved faster this time, and with more purpose, and the bags banged out a more joyous rhythm as he went: *pass it by, pass it by, pass it by,* the bags seemed to sing, and *go home to get home, hurry, go home to get home.*

That afternoon, he'd written an apologetic letter of rejection to Sturm, all the while thinking he was making both the best and worst decision of his life. *A sure thing,* his father had told him over and over in his youth, *is the best thing. Some people struggle their whole lives and never find a sure thing.* But Teddy knew a sure thing was a lifeless thing, too.

He let himself into the little apartment on Jane Street with the recovered keys. He tossed his bags onto the bedroom floor, put his hands around Andy-the-dog's muzzle, stuck his nose into the fur behind his ears and inhaled deeply, relishing the familiar smell of the little dog.

Afterward, after he had opened all the drawers and replaced his clothing in the closet, after he had pet the dog and brushed his teeth in the bathroom—*his bathroom*—and after he had spent long minutes standing at the open window in the living room, listening to the wind buffet the curtains, he slipped the keys into his hip pocket and left for the bakery.

Once he arrived, he pushed his way behind the counter, ignoring 'Trice's call, and slipped into the kitchen, where Jules stood at the prep table, stirring batter and humming to himself.

"I've left 'Trice's house," Teddy announced, and Jules, for once, didn't ask for clarification, but dropped the whisk and the bowl, wiped his hands on a damp tea towel, and pressed Teddy against the edge of his desk to kiss and to kiss.

'Trice soon left for the afternoon, slamming and shouting her way out the front door, and Teddy and Jules were left alone in the kitchen to talk in low voices that barely reached over the hum of music from the radio. It was a small, quiet evening.

"I got a job offer today," Teddy said.

"You what? You what?" Jules hurled himself around the metal prep table to fling his arms around Teddy's neck.

"I turned it down," Teddy said, and explained about Sturm, the ties and the prestige and money and big gray block of a building into which he could not imagine creeping every morning, from the gray street to the taupe interiors, and back out again in the evenings. The prospect was entirely too colorless to bear.

We are certain you can see, as clearly as we do, the solution: Teddy should help to run the bakery, set up shop at the messy desk in the kitchen or, better yet, learn to bake alongside Jules, with the smell of citrus rising up around him on the early morning air and the deeply colored jewels shaking on their strings and spattering the shop front with the light of indigo and garnet and topaz.

We can tell you that he does this for a short while, leaning against Jules in the gray dawn light of the kitchen, and he is blissfully happy to be with this man, moving around him in a fine dance of familiarity and routine and frictionless ease; but it somehow will not be enough. It is not enough to be in love like this, to be held so completely in the light-spattered little bakery. It is safe and beautiful and steady, but it is not enough.

And so, though it may disappoint you, Teddy will leave. Not entirely, no, because he will still love Jules, and the two will still make a home together and a small, quiet happiness, but that will only come with a bit of distance, a bit of difference, perhaps even a little dissonance.

In the darkness of early mornings, Jules will creep to the bakery and leave Teddy to sleep on his own for a few hours. Those few hours will mean everything to them both; those few hours are when they will each build themselves into something new for the other to love. Teddy will rise much later, stumble to the desk in the hall and work for most of the day on the books for his clients—the strangest and most wonderful mix of bodegas and dollar stores and freelancers and music teachers.

He will, of course, offer to do the books for Buttermilk. Jules will, of course, turn him down.

But this is all in the near future; in the meantime, Teddy has found Jules again, has walked back into the bakery and, in the space without 'Trice, Jules and Teddy have quietly remade their togetherness.

And when they left that evening, Teddy and Jules stood for a long time at the front door while Jules fumbled with his keys at the lock. Teddy, for his part, impatiently flipped his own set of keys over his fingers in jangly rotations.

"Stop it," Jules said, putting his hand over the keys, "or I will truly go murdering-crazy."

"Sorry," Teddy said, and dropped the keys back into his pocket.

And as he kissed Jules's cheek lightly, Teddy could have sworn he saw all the hanging jewels inside the bakery shake, shifting the streetlight into golds and reds and greens all over the little store.

Andy-the-man would not reappear for many days and only came back to the bakery to smile at Jules and nod, approvingly, when it became clear that Teddy was to stay for good. He showed himself less and less frequently, until one day became the last day he appeared, and he did not come again, but lingered silent and invisible in the empty kitchen at night.

❧

This is the way the story ends: on this night when Teddy and Jules shared a small, happy kiss at the door of the bakery, while the rest of the city went its darkening, evening way. Lights began to shimmer up in the house windows across the street, and the cars grew numerous and slowed, puttering and honking and cursing their way out of the neighborhood.

It would be several days until Jules showed Teddy the slender gold Hope Key on Teddy's recovered keychain, which, Teddy would find, fit the bakery door perfectly. But *that* moment matters less, in the scheme of things, than their first night together again (though perhaps you may find it to mean more, metaphorically, that Teddy's Hope Key will unlock the door to Jules's bakery. But maybe the coincidence of Jules losing the key which Teddy would eventually find, then lose, only for Jules to find it again, is too perfectly symmetrical to bear telling). For tonight, that key would hide in Teddy's hip pocket as they walked home to the snug apartment on Jane Street. For tonight, Jules would let them inside, and Andy-the-dog would greet them with his excessive snuffling and wiggling, and they would eat a dinner of cold fruit cut over the sink with a paring knife, and leave the lights off and let their home be lit by the bright gold of the streetlight pushing through the curtains; and they would sit in recovered and imperfect joy and feel grateful for the streetlamp and the paltry breeze, the broken blue lamp and Andy's wheezing snore, the whirling curtains and the breeze that took them up, the fruit, the knife, their hands and the inky dark that twined them together and hid them, for once, from everything else.

Acknowledgments

THANK YOU TO CANDY, ANNIE and Lex for your intelligent and unwavering support, your kindness, your belief and your help and advice. And thanks to everyone who offered inspiration, motivation and friendship as I wrote. Most of all, Lex, you are missed; this book will always remind me of you.

For a reader's guide to Sweet and book club prompts,
please visit interludepress.com

Also from interlude press

Black Dust by Lynn Charles

Fifteen years after a tragic car crash claimed a friend's life and permanently injures his then-boyfriend, Broadway musician Tobias Spence reconnects with his former love. As Emmett and Tobias explore their renewed relationship, the two men face old hurts and the new challenges of a long-distance romance. Will Tobias lose his second chance at love to the ghosts he can't seem to put to rest?

ISBN 978-1-941530-63-4

Speakeasy by Suzey Ingold

In the height of the Prohibition era, recent Yale graduate Heath Johnson falls for Art, the proprietor of a unique speakeasy tucked away beneath the streets of Manhattan where men are free to explore their sexuality. When Art's sanctuary is raided, Heath is forced to choose between love and the structured life his parents planned for him.

ISBN 978-1-941530-69-6

interlude press
now available...

What It Takes by Jude Sierra

Milo Graham met Andrew Witherell moments after moving to Cape Cod—launching a lifelong friendship of deep bonds, secret forts, and plans for the future. When Milo goes home from college for his father's funeral, he and Andrew finally act on their attraction—but doubtful of his worth, Milo severs ties. They meet again years later, and their long-held feelings will not be denied. But will they have what it takes to find lasting love?

ISBN 978-1-941530-59-7

Small Wonders by Courtney Lux

A pickpocket who finds value in things others do not want, Trip Morgan becomes involved with Nate Mackey, a down-and-out Wall Street professional who looks like a child in a photograph Trip found years before. In confronting their own demons and finding value in each other, Trip and Nate may find that their relationship is a wonder of its own.

ISBN 978-1-941530-45-0

Sotto Voce by Erin Finnegan

Wine critic Thomas Baldwin can make or break careers with his column for Taste Magazine. But when his publisher orders him to spend a year profiling rising stars of California's wine country and organizing a competition between the big name wineries of Napa and the smaller artisan wineries of Sonoma, his world gets turned upside-down by an enigmatic young winemaker who puts art before business.

ISBN 978-1-941530-15-3

interlude 🧩🧩 press™

One **story**

can change

everything.

interlude**press**.com

Twitter: @interludepress | **Facebook:** Interlude Press
Google+: interludepress | **Pinterest:** interludepress
Instagram: InterludePress

CPSIA information can be obtained at www.ICGtesting.com
Printed in the USA
LVOW11s0421200216

475911LV00003B/69/P

9 781941 530610